VENTRY

VENTRY

Daniel Caplice Lynch

An Irma Heldman / Birch Lane Press Book
Published by Carol Publishing Group

for Clellie

Copyright © 1990 by Daniel Caplice Lynch

A Birch Lane Press Book
Published by Carol Publishing Group

Editorial Offices
600 Madison Avenue
New York, NY 10022

Sales & Distribution Offices
120 Enterprise Avenue
Secaucus, NJ 07094

In Canada: Musson Book Company
A division of General Publishing Co. Limited
Don Mills, Ontario

Queries regarding rights and permissions
should be addressed to: Carol Publishing Group,
600 Madison Avenue, New York, NY 10022

Manufactured in the United States of America

Library of Congress Cataloging-in-Publication Data
Lynch, Daniel Caplice.
    Ventry / Daniel Caplice Lynch.
      p.   cm.
    "A Birch Lane Press book"--T.p. verso.
    ISBN 1-55972-049-2 : $16.95
    I. Title.
  PS3562. Y4173V46   1990
  813'.54--dc20

                                                    90-2170
                                                    CIP

Carol Publishing Group books are available at special discounts
for bulk purchases, for sales promotions, fund raising, or
educational purposes. Special editions can also be created to
specifications. For details contact: Special Sales Department,
Carol Publishing Group, 120 Enterprise Ave., Secaucus, NJ 07094

1

I hung up on him and went back to sketching on the porch.

The rain in that early June morning had left the grass drenched and at two in the afternoon, the damp, almost chocolate, smell of the loamy earth rose up and hung in the air. There were puddles in the ruts of the dirt road in front, the house wrens were flying down to drink from them, and water was dripping from the century-old eaves of my farmhouse overlooking the pond and the wooded valley.

My neighbor, the local newspaper publisher, Calvin Conklin, was on the porch with me, leaning back in a firehouse chair I bought at auction the week I moved in, a year and a half before. It had a lot of good lean in it.

"Who was that?" Conklin asked. Clouds were drifting eastward over the valley toward the Berkshires, where a helicopter swept along the ridge of hills. The sun was shining down benignly on my flower garden. The blue-white irises tottered in the breeze.

"Someone who wanted to talk about a murder," I said.

He took a long sip of his vodka. "I thought you were done with all that," he said.

The very last of the lilacs were soggy and nodding from the ends of the large shrub by the driveway. To paint them, I'd use cobalt violet and rose madder, then some white. For the leaves ultramarine mixed with yellow ochre and a touch of alizarin. Maybe tomorrow.

He'd be here in a few minutes.

I saw a worker bee crawl into one of the irises, deftly, like a crackhead slipping through an apartment window.

"I am," I said.

"Nice flowers, Ventry," he said.

"I don't think I discouraged him," I said. I moved the pencil across the page. I had a good central line flowing from the hank of gray blond hair hanging like a cockatiel's injured wing from Conklin's forehead, down his strong, lanky frame, slung in the chair, down to the long legs pressed against the top of the porch railing.

"I've been growing irises," Conklin said in his just- sippin'-and-talkin' tone, "ever since I took over from Dad, and I've seen them opening just once. Keep looking, my father said. He was nuts about flowers. Did I tell you this? When the lower petals first arch downward, at that moment, they shudder, boy, like a virgin. Beautiful."

"I'll be sure to keep an eye on them." Conklin's a pal. His father had been the congressman from up here forever. He'd died a decade ago. From something he said I gathered his mother had been an alcoholic and died in a sanatorium. Calvin still ran the family newspaper, the *Vigilant*, but said he was too lazy to run for office.

"Damn," I thought to myself. "Damn!" I had been "serious" for over a year and a half, lived on my own terms and done some good work. On this one day, I should have been as happy as God in France. Jack Giresse, who was born in Paris and taught me what I know about painting, used to say that. Now my father calls from his limo phone to tell me he's just a few miles down the road.

A wasp with threadlike legs of bright yellow hanging beneath it hovered by my head before circling lazily up to its paper nest under the second-floor window. A hummingbird appeared next to a bright red salvia below us, drank its nectar and zoomed off. I know just how he felt. I wanted a drink and a way out of what was coming.

I thought about a gin and tonic. About vodka. About the bottle of Moët and Chandon champagne Conklin had brought with him, chilled, along with an advance copy of *Art in America* that had a review of my first show. I hadn't had a drink in a year and a half.

We had been there on the porch for a couple of hours, ever since Conklin drove up in his mud-splattered van with the magazine and the bottle. I don't know how you feel about painting or critics or galleries or reputations. Conklin felt it was an opportunity to indulge in a previously hidden penchant for cruelty. He read it to me. Every word.

> Into the current debate over new directions in the downtown scene and the repoliticization of the surface comes the VEN-TRY show at Handasyde and Beaky on Prince Street. His years as a policeman and photojournalist—El Salvador, Ulster, Lebanon—have left him a stock of obsessional images of violence and betrayal that roll onto the canvas like a grenade. His best works have the moment-of-gunshot impact of a Capa, see his "The Bekaa: Israeli Casualty." At the same time they skirt the excesses of mawkishness and propaganda this kind of material often engenders.
>
> The canvases show a directness that belies, in a bold self-referential manner, the layers of reworking evident in the larger works. This emphasis on process reveals the mute pain in "Nuns in Hiding: El Salvador." The non-suffering onlooker is made into an accomplice.
>
> Political and anecdotal, yes, maybe too journalistic, yet he does know how to use paint. The creamy sensuousness of the broad strokes in his flowers, like the hibiscus in "Carmen with Cadillac," live in a lyrical world utterly apart from the man-made violence we see in the dagger-like strokes he uses to build up the old boxer's face.
>
> He handles these images of strength with boldness. In a self-portrait, "Tugboat Man Splicing," we see Ventry himself as a stocky tough in jeans and T-shirt on the deck of a tug, the *Helen B.*, wrestling with a hawser. A curly mass of coal black hair falls down over dark brows and fair skin; his gray eyes concentrate on wielding the marlinspike.
>
> This forceful, rough and confident show demands attention. We look forward to seeing more of his work.

He had to go on to say that my values were, in some works, uncertain, but overall my work was a necessary corrective to the last few shows he had seen. I represented an important turn away from European non-objectivism since I owed so much to Eakins, Bellows, and Hopper. I don't know how my mentor, Giresse, was going to take that. He immersed me in Delacroix, Degas and Picasso.

Being written about like that, as if I were following some script, is creepy. In addition to Jack, the person I really *owed* was my friend and advisor, Lou Darmstadt, who had used her clout at the gallery as their most successful painter to campaign for a show for me. If the show sold out, I could live up here for at least another year. If it didn't, I'd starve. I had used up all my money. I was almost broke.

I heard the sound of his car. My father's dark limousine was swerving through the mud and bouncing over the ruts of the road. The car shone like a beetle's carapace. I slapped my sketchpad down and stood up on the porch to glare at him. Conklin just sipped. The new Cadillac slid into a soft spot on the side of the road, tore up a few feet of lawn and came to a skewed halt. The window rolled down and my father's ruddy, tight little ferret face, peered up at me.

"You hung up on me!"

I kept quiet.

"Do you ever go to the goddamned post office and pick up your mail?"

I put on my sunglasses.

"How is anyone supposed to get in touch with you?"

I snapped my pencil in two. "What do you want from me now?" I asked, coolly, I hoped. Perhaps the murder he had mentioned on the phone was only a ploy to get my attention.

"Jesus Christ!" He got out of the car. "Jesus Christ!" He stamped his foot. He groaned. "Are you going to ask me in, or do I piss in the middle of the road?"

"Okay, come in." I turned and held the screen door open for him. He walked stiffly up the driveway and climbed the steps holding onto the railing. Nodding to Conklin, he kept on going. He was showing his age. He was born in 1912.

He came in, tore off his Burberry trenchcoat, took off his snapbrim fedora, and walked past me into the bathroom. He had never been in the house before, but he instinctively knew his way around places, though he was looking less like Dick

Tracy than the aging gossip columnist he was. I went into the living room and sat down next to the fireplace where the day before I had put some fresh green white pine boughs on the grate that I had cut in the grove further up the hillside. The resinous odor filled the room. Barred owls nested back up there. I would hear them at night hooting to one another. Some nights I hooted back.

Conklin slipped into the room.

I looked out the low-slung window to a meadow guarded by ash, maple, hickory and white pine. I wanted to mess with my canvases in the mornings, and scrabble around in my vegetable and flower gardens in the afternoon.

My father came out of the bathroom and looked at Conklin quizzically.

"This is my father, Vince Ventry. Pop, Calvin Conklin. You're both newspapermen."

"I run a small local paper, Mr. Ventry. You know, we met once."

"Yeah," Pop said, "You're Peary Conklin's kid. I met you in . . . in . . .?"

"The Stork Club," Conklin said.

"Yeah, in the fifties sometime. You were in uniform."

"Just back from basic."

"I knew the congressman quite well. And he was highly thought of. Highly."

"And he thought highly of you too, sir."

"Call me Vince."

I had grown up listening to this crap. I did what I always did, drifted away while Pop charmed. I went back on the porch and looked at my hilltop. I liked playing in the dirt. It's like paint, which is just dirt suspended in oil. I wanted to spend the long winter nights reading and the short summer nights in a bed sleeping, dreaming of pictures. In the past I had my fill of "excitement," certainly enough to last me out. I didn't want to leave this very quiet life for a long time, if ever.

I was a cop once for two years. In the Ninth Precinct, actually, the Lower East Side, not far from the gallery where my work is showing now. I was one of the Finest. Had the gun, the tin, the hook, the rabbi. It wasn't for me.

After I left the job, I'd done a lot of things in a lot of places, though never on the harbor. That self-portrait came from a photo of my grandfather's tugboat, my reflection in a mirror and a daydream. I left New York as a photographer for *Newsweek*. In Soweto, Belfast, Beirut, Managua, back to Southeast Asia, Chad. Intermittently, I took some breaks. Vacations, the office called them. It's a term of craft meaning a particular journalist is drying out somewhere. I spent three months studying drawing in London at the Slade and found British art students see their way of life as a permanent calling, very like unemployment. This led to six months minding the house of an art dealer in Provence, sketching olive trees and stone cisterns.

I delivered a Cézanne by hand to one of the dealer's customers in San Francisco and then didn't go back. I got a job part-time with a detective agency. I gave them a number to call at the NYPD and I worked there for two years, skiptracing, checking out disability claims for fraud, and bounty hunting repos. I thought I could paint by day and skulk by night. After the first year, I thought my nerves had been blowtorched. I should have left then. After the second, I lit out for New York to see Cheech and Lou and talk them into taking care of me. Lou is brilliant, talented and very special.

The three of us had met at an anatomy class at the Art Students League that Jack was teaching. Lou is Austrian-born. She has dark, dark eyes and light brown skin. Her father was a black GI, a tank driver from Alabama stationed in Germany. While on leave in Vienna, he met her mother whose name Lou uses. She has no reservations at all about speaking her mind in any of the several languages she speaks fluently. She learned Italian faster than I could learn rummy—*una notte*. She has a generous, ample figure that will grow Junoesque unless she tempers her taste for junk food and pastries *mit schlag*.

Her husband Cheech has a heavy, squat earthbound body, his inheritance from ancestors who had spent the last two thousand years in Calabria tending olive trees and grape vines. He had a wild and troubled adolescence. His erratic behavior caused his parents to take him to a psychiatrist who, after one unsettling conversation with his patient, urged them to commit him to Creedmore, a hospital on Long Island, where his therapy fortunately included free-form ceramics. He was enthralled. When he was discharged, he headed for Manhattan and art school where he met me, who introduced him to Lou. They sorted themselves into an affair and then marriage. He abandoned ceramics for conceptual art, and the resulting mixture of zaniness and vulgarity won him a downtown celebrity status he utterly ignored.

Lou came to America as a child in the late Fifties. For a time, her parents operated a shooting gallery concession at the old amusement park in Palisades, New Jersey. Maybe there were fewer hassles about an interracial couple on the midway. I had told her that as a kid I'd cut out admission and ride coupons from Superman comic books and bicycle there, up Riverside Drive and across the Hudson on the GW bridge. We didn't remember each other. Lou still claimed to be a crack shot and could also spiel a pitch at the marks like an old-time carney, which she did for one of Cheech's video bits called "Even Break."

Lou set up a three-card monte game on a cardboard box near Bryant Park behind the Forty-second Street library. She got her crowd together using me as a shill. Then she played the game, slowly and honestly, paying off everyone who won. When people caught on, there was damn near a riot. Even before we ran out of money, the regulars chased us out of there. Cheech got it all down on videotape.

Even in school, the other students crowded around her work. Now she's in MOMA, the Whitney, the Met, and her last series, "Five Love Songs for the Women of Darrah," had been featured in a spread in *Time* that predicted crassly, but accurately, that she would be the first in her generation to sell a painting for a million dollars.

After arriving back in New York, I worked for her for a few months. The job involved much heavy lifting. After a while I finally got up the courage to show her some of my canvases.

"Ventry," she asked me, "you like the good things? You like what money can buy?"

"Yup," I said.

She shook her head and walked away, calling out, over her shoulder, "Paint better." I thought she was putting me down, but over the course of a couple of days we kept talking and what it finally came down to was that I should invest a year of my life and just paint.

Working with Lou was good for the biceps, and Cheech has a mind like a funhouse, so the decision to leave was difficult, but I knew I had to eventually go off on my own. About this time, my father tracked me down in her studio by phone. Another one of his talents. His secretary, Sadie, spoke to me first. I was polite to her. Then he got on.

"You need some money, kid? Clamolas?"

That's the way he talked. Like he wrote. I hated it. He was going on about needing me for something. He sounded urgent, but I cut him short and hung up. I wasn't going to be a help to him with his damn column and I wasn't going to get involved in any of his schemes.

That was it. I decided this might be a good time to hand in my notice.

"I'm leaving, Lou"

"You're always leaving someplace, Ventry. The point is: where are you going?"

"Beats me."

"Let's go out and talk."

We went to the Grand Street bar nearby. I ordered an Irish whiskey, so did she. We talked and drank and ate hamburgers. We talked some more. Over our after-dinner beers, she suggested this county. She knew people here, painters, sculptors, film makers, even art dealers. She reminded me Jack was up here.

"No terrorists?" I asked her.

"Not a one. Get your ass up there, Ventry. Be serious. Drink up. It's your last for a while. That's an order."

It turned out to be a good idea, being serious.

Next day, this was in February, a year and a half ago, I left Soho with all my worldly goods, and drove north. I had some money in a pension fund I had contributed to when I worked for the magazine. There was also some money from my grandfather's estate, the tugboat man.

I drove to the end of the Taconic Parkway, which rolls through the hills east of the Hudson, and I kept on going. I spoke to a real estate agent in a small town where there were more pick-up trucks than Volvos outside the hardware store.

The agent, a sweet lady of about the same age as my mother and Aunt Helen, took me out to this once-upon-a-time farm. The large blue house that sits on this hillside above the Lebanon Valley looked to me like a great big blue hen on the cover of a fairy tale. Ten acres and a pond. I bought it, thinking that if I were frugal I would have enough to get by on for a year or two without working for wages. That had almost run out.

I have always had a very picture book view of rural life. I remember how I would sit home as a child in our big old apartment on Riverside Drive, while my father was sitting at a table somewhere downtown, at the Stork Club or El Morocco or the Copa, chatting up the captains, looking for material for his column, and I would page through my mother's coffee table art books, looking at Constable's oxen hauling haywains up country roads. The animals looked big, strong and friendly. Or at Winslow Homer's farmboys playing at snap-the-whip, or Eakins' kids at the old swimming hole. Somewhere between my childhood interest in Greek mythology, age seven or eight, and nudes, eleven or twelve, I had an active fantasy life under the spell of these outdoor scenes, and I remember thinking how fine it would be to live somewhere with cows nearby.

If I had turned on the radio, instead of looking at reproductions, maybe today I'd be a rock star. I spent those years drawing the oak trees in Riverside park, opposite our apartment on 107th Street, putting in silos and stiles and cows sipping at the millpond on 108th street.

That's why, years later, after being a cop and a guy with a camera and experiencing a hundred different airports and a hundred different stories, after a few false starts, I was on my hillside painting. It beats what I was doing before or anything to do with my father.

I had to stay. He had to go.

I went back inside. They seemed to be having a good time.

He broke off his conversation with Conklin. "We thought you were lost, Son."

"How long you going to be staying, Pop?"

He looked directly at me with that phony, sincere look of his. "Son, just tell me one thing. Are you happy?"

"Sure am."

"God, aren't you the lucky one? No worries, no problems."

"What time are you getting back to the city?"

He ignored me. "Kid, you know you could always count on me. I was always there when you needed me."

He had never been there when I needed him.

"Look," I started to say, "I can push your car out . . ."

"All right. All right, so I might have spoiled you some."

"Spoiled?"

"Did I object when you entered the Golden Gloves?"

"Yes." I'd been in the Golden Gloves all right. As I recall, it was straight out of Bellows' "Dempsey against Firpo," only that was me getting knocked out of the ring. I was no Dempsey, that's for sure. Pop knew him pretty well. He knew all the Broadway crowd, and they were the Broadway crowd because he knew them, so there you are and what does it matter?

"I could have fixed you up with lots of good people, big people, kid. Did I object when you took all those dumb jobs. Did I?"

Of course he did.

"Didn't I put the word in with Sonny Ehrlich when you joined the Finest and you needed a rabbi?"

"Sonny is a good guy and a good detective and I didn't want any help."

"So, he quit," he said to Conklin in disbelief and then turning to me said, "just when Sonny was lining up a gold shield for you in Manhattan South. Quit. I'll never understand it. He goes and takes his pictures. 'A freelance.' " To my father this meant "bum."

"What can I do for you, Pop?" I'm an idiot. I was being polite. To *him*. He reached into his side coat pocket and took out a gold cigarette case. Extracting a Chesterfield (was he the last man in America to smoke those things?) and tapping the end lightly against the table top, he looked sidewise at me as if I were a press agent who had just told him to name his price in exchange for a leadoff paragraph in his column. Conklin seemed in no hurry to leave.

"Kid," he said softly, "you got any dough?"

"What's this, a touch?"

"Cute. You're still cute. You sell many pictures, huh?"

"They're doing okay."

"Okay is one."

"Yes."

"One. You sold one picture." I didn't ask him how he knew.

"Kid, did you ever hear me talk about Mrs. Barrett?"

"No. Yes. Probably. You talked about everybody. Who . . ."

"Mrs. India Wentworth Barrett."

"No. I never heard you talk about her. I do know she's the one who bought my painting, 'Carmen with Cadillac.' What's going on?"

He lit the cigarette with his gold Zippo, snapped it shut and continued on, squinting through the smoke. "The grand-daughter" he exhaled, "of the Secretary of State, on one side, her other grandfather told the DuPonts about nylon or something; she's the great-granddaughter of Jay Gould's lawyer, and, as far as I know, the direct descendant of two generals in the Revolutionary War, both sides. Her husband was a paint-er."

"Barrett? Barrett? Yes, of course. Barrett, the abstract ex-pressionist."

"Right. You have an excellent memory for names. Perhaps you should have been a newspaperman. Peter Freeman Bar-rett."

"He died, didn't he?"

"Kid's a card, isn't he, Cal? A painter was dusted not twenty miles from here and he doesn't know it? In October last."

"October 18th, Vince. The *Vigilant* covered the story."

Pop looked interested. "What did you have?"

"The crime scene photos, but we didn't play up the grue-some side. People around here'd get nervous."

"Yeah?" Pop said, leading him on.

"Frank Van Deusen, the chief investigating officer for the county, the guy in charge of the case, showed them to me. Frank died of a stroke in January."

"Anything in the photos?"

"Couldn't run them, of course. Barrett was hung up like Jesus on a big easel. Blood sprayed everywhere. Just the body being carried out in the bag. That's all we ran."

"Yeah, well, I don't read the newspapers much, anyway," I said. They both stared at me.

"You were working for that colored paintress, then, weren't you?" Dad asked.

Paintress? Colored?

"No, by then I was here. Get to the point, Pop."

"What do you know about Barrett?"

It came back to me. In his time, Barrett had been highly thought of. He had started out as an illustrator. An image came into my mind from a book on graphics Jack had given me: a fashionable woman with marcelled hair holding a white telephone. Barrett had done it or something like it. Then, after the Second World War, his style changed. He had a famous show that bowled over the major critics. Greenberg and Rosenberg had both written essays about it. It was a very raw, angular kind of painting, fierce abstracts, blacks and grays, something like Kline, as if he had turned steel I-beams into paint and hurled them at the canvas. He was touted as one of the major figures in the postwar abstract expressionist movement. Except for that show, I didn't remember anything much more about Barrett.

"Long career. One big show. Did you know him, Cal?"

"Not exactly. My mother had her portrait done by him years ago. She's in a blue gown. It hangs in my bedroom."

"I'd like to see it."

"He did it way before the war, back in her debutante days. Anyway when I heard he had moved up here I thought I'd look him up. Thought there might be a piece for the paper. Called him. Told him who I was. He said to leave him alone."

"India said he was kind of a recluse," Pop added.

"Finally got to run a piece," Conklin said, "but it was the obit."

"We'd like you to look into how he died, Son," Dad said. Conklin looked surprised, then interested. Here was his story at last. Well, he could keep it.

"It happens to all of us."

"How and why he died."

"Does this look like a squadroom?"

"And who did it."

"No."

I stared at him. He looked as calm as a West African customs officer I tangled with once who wanted to impound my camera equipment on a sweltering afternoon in the airport at Yaoundé in the Cameroons. "Go ahead," that look said, "argue, I'm not going anywhere, and neither, my frustrated, angry friend, are you."

"What about the police? Why me? Why you? Leave me alone."

"Leave me alone, he says," Pop spoke as if his millions of readers were in the room, clucking their tongues at me. "Kid, you don't know dingus."

"Don't you think you're being unrealistic? I'm not a cop any more."

"You were."

I had been a detective the way he had been a journalist, but I didn't say it. "I was lousy at it anyway."

"I think you're all we've got."

"You want a car repossessed? You got a gay lover you think is going to the baths?"

"Watch your mouth. Just listen to what I have to say."

"Pop, maybe you haven't watched enough television. Hermits don't investigate these cases. The goddam police force up here collects a salary for just this sort of thing. Got that?"

"We need you," he said, like a man who didn't really want to admit he needed me much at all.

"I thought, Pop, you knew every cop in Manhattan. I mean, hell, I'm sure there's a police radio in that Caddy out there you just used to plow my lawn up. In other words, Pop"—I was getting steamed up. I had to slow down to keep from sputtering—"why do you come up here, interrupt my life and ask me to go investigate a death?" I started to shout, "What makes you do these things?" I think I was shrieking.

"Calm down, kid. Why don't you give me a club soda with a twist, another drink for Cal here and I'll lay it all out for you."

I went fuming into the kitchen where I got two glasses of water from a plastic jug I fill at a nearby spring which drips out of a pipe on the side of Route 22. I brought them back into the living room where he was lighting up again and set them down on an overturned crate that serves me as a table, next to the broad, low file cabinet that holds my drawings. I took Cal's glass since he looked like he was going to stay around and went back to the kitchen, dropped cubes in it and filled it with vodka the way Cal likes it, to the brim.

"Here," I said.

"Thanks," Conklin said. He was being quiet. Maybe I could get them to leave together.

"Pop, what is going on? Why am I all you've got?"

"I ran into India Barrett at the beginning of May, and I wrote a small piece about her: brave widow, going it alone. I've known her for years. Used to see her at the Stork in the old days. The paper ran it as a feature. I said she wouldn't rest till she found the murderer of her husband. Maybe I got carried away. She had been pestering the cops but they had pretty much drawn a blank. The case is still open, but going nowhere. Then she gets this call. These threats. They told her to forget about her husband's death if she didn't want the notoriety to detract from the memory of her so-called genius hubbie."

"Did they call him that or did you?"

"Well, me. They told her to lay off."

"And she called the police."

"Yeah, but what could they do? She's livid. Then she called me."

"Why?"

"They mentioned me, on the phone."

"Because of the article?"

He told me the story in his best ratta-tat-tat delivery, a mixture of clichés and thirties slang, sprinkled with an argot he invented.

When Mrs. Barrett called Pop, she was distraught. She needed to turn to someone. He had helped her years before, in the forties when one of her pre-Peter Barrett boyfriends had gotten into a snarling contest with one of the hoods who haunted the Broadway scene. Pop had squared it away. India sent him a Christmas card every year. He had written the article. Then his name had been mentioned in the calls. She called him at his office in New York and told him about this telephone assault.

"Some creepolas are doing a number on this grande-dame, buddy boy, two guys doing the old Mutt and Jeff, good guy-bad guy. Three calls. First a maniac screaming at her. Then a few hours later a real smoothie, saying everything's jake, long as it all stays on the Q.T. He was the one mentioned yours truly. 'No leaks,' he told her, 'Especially to Ventry.' Then the maniac, again that night, on the horn with the death threats. Kid, she is unnerved."

"What did they say? What do they want?"

"Mutt finished up with detailed descriptions of what they were going to do to India and me, too, if any of this got out."

"What's that?"

He looked very uncomfortable.

"Well?"

"When Barrett was found in his studio, he had been stabbed twenty, thirty times. Sliced up bad."

"It was awful," Conklin said.

"Whoever it was had probably used a knife with a short blade, maybe two and a half inches long. Like a pen knife. Wasn't found. Now, get this. The autopsy also revealed Barrett had been sprayed in the face with oven cleaner. Nice, huh? The lenses of his eyeballs were destroyed. If he had lived, he would have been blind."

"Jesus!"

"The police never released that information," interrupted Conklin.

"They told the widow, though. Mrs. Barrett told me that the voice on the phone said if we didn't let things drop, well, they would come by and clean our ovens."

"So the callers know this detail," I said.

"Yes."

"So they probably did it."

Pop looked at Conklin. "I admired your father. Hoover used to tell Sherm and me at the Stork what a fine American he was. I hope you take after him. But you're a newspaperman and a damn good one, I'm told. So you see why I sort of have to keep the lid on this one for a while. A word to the wise."

"Got you. *Verbum sap, sat.* Well, if that's the way it is I better go to work. I'll see myself out. Nice talking to you, Vince. Let me know if I can be of any help." We stood up, Conklin threw back his drink, shook hands with Pop and walked steadily enough out the door. Pop and I sat down again. We heard Conklin start up and drive away.

"If he takes after his father," Pop said, "maybe you could give the silverware a quick count."

"What was all that about Hoover then?"

"Oh the old man was a rabid anti-red, okay, but a greedy son of a bitch."

"Calvin worships him," I said.

"Just to be safe, give him a call later, and ask him not to print anything about me being up here."

"Why not?"

"Maybe those telephone maniacs take the *Vigilant*."

"So they're the killers?"

"Nah."

"Why not?"

"They had American accents."

I fell for it. "So?"

"The killer's Australian. Everyone knows that."

2

"Is that all everyone knows? Or does everyone know the name, too?"

"Cyril Hart."

"Just who's this guy, Hart?"

"He was the walker, twenty-five or something, you know, a companion. Mrs. B. had met his father years ago, traveling in Australia with her grandfather. The lad grows up, gets restless and writes to the name on the Christmas card from America. Mrs. B. says, 'Sure, I'd love to see you.' When the boy looked her up, she looked him over and they hit it off."

"Satisfaction at first sight?"

"He'd have a room in her town house in New York, help her with this and that, drive her up here to the Barrett's Kinderhook estate on Fridays and drive her back on Mondays. Peter Barrett stayed up here all the time. Cyril would escort her to dinners, the theatre, gallery openings, down the corner for a pizza, wherever she wanted to go."

"What'd he get out of it?" I asked.

"Five thousand dollars to buy clothes."

"Nice threads."

"A salary of $275 a week."

"Did they haggle?"

"And an introduction to any of her wide range of acquaintances in the social and art world."

"Hey, a fella has to get out once in a while."

"I forgot. You don't like introductions."

25

"Was killing her husband part of the job description?"

"No."

"Then how does everyone know he did it."

"Barrett was working on something to do with Indians, a mural or something and he wanted some books. The kid brought them up. The next morning the caretaker finds Barrett trussed up, hung upside down like a hog, stabbed, and very, very pale from the absence of most of his blood."

"And Hart?"

"Not there. Gone. Absent. But the package of books was there. Even opened. The lad has never returned to pick up his check."

"If he did it, why?"

"Hey, you're good. You should be a detective."

"Okay," I said, "forget it."

"He didn't seem to have an obvious motive. The local constabulary would sure like a chat."

"He never turned up?"

"Nope."

"Why don't you report the calls to the police?"

"I told you that got Mrs. Barrett nowhere. Calls? I told Sonny about them. He said there was nothing anyone could do."

"But what about up here?"

"As you heard, Van Deusen, the local cop, died. Anyway, there might be leaks, and I tell ya, kid, I don't like that business about the oven cleaner."

"Why three calls? Why such different messages? They don't sound very organized.

"That's what's got the wind up, boyo."

"What do they want from her, from you?"

"Silence."

"That all?"

"I have to admit she's afraid. For that matter, so am I. Then, too, she wants the killers punished. Can we count you in?"

"No, I don't think so."

"What do you mean, 'You don't think so'?"

"Just that. Look, this isn't my table. I'm sorry, but leave me alone."

"What would you do if you found me dead?"

"Pull a tear-spattered sheet over you to keep the flies off," I said.

"Can't we talk about this without your smart aleck remarks?"

"We never talked all that much about anything. You said 'Do this, do this, do this'. Then I did something else. Then we yelled at one another. Then you went away. When I grew up, I went away."

We looked at one another for a while. He had gray eyes like me. Took the thrill out of self-portraits, believe me.

"I may be in danger. Help me."

"Why?"

"Why?"

"Pop, you know more cops than a crammer for the sergeants' exam. What do you need me for?"

"Mrs. Barrett knows about you. We've kept up. And after all, she bought your painting."

Carmen. Years ago, I was hitchhiking near Syracuse in freezing weather. This Cadillac stopped to pick me up. After running up to it and getting in, the driver asked me where I was going. I said into town and he said he'd take me in. I saw right away that it was Carmen Basilio, once middleweight and welterweight champion of the world, then retired. I had seen films of his fights, and in my adolescent daydreams I thought I was like him. A tough guy. Basilio. Fighters have styles. Some are quick and rapierlike, men like Sugar Ray Robinson or Muhammad Ali, who move in, pop you and move away before you can react. Then, I once thought, there are the workmen of the ring, pugs like Carmen, and, I hoped, since I didn't have catlike reflexes, me.

I was strong enough for a kid, but slow. What I tried to do was push my opponent into the corner where he couldn't maneuver, practically ask him to wait, then slam away at his body with my right hook to slow him down. If he put his arms up, I would pound them to make him sore and too tired to flick the jab. Unfortunately, while I was trying to do this, the other guy might lack the training to do his part and use his fists to beat riffs like a jazz drummer on my face.

In my first two fights, this didn't matter too much. They were only three rounds, and the guys weren't doing me much damage. I was sixteen, big for my age, and had the tugboat captain's shoulders. I won and thought I was pretty tough. I must have been impossible to live with.

In my third fight, I chased this Italian kid for the first round. He danced in front of me. I jabbed and he slipped it, and stung me with the counter. I crowded him and he spun away. I thought he was scared of me.

In the second, I stalked him, and when I crowded him into a corner, he exploded with a hook to my side that knocked me spinning and stumbling, clear across the ring. When I got up and the ref moved away, he came in again: bam bam, bam bam. He was beating on my face. He opened up my eyebrows and the blood poured over my eyes. They don't hurt that much, eyebrow cuts, but blind fighters aren't all that effective. That's why pros have ringmen who use Monsel's paste, which seals the capillaries by burning them. After I took a wild swing or two, the ref stopped it.

When my cornerman and trainer, an old fighter from Pleasant Avenue in East Harlem named Vinnie, cleaned me up back in the dressing room, I still had some bravado left. "Why'd the ref stop the fight, Vin? I coulda nailed him."

"Kid," he said, "let me give ya some advice. Ya listenin' to me?"

The tough kid nodded through the tears and disappointment.

"I think you should learn to be polite to people."

Looking at Basilio's scarred, lumpy eyebrows behind the wheel of that Caddy, I remembered that night and what Vinnie had said. I told Carmen the story. He looked at me and laughed. We talked boxing all the way into Syracuse. He told me he didn't like the cold. Next time, he said, he'd settle somewhere warm. When I painted him into a picture, "Carmen with Cadillac," I put him and the car under a palm tree surrounded by tropical flowers, like hibiscus and bougainvillaea. That was the picture Mrs. Barrett had bought.

"I think this goes back a long way, kid. I got that feeling. This was no robbery. Who sticks up painters? I think they were after Peter to shut him up about something. Why else are they so scared of us? Look, go down to New York. Talk to Mrs. Barrett. She's in the townhouse. I'll give you the address.

"I guess I owe her."

"Yes, and kid, that's your only sale."

"Notices are good though." He ignored that.

"Yeah. And I figure you for tapped out. Am I right?"

"Maybe."

"Kid, she'd be good for twenty, thirty large."

"Oh, Christ."

"Hey, you need it. Do something for her, like find out who these characters are and where's Cyril and she'll give it to you."

"Thirty thousand?"

"Yes."

A year up here or more. Another show.

"Okay."

"Thank you, son," he said with relief.

"You know, if this does go back a long way, it might have something to do with that sleaze you publish."

"No one ever gets upset about that," he said with a dismissive wave of the hand.

"You have all those files?"

"Yes."

"I might have to look at them."

"That is raw data! Absolutely confidential."

"Hey, I looked through them all the time when I had to go down to your office. Sadie didn't mind."

"I never knew that." He appeared shocked.

"Now you do. I'll need your cooperation. I'll need your knowledge, your contacts if you still have them."

"I got 'em."

"Okay then."

"I knew you would come through."

"Who should I talk to?"

He held his fist up and cocked it, like a coach exhorting his players. "This is the deal. We got something for you. The Hart kid's cousin has come to New York on her own. Showed up in April. She called Mrs. Barrett. Her name is Moira Hart. Go see her, talk to her, she'll lead you to Cyril. Leastways she'd know something. But first you got to get down to New York, talk to Mrs. Barrett, right away. Then the kid's cousin. Maybe they were after him. Who knows? And the rest of this is just a smokescreen. See what Barrett was up to. What kind of people he was involved with lately. Talk to your pal Conklin. And remember . . ."

"Remember what?"

"Word can't get back to Mutt and Jeff? They'd target me. Above all, be discreet. Don't tell anybody you're a detective."

"I'll need a cover."

"Tell people you're writing a biog."

"No, hell, I'm a painter. We can say his wife wants a portrait of him from a photo and I want to get a sense of the guy behind the photo. I'll think of something. You going to stay here or what?"

"No, I'll be going back now." On the porch, as he adjusted his fedora, he turned and offered his hand. "I'm glad you're helping." It was an odd moment for us.

"How's it going these days, Pop?"

"Believe it or not, I'm doing a little PR." This was puzzling.

"Are you allowed to be a flack? I mean do you plug your own clients?"

"Naw, it's not like that. I'm more of an advisor on strategies and such like." He looked at me sideways. "Mrs. B. has me on retainer. I've done a little work for her. It keeps me in prune juice." The only strategy I can remember him planning was always raising on ace, king showing in the Friday night games. "The column doesn't bring in much any more. Syndication is way down." So his interest in Mrs. B. is way up, I thought.

"I might be getting involved in a show, too," he continued. "Mrs. Barrett has a friend who wants to do a musical with Indians or cavemen or something. We get the right people together, we'll do all right. That's what you should have gotten into. At least you could have designed sets or something."

The world of the Broadway musical was an overgrown ego

garden that he had tended devotedly all his working life. I had no interest in it.

"I'm glad you're helping us. You won't regret this." Yes I would.

He walked down the flagstone path, got into the mud-spattered car and drove off.

I wouldn't drink the champagne tonight. At the thought of leaving, the wine would turn to vinegar in my mouth.

3

Mysteries have solutions and so do good paintings. This was in my mind the next morning when I woke up from the bubble dream. It's a bad one. I see a soul, desperate, escaping from the tortured lungs of a drowning passenger on the *Titanic*; it bubbles up through fathoms of the wintry Atlantic Ocean to find a high and dry transmigrational home in my grandmother's Colorado rooming house at the moment she is giving birth. The soundless screams, then the bubbles. I have it after almost every meeting with my father.

I had plenty to do before leaving. The sun was just lifting up over the Taconic hills to the east. The catbirds were mewing in the dense thicket behind the house and outside my window a cardinal was whistling as loudly as a traffic cop in Naples.

I stood in the shower long enough for the small heating tank to send me the cold water message.

In the old days I had a camera bag and a duffel always packed and I could be on my way in a minute. Now I threw enough in a bag for at least a week. I didn't figure on giving it any more. Today was Tuesday, June 7th. In the way of live-stock, there wasn't much that depended on me, just the songbirds in the trees. Lou had wanted to give me a parrot once, but I turned her down.

I wanted to visit the vegetable garden before I left.

Spider webs glistened with dew on the grass. I walked slowly along the paths of the garden, stooping to pluck out quack grass or purslane. I had planted enough in the spring to get me started toward self-sufficiency. There were egg-plants, red cabbages, cauliflower, green peppers, frying pep-pers, potatoes, head and leaf lettuce, opal and small leaf basil plants, bush beans and snap peas, carrots, which were a washout, onions, garlic, asparagus beds, and scarlet runner beans. I had planted chives and parsley. There were my brave Early Girl tomatoes, resistant, I was promised, to every kind of wilt and plague. I had started them from seed in February, keeping the small peat cups moist and turning the plants daily so the stalks would grow straight. They did too. I had painted the garden from two perspectives last week. I didn't want to lose it to the slugs.

Slugs are creepy, unlovable, and eat my seedlings. I hate them. Slimy and skinless and loathsome creatures.

From my garden basket, I took a jar filled with salt. I unscrewed the top of the jar and, taking the smallest pinch between thumb and forefinger, took careful aim and sprin-kled some salt on the back of the largest slug, which contrac-ted at that point, turned color, shriveled, and leaked onto the ground. I spent the next quarter hour carefully searching for slugs, taking care to brush them off plants with a twig before dissolving them.

There were seventy-six. If I were to go back an hour later, the ones I missed would be feasting on the messy remains of these. It occurred to me that where I was going I might need a weapon with more impact than a pinch of salt.

I screwed the cap back on the salt jar, put it into the basket and, after tying the chickenwire gate in place, walked toward the back door of the house.

In the kitchen, I put the basket in the space under the sink. I poured a cup of coffee and sat down on my firehouse chair which I had brought in from the porch. The blond wood of its seat and armrest were worn smooth by generations of sto-rytelling retirees waiting for the alarm. They rubbed it, I'd bet, just before the punchline.

In my workroom and studio, I cleaned my brushes again. I wrapped my untouched canvases in heavy black plastic to protect them from any roof leaks. My finished work was already leaning against the wall, paintside down, in various rooms about the house. I put cellophane on top of the larger paint cans and banged their lids on before placing them beneath the counters. I wrapped the power tools in plastic, put them in their boxes and also set them under the counter. I stacked the stretchers in a corner and swept the floor. I pulled the curtains on the windows. Before turning out the lights, I reached up to open a cabinet built high into the opposite wall. No one ever noticed it. For a handle it had a bent nail and the cabinet's plywood front matched the walls.

"Hide high, Ventry," Jack Giresse's mother, Madame Rachel, had told me years ago. People searching always look down. I suppose it has to do with our primate origins. She acquired her skills when the Gestapo was in Paris. She never told me much about that time. I guess people hide their memories high too. I felt my cameras up there, and behind them a glass jar stuffed with twenty dollar bills, which I now stuffed into the front pocket of my jeans. My passport was there, too, and a key to my safe deposit box in Manhattan. I took down a child's lunch box, with Little Lulu, Tubby and Iggy printed on the side and an Adidas shoe box. Inside the lunch box, wrapped in an oil soaked tee shirt, was a Colt .45 Automatic, the 1911 Government Model. A half-box worth of shells were in a baggie inside a thermos bottle. Some lunch. The gun was designed for the Army by John Browning to deal with Filipinos running amok during our occupation of those islands. The heavy bullet would stop a machete-waving zealot in mid-hurtle and the mechanism was so loose it would fire with half a pound of sand in the works.

It certainly scared the bejesus out of my grandfather F. X. Brunnock's tug crews. My Aunt Helen said he used to wave this cannon around whenever mutiny came up as a topic in the foc'sle in the Lower Harbor. Evidently there's a lot of waiting about in the cold on tugs and, in those days, during the First World War, professional decorum did not forbid getting tanked up on hootch and bashing the skipper about if you wanted to head in for shore and a warm bar. This from the bedtime tales of my youth. New Yorkers see these tugs in the harbor all the time and cherish the myths they create around them and their crews.

When Aunt Helen and my mother moved to New Mexico, they gave me the automatic. When I moved up here, I cleaned it and got a handgun permit from the county. The sheriff gave it to me because I owned land, was likely to vote and Conklin had signed a form claiming I wasn't likely to shoot myself or anyone else. It had no validity in the city. I used the pistol to plink at Pepsi cans and tennis balls. No one could hit a damn thing with it at ten yards and the recoil was too much, even for me, shooting two-handed. Historic, though.

I put the lunchbox with the antique back on the shelf and opened the shoe box where the Smith & Wesson .38 Chiefs Special lay in its holster, two boxes of bullets next to it. Two-inch barrel, nineteen and a half ounces, checkered walnut handle. My Ninth Precinct gun. No romance about it. I put the holster, revolver and shells in my jacket pocket. Back to work.

It was time to call Lou.

I dialed. She answered right away, even though it was just past eight in the morning.

"*Guten Morgen, gnädige Frau.* How are you, painter lady?"

"I am working. How are you?"

"My father was here yesterday."

"Take an aspirin. Drink some water. Go back to sleep. Later, work harder."

"I don't have a hangover."

"Perhaps you are growing up. Your show was good. I hear you sold the Carmen picture." I could hear her red-throated Amazonian parrot, Pedro, shrieking in the background.

"That's why I called. My father wants me to do a favor for the woman who bought it."

"Mrs. Barrett."

"How do you know?"

"The gallery told me."

"Do you know her?"

"No."

"Or Peter Barrett?"

"He is dead. I knew his work. He was past it."

"I'll be coming down to New York this morning to see Mrs. Barrett. Could I stay at your place?"

"Of course."

"I'd like your take on Barrett."

"Don't talk like an L.A. dealer, Ventry. I've had enough of that. You mean my opinion?"

"Yes."

"Could you ask around about Peter Barrett? Maybe someone has heard something."

"I have no time for asking, but should I learn anything, I'll tell you. Some of us are serious about our work. Cheech is more likely to have heard something. I will ask him."

She didn't have a split personality: she had a spectrum personality. In the morning everything was work-work-work with Schubert playing endlessly on the sound system. As the day rolled on, she became more open to the nuances of personal relationships. And when the demands of labor and duty ceased, the party girl emerged. Schubert gave way to the Shirelles. "We'll see you when you arrive, Ventry." She hung up.

I loved her. She loved Cheech. So I loved them both.

It was time to leave. I took one last look around, closed the flue in the fireplace, turned off the water, locked the doors, and threw the bag in the car. I pulled out of the driveway and headed south.

4

Three and a half hours later, at noon, I was on the East Side of Manhattan in front of Mrs. Wentworth Barrett's townhouse, a narrow, unadorned four-story brownstone on 61st Street. It was humid, my clothes were sticky and there wasn't a pond in sight. I had called from the parking lot in Queens where after my three-hour drive I had dropped the car. She was expecting me.

There was an outside set of steps running up to the main entry on the second floor, but I had been told to go through a little gate on the side and walk back underneath the stairs where I found a barred metal gate; above that, a mounted television camera pointed down at me. I pressed the button, and Mrs. Barrett herself answered my ring.

She had been a beauty. Cool, dressed in green silk. About five eight, maybe a hundred and twenty pounds. Not yet sixty, I'd say. Her hair was that snowy white that blondes turn if they're lucky and it was pulled straight back in a bun, framing her ruddy face. She looked something like a Romney portrait of an eighteenth-century general. The chin tuck had been a good job. There wasn't much of a seam and the skin didn't have that Saran wrap tautness. She extended her hand to her newest recruit and said hello. After making sure the gate was closed behind me, and the alarm reset, she led me down a narrow hallway. You could have dropped a plumb line from the back of her head to her heels. We went through a dining room into a large room in the rear of the house. I was dressed appropriately, if she was looking for someone to do the windows. I was wearing blue jeans, a T-shirt and running shoes.

She sat down on the sofa and indicated a wing chair next to the cold fireplace. There was a low mahogany table between us and on it were some blue and white irises, like my own, in a Baccarat vase, and a china plate with small, yellow cakes.

"That's a very beautiful mantelpiece," I said nodding towards the exuberantly carved foliage above the fireplace.

"Thank you, Mr. Ventry. It's a Grinling Gibbons. It was taken in the nineties from the Chalmer's townhouse in Grosvenor Square in the dispersal of Lord Chalmer's estate after he went bankrupt. My great-grandfather was in London at the time on shipping business and learned from Lord Chalmer that the mantelpiece had been made for the Wentworth family's house in Surrey, so we like to think it's at home here. A drink, Mr. Ventry?" She handled the tour guide's recital with as light a touch as Gibbons had with his chisel.

"Something with lots of ice in a tall glass, if you wouldn't mind."

"Gin?"

"A soft drink, or water, please?"

While she went off to the kitchen, I looked at the pictures. There was one long-necked thoroughbred with gleaming flanks by George Stubbs. Most of the other paintings on the walls were nineteenth-century American: merchants and merchantmen, the Wentworth ancestors with their Bibles and their ships which had brought the wealth from the mills of Europe or the China opium trade to the South Street docks.

Above the mantel hung a John Singer Sargent portrait of young girls at a cotillion looking about them proudly, but shyly, the younger girl half hidden in shadow. The Secretary's daughters, I would guess.

On another wall was a William Merritt Chase scene of a mother and two young girls, the sisters again, picking flowers on a breezy summer afternoon on the east end of Long Island. See what you can aspire to? the room asked. One could imagine TR stopping by with Alice for tea and a bully chat about dreadnoughts, comfortable in the surroundings, the appurtenances of old New York. Who would you be if you grew up in a room like this?

There were none of Barrett's works and I didn't think he would have spent time here. No "Carmen with Cadillac" either. The old bruiser wouldn't have made it this far.

She returned with two tonics on a tray, which she set down on the table with grace. Moisture was already condensing on the glasses. She wrapped hers in a napkin, as did I.

"Cheers," she said.

"Cheers," said I. She put her glass down and started crying in big, gasping sobs. I put my glass down quickly and sat down on the sofa beside her. I held one shoulder and patted her on the back.

"It'll be all right," I said. "All right. Everything," and so on. She stopped and sipped her drink. After a sob she brought herself under control. She reached out to adjust the irises. On the ring finger of her left hand was an emerald-cut diamond, half an inch long and a quarter-inch wide, set in platinum. Carats by the tubful. The ring was too large for her finger now and kept flopping to the side. She adjusted it continually as we talked.

"I feel lost and I was terribly upset by the phone calls. I don't know what those men want."

"Just tell me what happened. Tell me all of it."

"You're Vince Ventry's son and you're an artist, like my husband. I have a sense that I can depend on you if you are willing to help me."

"How?"

She paused. The room was still. Dust motes floated in beams of light shining in through the heavily barred French windows.

"Come with me," she said, as if she just then had decided on a plan of action. "Come. I'll show you."

We walked up the stairs. She led me to a rear bedroom, with windows onto the garden. She turned on the lights. Several Barrett canvases hung on the walls.

One was a full-length portrait of a tall, slender young girl, Mrs. Barrett in her golden youth. *La jeunesse dorée*. She was caught in the act of walking quickly along a city street. She is glancing up at the viewer. In her haste and absentminded- ness, she is, in just that fraction of a second, recognizing you and her features are just about, but not quite, moving into a greeting. The buildings in the background are gray and brown, the passersby indistinct, mere shadows. The girl her- self speeds through space, aglow with youth, color and ener- gy.

This was Barrett, early on. Barrett before he changed his style to abstraction. Perhaps his talent was sparked by his feelings for the woman. Now I very much wanted to take a look at his portrait of Conklin's mother. Barrett felt how the body filled space and moved through it. His color was lush. The yellows and whites of her clothes were an explosion out of the drab background.

"I look at that every morning," she said, "and he's here. Do you know what I mean?"

"Yes, I do."

I kept looking at the painting. We didn't look at the other paintings, but, after a while, went downstairs. Mrs. Barrett motioned me to go ahead, so I went back to the sitting room and took my seat again. I drank some tonic. After a few moments, Mrs. Barrett joined me, her face still moist where she had sprinkled water and dabbed at the tears. We sat there in silence for a long minute. I looked out through the barred windows. The view was of the sooty brick of the upper stories of her neighbor's townhouse. A six-foot garden fence lay between them. Finally, she spoke.

"If you help me, I will pay you twenty thousand dollars. If you find my husband's killer, another twenty thousand. What do you say?"

"Yes."

"I'll be back in a moment, Mr. Ventry."

I studied the room. It was designed with power in mind. It was a stage set for the ruling class and had all its decorator icons. It was dusty, in need of a scrubdown, but that room had a lingering jauntiness. Let's say you wanted to meet with the Saudi Minister to OPEC to dress him down, tell him that this cartel business among the producers had been all very well in its day, but we in the West had had just about enough and were going to buy the upstarts out and start running the world again, secure in our position of, harumph, leadership and, ahem, vision. You might do well to choose that room in which to recapture your historic role.

Like the Stubbs, the furniture was eighteenth-century English and museum quality because the directors of museums had their meetings in rooms like this. There were some Hepplewhite chairs, done, I would bet, from Cuban mahogany and not the heavier wood from Honduras the craftsmen had to use later. The chintz cover on the sofa had the faded country house look to it. On a table by the sofa was a pile of books. I noticed several on American Indian art.

Leather-bound books with gilt lettering were lined up in well-oiled rows in the Sheraton breakfront. There was an Aubusson on the floor and, twelve feet above, an Adam ceiling, where the world-inheriting Wentworth eye could amuse itself with the deft plasterwork. The fireplace was framed like a grotto by that lovely limewood mantel.

When she returned, she handed me a thick manila envelope. "Here's the twenty thousand dollars. Just find those men. Stop them."

"Could you tell me more about your husband?"

"I'll try. It's difficult to capture him. His vital essence was overpowering."

"Try."

"A friend of mine once said he reminded her of Sterling Hayden. Do you remember his films? Peter was brash, good-looking and . . . physical. After the Second World War, Peter came back from Europe, troubled, looking for a different way to paint. He told me he had visited Picasso in Paris after the Allies had liberated the city, but Picasso's style wasn't right for him. He had been very impressed by him, though. We met when he came back to New York.

"He seemed to me like a leader of other men in their search. He met some Europeans, like Hans Hofmann. With them he talked endlessly, exploring the possibilities in abstraction." (Just as he helped the Wrights explore the possibilities of powered flight, I thought. Well, he was her husband.)

"Suddenly he was charged up. He would go on for hours about what Pollock had done during the war: giant canvases, like a fist slamming into the paint, my husband said.

"I remember him telling me the new work was strong, like a steel bridge, and that American artists had to be strong. He became fanatically interested in his own physical condition. From that time to the end he lifted weights. His arms, Mr. Ventry, what power in those arms." She blinked back more tears. "He had an accident, slipped on the ice while helping a friend home who had drunk too much. He told me that when he was laid up, he had the time to see his way into a style of his own. He was like an evangelist. This was the new religion. He and de Kooning had raging arguments over the figure on the canvas. What fights they had over that! It was all so exhilarating. Those turbulent nights, so long ago.

"With abstraction Peter could express his inner self: the high voltage tension and the anxiety we were all learning to express in those days. Others understood. He said he felt they had to go beyond technique, to talk to the paint, to make love to the canvas, but he used a stronger expression. This was the best time. We were together. Out of it came one of the most talked about shows of the twentieth century."

"Yes, I heard of it."

She sipped some of her drink.

"And after that, Mrs. Barrett?"

"Peter never stopped experimenting. He tried everything. Picasso was like him in that regard. We would see Pablo and Jacqueline at *La Californie*. Both men were so restless, looking at everything. In the early seventies Peter became passionately interested in American Indian art. Both of us did, actually. I'm on the board of the Dawnwalk Foundation. In fact, I'll be leaving tomorrow for Alaska on foundation business, so I'm glad you could come today."

The rich were nomads and their charities as numberless and remote as the stars in the Milky Way. "I'm sorry." I said, "I don't really know much about the Dawnwalk."

"The foundation is concerned with the earliest American art. We're working toward a museum and a memorial. And," she leaned forward conspiratorily, "maybe a musical. Morgan Kavanaugh is lining up backers. He is so charismatic. But, really, the period, the Indians, everything has been so neglected. We wanted to change this. Peter offered to do a pair of large paintings for the foundation."

"It sounds ambitious."

"Oh, yes. Morgan is the director and has prepared a video cassette that explains it all. I'll give you a copy before you leave. Frankly, it's very promotional. I've handed it out to all my friends. So much needs to be done." Quite, and last year it was the whales, and next year it will be the Amazon forests. All worthy projects, I'm sure.

"Tell me, Mrs. Barrett, who was Cyril Hart, exactly?"

"Oh, Cyril. I'm sure he didn't have anything to do with my husband's death. Why should he?"

"He was there."

"He was delivering a package to him that night, that's all. I asked him to."

"What was in the package? Was it valuable?"

"Some books on American Indian pottery. I assume it had to do with the large paintings."

"Was there any urgency? Any reason why Cyril would go that particular night?"

"October 18th? I don't know why, but Peter had an urgency about wanting those books. No. I wanted Cyril to go up with them and be back in time to take me to dinner with my cousin Hadley, his wife and Morgan Kavanaugh two nights later."

"Peter never explained what the rush with the books was about?"

"No. Perhaps because he was anxious about the new paintings. His last works are still in the studio. I haven't been able to go there."

"I understand."

"You go. Then you'll know what kind of an artist he still was."

"I will." It meant a trip back upstate but I could talk to Jack about his late contemporary while I was there. "Now, Mrs. Barrett, how did you meet Cyril?"

"I knew his uncle in Australia. My grandfather took me there just after the war, some trip connected with the fabric factory. Trevor Hart showed me about. He was quite handsome. He said he had gone to high school with Errol Flynn. Funny the things you remember. He and I got along. Well, anyway, he married and his children are grown. Cyril told his uncle he would like to study here. Trevor wrote to me. I wrote back and told him to tell the boy to look me up upon his arrival, which he did. Cyril hadn't gone to school with any movie stars, but we hit it off. I hired him as an assistant and a companion. My husband was impossible, socially. So great many men are."

"Pardon?"

"I mean so many great men are." Once she sorted out what she meant, she pronounced "great men" as one word, as if the term fit between Capricorn and Aquarius.

"What was Cyril like?"

"He was a polite, engaging, funny, trustworthy scalawag. Pushy, but perhaps that's just being Australian or young. I enjoyed spending time with him. I liked to think . . ." she paused and swallowed. "I liked to think I had something to offer him. Show him possibilities." She made the words sound grand. "Cyril knew instinctively that there was more, just as I had known at his age when I took up with my husband. There was a world, or many worlds, just . . . there." She gestured with her hand toward the hallway. I looked over. There was only the carpet.

"You do know what I'm talking about? And they look so much more lively and exciting than whatever drudgery you've been set to by parents and schools. The wall is low at times," she intoned in a lower voice as if she were quoting, "but there *is* still a wall between."

"Yes," I said. Pausing as if to meditate on all the barriers she had found in her life and what she had to do to cross beyond them, she sat very erect on the edge of the sofa. Good bones. What kind of barriers had she known, I thought, with sudden irritation? What was she doing with this Aussie kid? Did this "scalawag" kill Barrett?

"Did Cyril have any criminal record? Any history of psychiatric trouble?"

"The police talked to Australia. Of course, there was nothing."

"What did your husband think about Cyril?"

"I suppose he liked him. My husband lived only for painting, so he painted. When I was up in Kinderhook, I was content just to be with him. But here in New York, I was alone and I needed an escort. Cyril was fun."

"Your husband was working hard on the foundation paintings?"

"I do know he was on the verge of a breakthrough. Once before in his life he was as sure of himself. In that good time, when he did both that picture of me and started working in the abstract. For years now he had been working like a bricklayer putting up a wall, a thousand bricks a day, twenty-four canvases a year. Just before he died he was on the threshold of something powerful. I know." She looked at me triumphantly: "I'm proud of our relationship. I was his muse, his lover and his friend. He needed space to work. I gave it to him. All that good work is unfinished. I want you to find out who killed my husband."

"I'll try."

"They stole so many of our favorites that night."

"What was taken?"

"A Fairfield Porter, a de Kooning, a Franz Kline, two by Roy Lichtenstein, a drawing by Louise Darmstadt, a painting of Porter by John MacWhinnie and a Lee Krasner. Here, I have some photos of them for you. The insurance company has duplicates." She handed me a small stack of color prints. I glanced at them, whistled at Lou's drawing and put them in my jacket, next to the .38.

"The police have done nothing. 'Cyril,' they say, That boy couldn't have overpowered my husband. Barrett was a man! 'A burglary!' " she shouted, " 'A burglary,' they say. Does a burglar *torture*? 'No leads,' they tell me. 'The case will break when we get a tip off, when someone confesses, when the other paintings come on the market.' Now they don't take my calls seriously." She was winding down. "I'm an old woman." She stopped.

"Mrs. Barrett? How did people feel about your husband?"

"They envied him, the way any man of talent is envied. He didn't care about reviews. He was above them." (I couldn't believe that.) "All he cared about was his work."

"Who do you think killed your husband, Mrs. Barrett?"

"The men who called me, threatening me, telling me not to make any more investigations."

"What do you think happened to Cyril?"

"I sincerely wish I knew."

I didn't know where I was going after this. I needed leads.

"My father said something about a cousin from Australia?"

"Oh, yes, Moira Hart. Trevor's daughter. She wrote to tell me how upset the family were. Then she came to New York to study at Columbia. We talk on the phone occasionally. Naturally she's quite anxious about Cyril."

"I think it might be useful if I talked to her." This seemed to annoy Mrs. Barrett.

"Mr. Ventry, the envelope on that table by your side and your acceptance of it suggest you are the detective, not I. I will give you her number, but you must decide what you are going to do."

"Thanks. And who can I talk to at your husband's gallery?"

"Justin Schreier. He's the owner."

I asked her if her husband had any friends I could talk to.

"My husband was reclusive in these last years. Vietnam upset him terribly. He stayed to himself. He didn't see many of the old gang."

"Who did Cyril see?"

"Well, coming from Australia, Cyril knew few people other than those he met in my company. He did speak of one young man he met upstate who owns a gallery or, no, an antique shop in Hudson. Royal Antiques. Affected, but memorable, Cyril said. His name is Valentine Royal. I have a card somewhere. Perhaps he could help you. Cyril would occasionally drop into his shop. He bought some lovely things, though I don't really have a taste for old farm implements and crocks."

I made a note of the name. "Now this is the hard part, Mrs. Barrett. You are going to have to tell me about those calls you received."

Her narrative didn't add much to what my father had told me. The first caller was gruff, threatening, spoke ungrammatically. The second was calmer. They hadn't mentioned any demands or affiliations with political groups. She was unable to place an accent. If they read my father's article, they must have known Mrs. Barrett was rich, yet there was no demand for money. What did they want? Just silence? Why call attention to themselves?

How would you go about solving a murder? a disappearance?

You would ask all the questions you could. Then you'd think about the answers. Then you'd talk to more people. Jack always said that in painting you should begin with the shadows. I needed to know who might want to kill Barrett, or snatch Cyril, for that matter. That they didn't have too much to do with one another compounded the problem. If it had been a break-in gone wrong and the killer or killers didn't know either Cyril or Barrett beforehand, then the police were right: there was no way to crack the case without a voluntary confession. There had been no stray fingerprints. No hat dropped with the maker's name. No pistol with a traceable serial number. Just carnage.

I didn't have a computer or a police lab, a badge or an informant. What I had was a motive, my own: to live off Mrs. Barrett's envelope for a year or more. I didn't know the killer's.

Perhaps Calvin Conklin might be a good start. He had a fund of information about the area. Then I'd talk to this young cousin. I'd also see if any gossip was knocking around the art world. Jack and Lou might help there.

India and I spent most of the afternoon, poking in the corners of their life together, looking for a grudge, a feud, a name that would trigger a memory of an old injury.

"My father loved it there as a child during Grandfather's term as ambassador,"she said, explaining her unusual name. We dropped the Mrs. right about the time we left the Hepplewhite room and moved to the kitchen where she brewed up some iced tea. I became just Ventry. I asked her where "Carmen with Cadillac" was and she said she hadn't arranged to pick it up. I decided tomorrow I would go down to the gallery and look at my stuff again and find out what the prospects for sales looked like. She didn't know where she was going to be living, certainly not Kinderhook, but she knew she had to get out of this house. I asked her why she bought my painting. She said Carmen looked confident and tough, like her husband, back when they met.

She had lots of stories. Some of Peter's friends are in the art history curriculum now. They were certainly an illustrious company. These days, talents like Lou are the future of American art. At most I'll be a footnote in her biography, just maybe a reference to check in someone's monograph on the first titan of twenty-first century art. What's it matter?

India mentioned Jack Giresse. I told her I knew him very well, that he had been my first teacher. She said he would know the background of her husband's personal relationships in the art world as well as anyone. She said Jack had once worked for him and so would be a good person to talk to.

We talked money. I asked her about the kinds of contracts he had with galleries. I admit I was curious. Handasyde and Beaky took 60 percent from me. But then this was my first show. Because I didn't want to haunt the place, I hadn't been back there since the *vernissage*, a word carrying echoes of the days when painters brought their friends around to the gallery to watch them put the final coat of varnish on the work: Pissarro in from the country, Degas and Manet arguing, the Morisot sisters dropping by with Mama. Now it's just the opening party. Mine was a hoot. Cheech had brought the Moet. Everybody crowded around Lou.

Did India have any contracts? Indeed she did. She had all the papers prepared for me. In addition to the contracts, she had a large file dealing with the estate, and a photographic archive of all of his work, with accompanying notations as to present site and price.

She said Barrett had been obsessed with artist's rights. He said too many painters just had a spoken understanding with their galleries. Not Barrett. He was a demon for written guarantees.

I glanced through the contracts. They were boilerplate with straightforward terms. I didn't think I needed to examine the papers exhaustively. "Did the police go through these?"

"A pair of detectives talked to me, They didn't go through the papers. Their minds, I think, were already made up."

"Were they from upstate?"

"Yes. Van Heusen was the man's name who did most of the talking. No, Van Deusen. He doesn't seem interested any more."

"He died."

"Oh, I'm sorry. Anyway, no one else has been around."

"I see. Did your husband make a will?"

"Of course. I inherit everything. We have no children. My grandfather's interest in man-made fibers has left our family well provided for. There are no trusts. My husband didn't want his work to be a mausoleum for himself. He still had about a hundred of his own works when he died." I thought that was a lot for a successful artist. Sales must have been slow.

"I don't think there will be a Barrett collection," she went on. "The paintings will be sold or donated. Of course his work from the fifties, especially paintings from his first show, the big one, are all in museums or first-rate collections. Peter was eventually going to donate many of his unsold paintings to schools and colleges, and, believe it or not, labor unions, but he hadn't gotten around to it. I will dispose of his life's work the way he would have wished. He was horrified at the debacle surrounding Rothko's estate. The lawyer and I are the only executors. Peter trusted me, and after me, nobody. I trust the lawyer. He's my cousin, Richard Hadley. He and Mr. Kavanaugh will help me arrange a retrospective to benefit the Dawnwalk Foundation. Finally, if I should die before the dispersal, everything goes to the foundation and the National

Organization for Women, but they don't know it. That's about all."

"Did the insurance company send an investigator around?"

"Yes, but Hadley took care of it. They haven't as yet settled on the paintings that were stolen from the house that night. When those men called I thought it would be about them. The insurance company said not to be surprised by the thieves calling and to get in touch with them if they did. This doesn't seem quite what they had in mind though."

I told her I'd call her as soon as I learned anything. She could reach me through Sadie, my father's secretary. She already had that number. She had given me Cyril's cousin's number. She was very tired. I had been there for four hours.

"Perhaps you should hire a bodyguard?" I asked.

"Just a moment." She left and returned shortly with a booksized package holding the Dawnwalk cassette.

"Thanks. Be careful."

"About the bodyguard: If your investigation . . . falters, I'll fly to Geneva when I get back and then check into a health spa. The Swiss Army can protect me. Good night, young Ventry." She kissed me gently. "Get them for me." She saw me out, locking the heavy gate.

5

After I left Mrs. Barrett's house with the cassette and the envelope filled with hundred dollar bills, I stood on the corner, without ideas, plans or clues. It was 4:00 P.M. Cabs approached me slowly, then picked up speed when I made no move to hail them. I had no information and two telephone numbers. First, I walked down Madison till I came to a shop that sold magazines and souvenirs. I bought a canvas I LOVE NEW YORK tote bag for the bulky envelopes. Two hundred $100 bills don't fit in my jeans pocket. There was a phone on the corner, so I walked over and dialed the girl's number.

"Hello."

"Could I speak to Ms. Moira Hart, please?"

"This is she." She had an accent, rich and clear. She sung her vowels into dipthongs: shee-ee.

"Hi. My name is Ventry. Mrs. India Barrett suggested I give you a ring."

"Is it about my cousin?"

"Yes. Can I come by?"

"First, I'd like to check with Mrs. Barrett."

"Fine. The name is Ventry."

"Right. I'll call you back after I speak with her? What's your number?"

"I'm calling from the street. Call this number instead." I gave her my father's office number. "You'll get a secretary, named Sadie. Give her the message and the address."

"Ta."

I dialed the gallery's number.

"Schreier Gallery. Can I help you?"

I said I was calling on behalf of Mrs. Barrett and would like to speak to Justin Schreier. His secretary was polite and got him on the line with a minimum of fuss.

"Mr. Schreier?"

"Yes?" The voice was wary.

"Mrs. Barrett has asked me to clear up a question or two about the estate. Check with her if you like." If I had just told him the gallery rent was doubled, he could not have grown more silent.

Finally he asked, "What do you wish to know?"

"Was Peter Barrett working on anything special when he died?"

"Everything he did was special." He had a precise, almost affected manner of speaking, as if words were precious and had to be husbanded. There was, as well, an undertone of something very like resentment. Maybe someone pissed on his cornflakes.

"Yes, Mr. Schreier, of course everything was special. Do you know of a commission?"

"Commission? No. Six years ago he did a maquette for a steel sculpture. It was, I believe, for the courtyard of an opera house in Brazil, but an austerity program in government put an end to that."

"Nothing recently?"

More silence from him. From the street the shriek of a whistle from a messenger on a bicycle, scattering pedestrians who cursed him as he went by, sack slung behind him, racing cap tilted low over his eyes with the brim turned up.

"Mr. Schreier?"

"You're from Mrs. Barrett?"

"The name is Ventry. Check it out. She's leaving on a trip tomorrow. Call her today and I'll get back to you tomorrow."

"Perhaps that would be best. You understand, I don't know you."

"Of course."

We goodbyed each other. The heat spread up from the sidewalk, baking me evenly. I called my father's office.

Sadie answered on the first ring.

"Vince Ventry's Broadway Beat."

Sadie is a Jewish woman of a certain age, with a silver-haired pixie cut. She is Lennie Bruce shrewd, keeps track of Pop's spies, insiders, tipsters and sources, is master of the archives of secret files, where the adulteries, peccadilloes and bitchy gossip of decades are buried. She types up his notes, and takes care of the calls. To call her a secretary only is to miss the point. They had an affair, once, I'm pretty sure, since I walked in on them before I was old enough to know what it was they were doing.

"Hi, Sadie, is this going to be a good day for me? Are my stars in order?"

One afternoon, alone in the office, decades ago, Sadie picked up a rival newspaper and saw that a daily horoscope had been made a feature. When Pop breezed in, she cornered him and begged him to use his influence with Buckley the managing editor to allow her to do the same thing for their rag. Old Smilin' Jack (he never did) was a pretty strict Catholic and didn't want any part of it, but Pop told him no one took that stuff seriously, so I guess he blessed himself and let it go in. She's still doing it, syndicated too, as "Estrella." She tried to explain it all to me once. It got terribly complicated, with terms of art like "trine" and "ascendant."

One day, when I was about seventeen, I got Sadie angry to the point of tears. I had told her, in my enlightened, unfeeling, self-involved way, that all this sign business, this Taurus and Capricorn crap, was really a form of prejudice. "Supposing you didn't want to be prejudged because you were a Taurus?" I asked, since I was one, born April 29, 1952, just after Pop turned 40. Wasn't it just another form of pigeonholing, like saying all blacks were lazy, all the Irish drunks?

Now, despite the fact she worked for my father, who firmly supported winners of any ilk and was a genuine forelock tugger, Sadie was a definite liberal. She came, she once whispered to me, from a progressive background. She bought Marian Anderson's and Paul Robeson's records. That meant something to her. She gave Christmas presents to her building super's kids. She contributed to every cause that had the words "Peace" or "Justice" in them. If there was one phrase she thought described her, that was "No Prejudice Here." And here I was, Ventry's kid, attacking her favorite sideline as an example of prejudice. Her self-image was crumbling in front of me. Seeing as how she was just about the only person in my father's life who seemed genuinely to like me, I felt bewildered and ashamed at the sight of her in tears. I was too shy to embrace her and comfort her. So I ran away.

I took refuge in Madison Square Park. I sat down on a bench in front of the statue of Chester Alan Arthur. I had my pad with me, and I drew Sadie. Not the sobbing lady I had just left in my father's office, but a confident Joan of Arc with Sadie's face, mounted on a horse, carrying a sword (I had just that week been copying the statue of Teddy Roosevelt in front of the Museum of Natural History) led by two figures, a Black, labeled Justice, and an Indian, labeled Peace. Above her head wheeled the signs of the zodiac, not many of them, in fact not even the signs, just the words I remembered: Taurus, Capricorn, Trine and Ascendant.

I brought the drawing back to Sadie, and that's how I made it up with her. She cried some, and after that we got along better than ever and I didn't tease her any more.

"There are no phones where you live, kid? You didn't want to call your Tante Sadie?"

"I'm calling now."

"Of course, for me to tell you that young English girl wants you to come over."

"Australian."

"Pardon me. She's probably soggy with longing, that one." She gave me the address. "You're working with your father now. That's nice."

"As much as you admire the patriarchal spirit and the concept of the closely knit, mutually encouraging family, Sadie, I am not working for him, nor will I ever. You know that."

"So who's the broad?"

"A source."

"Peter Barrett."

"Well, you would know."
"Oy. Watch yourself, kid. Come by and see me, sometime."
"Right. I'll be in touch."
I hailed a cab.

6

The cab, a veteran of the pot hole wars with no suspension, broken seats and a dirty plexiglass partition, took me up Madison to 96th, then across to Fifth into the park and over to Broadway and then to Riverside Drive where Moira lived. The fifteen-story apartment buildings over on the far West Side of Manhattan were built in the twenties for an affluent class with a hankering for chilly breezes, high ceilings, sweeping views of the Hudson's reaches and sunsets that the industrial output of New Jersey made more dramatic with each passing year. The cab stopped at Moira's address, just a few blocks north from where I first learned the rules of ringolevio and around the corner from the dentist, half-blind, but a friend of Pop's, who repaired a tooth I had broken biting into a frozen solid bar of Bonamo's Turkish Taffy.

The doorman called up on the intercom, and I took the elevator up to her floor. The woman who came to the door of the apartment was tall and lithe, about five-nine, in bare feet. Her eyes tilted delicately upwards at the corners like Modigliani's sad-eyed models. She had dark curls cascading around her head. She was dressed in close-fitting, faded jeans, which favored her rounded hips, and a peach-colored silk shirt.

"G'day," she said, and proffered her hand, which I shook. "Won't be a sec. I thought we'd go for a bit of a walk."

"Not a walkabout?"

"Them's the blackfellas. We're for the promenade. Do you want to leave your tote here?"

"I thought I'd keep it with me."

"Fine." She went into the apartment and came back immediately with keys and shoulder bag in one hand and in the other a light, salmon-shaded sweater and a pair of leather-thonged sandals, which she dropped at her feet and then stepped into.

"Hold me jumper," she said and thrust the sweater at me. I took it and she turned the keys in the apartment's two locks and took back the sweater. "Ta," she said, and put it in the shoulder bag along with the keys. Her movements were quick and confident.

We took the elevator back downstairs and then crossed the Drive to the strip of park that ran along the river. It was a cloudless day, with the New York sky, for once, a limitless blue. The heat shimmered in waves above the blacktop of the road. Kids were playing softball on the narrow patches of grass; anybody who grew up here learned to hit straight away. A jogger with a bandana tied around his head and a belly hanging over his shorts came by us slowly, sobbing for breath, running in a kind of imaginary sand pit he could never escape. Mothers pushed canvas strollers with happy babies and straggling toddlers along the paved walkway. Out on the river a tug with a big letter M on the smokestack towed a barge upstream.

"Mrs. Barrett said you were working for her. What do you want to know about Bulk?"

"Is that what you called Cyril?"

"Bulk is what his mates called him, being on the small side."

"I'm sorry, Ms. Hart, about your cousin. I feel kind of awkward asking these questions. I'm only doing it as a favor to Mrs. Barrett."

"I understand. Call me Moira, if you like. She said you were a decent sort. I've gotten to the point where I feel like talking about him again."

"Have you heard from him?"

"No."

"Do you know where he is?"

"No."

"Do you know anyone who can get in touch with him?"

"No."

"Mrs. Barrett doesn't believe Cyril killed her husband."

"I don't either."

"If he came forward he could help us find those who did it."

"Do you really think so?" she asked. "You don't think he had an argument with Peter Barrett and killed him?"

"I don't know. If he didn't do it, why'd he run?"

"Perhaps he was taken?"

"Can you tell me something about what he was like?"

"Sorry?"

"Did he have many friends? Did you know them?"

"Bulk had rafts of mates and he was always at the center of the clique. I knew the crowd in Hobart, that's where we're from, but as for his Yank friends, well, I haven't a clue."

"Hobart? In Tasmania?"

"You're not wrong."

She had a quirky way of speaking. Not only were the rhythms unfamiliar but the expressions, too, made me mentally blink.

More joggers came by, probably students from Columbia and Barnard. All wore headbands, some had stereo headphones, and their eyes looked inwards as they pounded along in the heat.

"How long have you been here?"

"This April. I've been accepted in a grad program in Columbia. To study language theory. The apartment belongs to a professor at Columbia. I rent a room from him. He's gay."

"Tell me, how long has Cyril been in the U.S.?"

"A year and a half. He got along with Mrs. Barrett right away. She gave him some money every week to help with her papers and things."

"Yes, I know that."

"He spoke sometimes about this bloke who was finding him some work off the books. He liked America. Mrs. Barrett was going to use her contacts in the State Department to find some way to help him stay."

"What was the name of the man Cyril worked with?"

"He's an art dealer of sorts, somewhere out of town. Up the river I think. His name is Royal. Cyril mentioned him in a call he made at Christmas. Must have cost, that."

"Mrs. Barrett mentioned him too. Did Cyril ever explain his business with Royal?"

"No. Cyril could be secretive sometimes. He was fond of games. So am I, I reckon."

"Would you mind telling me about your family?"

"My father met Mrs. Barrett when he was very young, just after the war. The first civilian job he had was driving Mrs. Barrett's da about. The connection between the families goes back a long way, see. We'd never harm the Wentworths. Nor Peter Barrett."

"Are Cyril's parents still there?"

"Killed in a car crash in '82. My own parents were divorced. My mum runs a shop, antiques and crafts, near the Salaman-ca market in Hobart."

"Mine does too, in the Southwest."

"Anyway, Mum married again to a bloke who teaches an-thropology at the Uni. Da left Tazzi when I was eight, but Bulk and I would see him on holiday. Once Da took us to Green Island on the Barrier Reef in January. That was fun. Snor-keling and feeding the stripey fish among the coral, sun bathing. We all decided to become surfies. That was the last fun Bulk and I had together. That was about two years before he came to America. Da died since."

"I'm sorry." We walked along under the oaks. Squirrels looking for a handout kept a wary eye on us from ten feet up on the trunks.

"Why did Cyril leave Australia?"

"Oh, Bulk just wanted off the bloody island. If he hadn't hooked up with Mrs. Barrett, he probably would have gone to England. Most of us do. Go to the U.K. rather than the States." She looked at me questioningly, as if she were unsure wheth-er or not to explain the reverse emigration habits of her countrymen.

"To Earls Court," I said, naming a section of London well known to be a magnet to Aussies. "Vans. Backpacks. Hostels. Beer drinking, sunburned Australians singing in the streets." And throwing up on the sidewalks, I could have added.

"And chundering in the footpaths," she added, reading my mind. "The old stereotypes take a long time to die, don't they?"

Moira Hart's background and her speech suggested someone confident in herself, a bit saddened, maybe, about her cousin, but outgoing, not conspiratorial. Her firm, ample figure suggested fleshly wickedness in all its baroque forms, and her eyes in the June sunlight were a green that reminded me of the leaves in my garden, just unfolding.

Couples were stretched out along the grass by the path, entwined in themselves, waiting for a breeze from the river.

"Let's go somewhere we can sit down and be cool," I suggested, though to have offered to go somewhere to lie down would have been more in line with the current of my thoughts.

"Is there a pub nearby?" she asked.

"We'll find one. Have you eaten?"

"I could do with a meal."

"Let's go then." We started walking up to Broadway. "Did Cyril mention any hangouts, any pubs he liked to go to?"

"No, I'm sorry."

We found a bar on Broadway with good sirloin hamburgers, ice cold German beer and air conditioning that worked. It was the first drink for me in over a year. I decided to have another. There was a news show on the television above the bar. It was called "Live at Five" and the broadcasters smiled and flirted with one another. The jukebox was silent, but, after my second beer, tempting.

After eating we got back onto the subject of her cousin.

"If I sound too much like an interrogator, Moira, I'm sorry. I have to begin someplace."

"No lie."

"Can you remember the last time you heard from him?" Her eyes filled with tears. She blinked furiously, then took up a napkin and wiped her eyes.

"Yes. Another call. He said he was getting along with Peter very well.

"You see he was really supposed to be working as a sort of driver or secretary to India. But as I say, he remarked on his good relationship with Peter."

"What did he say?"

"He hoped he could persuade Mrs. Barrett to spend more time with Peter up in Kinderhook, so he could stay there, or else make an arrangement where he would stay with Peter. Also he liked the area, and he had a mate up there, this Royal."

"Why did he want to stay close to Peter?"

"He said Peter was going to start on an important project that was going to be very prestigious. It would bring Peter back in the public eye."

"Did Cyril know what he was talking about?'

"No, not really. Somebody else would have told him that and he would remember. He wouldn't have a notion of what the American public would want."

"Mrs. Barrett sensed he was working on something new."

"Did she tell you what it was?"

"No, did Cyril?"

"No. He mentioned something about Alaska and the sun-rise."

"What?"

"Since you called first, I've been trying to remember my last conversation with Bulk. We didn't talk very long. I don't think he mentioned coming back to New York or taking a trip with Mr. Barrett. In fact, as I said, he seemed to want to stay up in Kinderhook. But I recall he did say something about Alaska and the sun. Jogging in the sun, maybe? I don't remember. You septics jog all the time. I suppose even in Alaska in the morning."

"Us 'septics'?"

"Oh, you know. Tanks, rhymes with? Aussie slang for you lot."

I ordered two more beers. The TV sound was off, but the picture stayed on: a balding politician in shirtsleeves kept shaking his head behind a lectern he was gripping with both hands. Madonna was singing on the juke box, explaining to those unfamiliar with the story what her boyfriend made her feel like. I love the classics.

"Alaska. This project had something to do with Alaska?" I asked.

"I don't know, really. Perhaps I misunderstood. "What are you going to do, cobber?"

"Copper?" I said surprised, "How did you know I was a cop once?"

"I didn't. Were you?"

"Yes, for a couple of years. A long time ago. We can talk about it sometime."

"All right," she drank some of her beer. "I said 'cobber.' What are you going to do, cobber?"

"What the hell is a cobber?"

"Like a digger, but better."

"Oh. I'll drink to that." We did. "I'll find them." I said, "I'll find the ones that did it, see, and then they'll be found."

"No lie," she said.

"I'll find Cyril for you, too. Ask me how I'm going to find them?"

"How are you going to find them?"

"I'm going to ask questions everywhere. I'll talk to Barrett's gallery. See what's on the art world jungle telegraph about a big Alaska commission. Maybe it's their centennial or something. Upstate, I'll drop in on my old art teacher, see if he has heard anything. See this Royal."

"Are you an artist?"

"You can't tell?"

"Don't be cheeky. What is it you do, Ventry?"

"I paint. I garden. I resent my father."

"What about your father?"

"I resented him this morning for taking me away from my hillside. Right now I'm reconsidering."

"What does your father do?"

"He writes a gossip column for a New York newspaper— Vince Ventry's Broadway Beat."

"And you say he got you into this?"

"Mrs. Barrett asked for his help. He came to me."

"And this hillside of yours, is it good for gardening?" she asked.

"Well, you never have to reach very far for a rock."

"And for resenting?"

"Cold, hard, stony ground."

"Da liked to garden. Keen on it, he was."

The waitress brought us beer number six.

"And what do you reach for on those cold nights up there? A sheila and a Bud?"

"A pencil and a sketchpad. A book. I never get tired of books. There are libraries in Chatham and New Lebanon and bookstores in both places. People around there read a lot. It gets dark early."

"It sounds totally hedonistic."

"Not really. Sometimes I wake up in the middle of the night so depressed, angry and frustrated I want to take a rifle and go off and shoot up my past. Just blow it to hell. In the morning, sitting at the window with a cup of coffee, everything is calm, the fog drifting in the valley, the mist rising from the pond, sometimes wild turkeys, or deer, edging out of the woods, stopping for a drink."

"Do you get these midnight horrors often?" she asked.

"I used to get them all day long, when I was . . . well, working at jobs I should have not taken on. Now just sometimes, at night mainly."

"Good."

"Yeah."

"What's your painting like?"

"It's like me. Sometimes it's all shot up. Sometimes it's relaxed. Thanks to Jack Giresse, my teacher, I know something about how to draw and how to do what I want to do."

I reached over to an adjacent, empty table and took a paper napkin from an unused place setting. From my pocket I took a felt tip pen and slowly drew the pen across the paper; letting it bleed in where I wanted it to, and sketching quickly for thinner lines, I drew a caricature of Moira, the curly hair tumbling about her head, the eyes uplifted in the corner, the straight nose, the mouth, rich and full as a Rosetti. The Pre-Raphaelites left out the beer bottle as a rule. I didn't. Signing it

"Ventry," I passed it over to her, saying, "Just the thing to send back to Ma."

"Is this you, 'relaxed'?"

"It's a trick I learned from Giresse. It's kept me in beer."

She signaled to the waitress for another round and carefully folded the napkin and put it in her bag.

"Is that all you paint? Girls in pubs?"

"I paint what's in front of me. And sometimes what I think should be in front of me. Paint's funny stuff all right."

"Crikey, you're an odd one and that's no lie." More beer arrived.

"I give it orders and it shapes up, see?"

"You sound like a regimental sergeant major."

"I just flail away with the brushes, just to see what comes out."

"Now that sounds like anarchy."

"Why, bless your heart. You know what the hardest part is?"

"Knowing when to stop?"

I gave her a sharp look. "No, I can walk away from anything. Mixing color. You don't do it right, you get mud. Gobs of goo. Really, you need a degree in chemistry. Jack taught me what I know. *Cher maître*. You got to know mixing. That's it."

She took my hand in hers. "Your hands are strong but the skin is rough and the nails are chipped." I lifted her fingers to my mouth and kissed them.

"You're sweet, Ventry."

"Thanks."

"What's your first name?"

"I don't use it. Ventry's okay."

"Why?"

"When I was a teenager hanging around Jack Giresse, he always called me Ventry. Made me sound like an adult."

"Did you do anything else besides be a cop and paint?"

"Lots. I was a photographer."

"What kind of photographer were you?"

"For a news magazine." I sipped my beer. "You could say I was a tourist, like everybody else."

"What do you mean?" She looked puzzled.

"The places I went to take my snapshots with my Nikons just happened to have teenagers shooting each other at pointblank range with anti-tank weapons and AK-47's. So much for the poetry of the camera."

"A bummer, eh, Ventry?"

"One afternoon," I went on, "After ten years of it I woke up with a hangover in Atlantic City. Nothing unusual in that, but, God, this was awful. At first, I didn't notice the bruises on my head where I hit the table the night before, after I passed out the first time. When I looked in the mirror, the blood vessels in my eyes seemed to have ruptured, probably from heaving so hard."

"This is so romantic," she said. "You sound like Bulk and his mates talking about the night they won the Shield Final. So right for this moment. Do go on."

"Shield? Anyway—and that reminds me I have to ask you questions—my stomach was bilious and my head envied my stomach. Guilt showed up, of course, followed by self-pity. Some of my memory of the evening's festivities never returned."

"You certainly lived a glamorous life."

"The last thing I recalled was Hyland, this writer I'd been with, saying 'And then we crashed the car.' He said 'cah,' he was from Boston, 'and then we crashed the cah for the second time,' and I couldn't remember whether I had been *in* the car that had these crashes or whether he was just *telling* me about it."

"I see. Binge drinking, you decided, is bad for you."

"So I had a good think. I decided I don't like photography. I didn't like travel. I had spent too much time in airports to do it sober any more. And I didn't want to see any more kids with bellies distended from hunger, and scrawny little necks, and big eyes and hair falling out, selling me cigarettes, one at a time, or fruit, either. My capacity for indifference had eroded in a major way. To go on would have been suicide."

"You sound like you had given it a good try with the grog. What about your work, your friends?"

"Work was shit. My colleagues would do anything rather than grow up. We did drugs together and we drank together, got laid and were bored together. They weren't like me and I was becoming like them. Their egos would survive the grind, like cigarette butts. Useless, white and indestructible."

"Clever that. Were there any women on these trips?" She was casting her net.

"Yes. There were the whores. The wives, those I never saw, except the ones of American officials. I never even knew them. They have their own life, you know. The magazine didn't want any pictures of a swank house with servants cutting the lawn in El Salvador or serving the drinks in the Phillipines. That wasn't the story. The nuns were good people. I liked the nuns."

"All the nuns I knew at home were Irish and elderly."

"Yes. The best. Here's to the Irish and elderly ones. I met a lot of them. And young Americans and middle-aged French women. These people saw too much. What do you do when a jeep filled with soldiers rolls up in front of the little school-house you and the villagers built, jump out, grab the teacher, throw him on the ground and shoot him in front of the students and then drive off? Who you going to complain to? What kind of civics lesson did the kids just learn? Still they stayed and kept their mouths shut. Pretty much."

"I thought of being a nun once."

"Yeah? I painted a picture of them, the nuns. I'd like you to see it. It's in a gallery downtown. Handasyde and Beaky, will you remember that?" She nodded. "Will you go?"

"If you want. Yes."

"Here."

"What's this?"

"A card the gallery makes up as an invitation to an opening."

"And this fella?"

"A boxer I once knew."

"This is very good," she said.

I took the card from her, and wrote on the back "To Moira, who listens," and signed it, "Ventry."

She smiled when she read it and put it in her bag.

"After Atlantic City?" she prompted.

"Two years in San Francisco doing, well, a bit of this and a bit of that. Some painting. Then back to New York. I went to work for Lou, more about her later, but she is a great friend. Grand. The best."

"Did you see your father while you were in New York?"

"No way."

"So what did you do?"

"I ran away from stuff for so long. When I worked for the magazine, I was running away from New York, from my father. Now I was running away from chaos and stupidity and trying not to care when the Pulitzers were announced and I didn't get one, and other people's pain and hungry kids, dead kids. The third bloody world. No one is in charge out there, you know that? I couldn't deal with it. I ran out to the coast."

"Makes sense to me, cobber."

"Right. It wasn't self-pity."

"Oh no," she said with an ironic note and a bemused look.

"Really. It seems everything I had ever done up to then was accomplished while I was on the way to do something else. Offhand. It was safer in a sense that way. Things didn't fall together for me there so I figured it was time to hit the road again. I came here and I worked with Lou, until I could think of something I wanted to sit in one place and do. I decided that was painting. It seems to be. Then Pop found me and called me back. And, right now, I'm glad." I took up her hand to give it what was to be a gallant, sweeping kiss, but I'm a bit of a lummox and I banged her knuckle on my front tooth.

"Ee-ow." She grabbed her hand back.

"Sorry."

She sucked the back of her hand. There didn't seem to be any blood. She looked up at me and laughed.

"Well, what now?" she asked.

"I just got to the point where I was doing serious work and getting some recognition, and my father waltzes in with his story and here I am, and you know, maybe I did the right thing coming down here."

"I meant *now* now."

"Oh."

"Let's go back to my place. The professor has gone to Fire Island for the weekend."

"Fine." I paid the waitress with one of the Barrett hundreds, left a twenty as a tip for taking up the table for so long. We stopped off at a deli for more beer and I called Lou from a pay phone and told her that I'd stop by the next afternoon. We walked to Moira's apartment. We sat on a couch in the living room to watch the river traffic, the gulls sailing by and the sun going down over the Palisades. I took off my shirt and she took off hers. Her breasts were not large, but firm and white, with delicate blue veins and rose nipples, lovely to the touch. We caressed one another. "Ventry," she said. We kissed and stroked.

"Stay the night?" she asked.

"Yes," I said.

"Come on, then."

I followed her into her bedroom, which overlooked the building's interior airshaft. We took off the rest of each other's clothes and hugged each other tightly, before falling on to the bed, a mattress on the floor. Where she straddled me and put me inside her. I kneaded her breasts, luminous in the light filtering in from other apartments, and I rubbed her flat, sweaty stomach, as she throbbed and rocked above me, crying out, quivering, then I held her buttocks tight, holding her close to me, till I released myself inside her, and she sobbed and fell forward to lie on my chest. And that was my first night with Moira, who asked me many questions and answered few of mine.

7

The next morning, I was awakened by Moira, kneeling by my side in a blue chrysanthemum pattern kimono wrap, holding a large, white mug of steaming tea.

"Wakee, wakee. It's Wednesday morning. Up you come, mate."

"Hi," I said. "What time is it?"

"Just gone seven," she said.

I took the mug. The tea had milk in it and tasted sweet and strong. She watched me sip.

"It's good," I said, and I reached through the opening of the robe and touched her thigh. Soon, I put the cup down and we were making love again. The pleasure of touching her body chased last night's alcohol down into my nerve endings, raw as a sunburn, then we lay entwined, not quite ready to begin the tentative process of finding out how we fit into one another's lives.

"The shower"—she pronounced it "share"—"The share is through there," nodding toward the bathroom door. The water was hot but the shower curiously lonely. What's happening? I asked myself. The hot spray on the back of my neck didn't answer.

As I dressed back in her room, I heard her banging pans and cabinet doors in the kitchen. On a bureau was a family photo in a wooden frame. Cyril, I guess, and Moira. She was about twenty-two or three now, but was more slender in the photo, still somewhat girlish. Her father stood between them.

It was taken on the beach and the three of them are squinting into the sun, looking freckled, healthy, cheerful and Australian. Cyril was a good-looking kid, a bit impish, as if he were going to play a trick on the others. Moira called me.

I went into the kitchen and sat down at the formica table next to a window that opened onto the airshaft. She dished out buttered toast, a fried egg, bacon and grilled tomato.

"Nothing. Please." I said, "Don't eat much in the morning."

"Nothing?" she asked.

"Thank you, no."

"Well, I'll just put this lot to warm in the oven in case you change your mind." The kitchen was becoming suffused with domesticity, but she was beautiful in the morning in a cotton kimono, and I had been alone on my hillside for months. I drank more tea.

"What'll you do then?"

"I'll speak to people who knew Peter."

"While you were asleep I had some ideas."

"I noticed."

"Listen, you."

"Okay." If I smoked, I would have lit a cigarette and looked wary and thoughtful and a bit amused, too.

"Let's for starters say that the blokes we're looking for could have been after either Cyril or Peter, and one or the other got in the way."

"Why?"

"Because, they only knew each other for a short time and Cyril was spending almost all his time with Mrs. Barrett. We can't exclude one or the other as a target."

She looked at me from across the table, her left hand clenched tight in a fist, "Bloody hell, no one would want to hurt Cyril. He was a harmless fun-loving boy."

"Maybe he knew something . . ."

"He couldn't tell you the time, that one. I reckon his head was filled with dreams and fantasies. He had found the perfect layabout job, a companion for a rich, old lady. God, but he was wonderful, useless, but not a villain."

"What did he study?"

"Cyril sort of . . . hovered around the Uni, very popular, but didn't do a thing."

"Oh."

"Maybe we should talk to this Royal fella."

"Yes, *I* should," putting some stress on the "I."

"And the police up there," she continued blithely.

"Yes, I'm afraid so. Tell me, did Cyril write you any letters, gossiping about his employers, his new friends?"

"No, just the call now and then."

"What happened to his stuff?"

"I picked it up from Mrs. Barrett. Mostly clothes and shoes. Very fine they are too. It's all back there in my room if you want to look. I still think he'll walk in here some day. I kept the wallet and the passport. But I don't like the idea," she said in a louder voice, "of the lot that did him still muckin' about."

"Did him?"

"Took him or . . . whatever."

"I can understand that."

"Who collected Peter's paintings?"

"I don't know."

"Find out and talk to them."

"Good idea. I guess I should look at newspaper clippings about the murder before I talk to the police. I can get them from a newspaperman I know upstate."

"When will that be?"

"Today or tomorrow."

"Make your calls. Find out who was buying his pictures. Call your artist friend and whoever else you can think of. I have an idea of my own. I may have something for us, but it means I have to go out."

"When will you be back?"

"In an hour or two. You look pretty seedy. You won't leave, will you? Drink more tea." She went into her bedroom, and when she came back a few short moments later, she was dressed in jeans and a white cotton tank top with a tan linen blouse over one arm and a small, red nylon knapsack over the other. She was wearing flat leather sandals. Her eyes were hidden behind large, smoky sunglasses.

"I'll just switch the answering machine on. No need for you to take any calls."

"Right."

"Ta." She hesitated and then gave me a quick kiss.

"Ta, Moira."

I started sawing away at the fried egg but gave it up after a while as a bad job and munched some toast instead. I picked up the plate and carefully emptied the contents into an orange and white paper bag, from Zabar's Deli, by the sink, which I then put in a larger green plastic bag and tied off with the little wire that comes attached. I washed the dishes and mug in the sink and put them in the drying rack. The weather from the airshaft looked sunny, and the clock on the oven said 8:42. Time to crack the case.

In the living room, I sat down under a print of Larry Rivers' collage of Frank O'Hara in the nude, the poor, dead, young poet of the jazz clubs and galleries, "made in the image of a sissy truckdriver," he had written about himself, run over while he was sleeping on the beach, a clan totem of the lads around MOMA. I threw him a salute, and dialed Lou's number.

"Yes?"

"Lou, this is Ventry. I'm sorry we couldn't get together last night."

"You had a better offer?"

"Sort of."

"You took precautions, eh, Ventry? You were not impulsive."

"Again, sort of. Look, did you find out anything?"

"About Barrett?"

"Yes."

"I had heard there was something macabre about his death, so for you I asked around: some real types, the ones into chains, candles, feathers, and blood. I had to tell them who Barrett was. Not a smidgen of a rumor. Nothing.

"All the people I asked agreed he did some good work once. Since then . . . he was perceived as declining. Perhaps, now that he is dead, there will be a retrospective."

"Mrs. Barrett still has a lot of his pictures."

"That must be a great comfort for her." It was impossible to tell if Lou was being ironic in her early morning Teutonic mode. "There has been little interest among the important New York collectors in Barrett for some years."

"Who are they?"

"Oh, Ventry."

"C'mon, tell me, I don't know these things."

"Selma Marks, the Mahjoub brothers, Karl Fischthal and his wife, Grete, people like that."

"Don't know 'em."

"That is their misfortune. Now, I must feed Pedro and go back to work." She hung up.

I dialed the Schreier Gallery to see if the owner would talk to me today. The recording told me he wouldn't be in till 10. After dressing, I looked over the roommate's record collection. He was very fond of voice. Over a foot of Janet Baker records, almost as much Marilyn Horne, Peter Pears, lots of Bach cantatas and a few show tunes, Judy Garland, mostly, and Liza. I didn't play anything. I was in the mood for smokey saxophones and sixties cool jazz and he was fresh out. I tried the gallery again.

"Hello?" It was Schreier.

"This is Ventry. I called you yesterday about Peter Barrett."

"Yes, I spoke to Mrs. Barrett and she asked me to cooperate."

"Thank you."

"Well?"

"Can you tell me about Peter Barrett. What was his state of mind, for example, the last time you spoke."

"We spoke just prior to the . . . umh . . . before he passed."

"Yes."

"He said his health was good, and he thought he might still surprise people."

"What did you say to him?"

"Me? I told him we looked forward to a show of all new work in the fall."

"And?"

"He said he did, too." Fine.

"Did he talk about what he was working on?"

"Not precisely, no."

"Well, thanks. Who's been buying his work?" I asked bluntly, thinking of what Lou had told me.

"He's in the most important collections. There's a waiting list for his pieces." Mr. Schreier was hustling me.

"What about a retrospective of his work? Lot of interest there?"

"Undoubtedly. A major effort. I see a multi-city, traveling exhibit. Get a first-rate catalogue together. But not right away, I wouldn't think. Perhaps next year. I've written to the Whitney. They've got a knockout piece from the fifties. God, he was hot then. But, the time has to be right." His voice drifted off, maybe he was taking notes on himself.

"I see. Thank you, Mr. Schreier."

"You know. . . ."

"What?"

"It's probably nothing, but he asked if I knew any American Indian artists."

"Do you?"

"We don't usually show any American Indian artists. It's a specialized field. Anyway I couldn't help him."

"Then why did he ask about American Indian artists?"

"I'm sorry, I'm at a complete loss."

"Thanks for your help, Mr. Schreier. If you think of anything else, would you give me a ring?" I gave him Sadie's number.

"You're Vince Ventry's son."

I almost said, 'What's it to you?' but he had been helpful. "Yes, we are related."

"And that was your show at Handasyde and Beaky?"

"Yeah. Have you made it down there?"

"Yes, I have. Mr. Ventry, I liked your work. Should you ever be up here, drop by. We'll have a talk."

"Thanks, I'll do that." We said goodbye and hung up.

Moira's absent roommate had a coffee bean grinder in the kitchen. I found the beans in the fridge and ground them up, which made a noise like a cement truck. I boiled the water and poured it onto the ground up beans in the Melitta filter. Then I realized the professor also had a television and a VCR. I went into the bedroom, found Mrs. Barrett's cassette and brought it back. At that point Moira breezed back in. She had been gone about an hour and a half. "You look better, mate. Well, I may have some information for us."

"Oh?"

"First you."

"I pretty much struck out. Lou, my friend, hadn't heard anything. I called the gallery, the dude over there didn't know much. He said Barrett asked him about Indian artists, but he doesn't know why."

"Did you ask him who the big collectors of Barrett's work are?"

"No."

"Why not?"

"Because I forgot."

"Oh, crikey, you need a keeper, you do."

"Where'd you go?"

"To the University. I went to Avery library, and made some inquiries about their holdings, specifically anything to do with scholarly writing on the works of Peter Barrett." Reaching into her knapsack she took out some sheets of paper, "Here is the verdict on his life's work," she said. "I photocopied the three articles the librarian found for me."

"Librarians were never so helpful for me."

"He's from Brisbane," she said, matter of factly.

"We're not going to read this stuff, are we?" I asked plaintively.

"Listen to yourself. You almost sound Australian. Did you spend your childhood watching telly and scratching your toes?"

"I never watch it. I prefer renting old movies. Does this VCR work?"

"Yes, but all we have at the moment are gay blue movies. Not much fun for you, mate."

"Let's watch the video India Barrett gave me." I found the power switch on the VCR and pushed. A cheery red light came on. I turned the TV on and inserted the cassette, and we sat back on the couch to watch.

The tape opened with news footage of the centennial celebration of the Statue of Liberty. It was well edited, had good production values and a lively sound track. I saw the president, the aircraft carrier, the celebs, the Blimp race and the fireworks. Took about thirty seconds. Then a voiceover:

"This is what New York Harbor looked like the day before Henry Hudson sailed into the Upper Bay on the Half Moon." Quick cut from the teeming multitudes to an empty harbor: no ships, no buildings, not a blimp in sight, only the gulls wheeling above the surface of the water. Then a shot of a wisp of smoke, curling upwards. It was a very effective transition. Again the voice over.

"Native Americans—Indians, if you like—lived on this continent for ten thousand years before the Europeans came. Who remembers them? What monument marks *their* coming?"

Cut to a craggy faced, gray-haired man, almost gaunt, with jet black eyebrows, dressed in a dark blue suit and red tie, leaning against a desk in what appeared to be a library. To his right there were some bookshelves with a couple of ceramic pots and what looked like a peace pipe. To his left was a large map of North America.

"Hello, my name is Morgan Kavanaugh." He spoke with an accent that was hard to place.

"Is this guy Australian, Moira?"

"Nah, a pom . . . no, I'd say Irish who went to a posh school. Would know his way around Mayfair, this one. What is this thing?"

"It's supposed to raise money for some project Mrs. Barrett's hot on."

"If you love the fruits of this good earth of ours, if you revere the past, if even in the worst times, you have a secret, ungrudging hope for the future, why not give me a few minutes of your time? I think you'll be interested in what I have to say."

Kavanaugh spoke well. He was a spellbinder. You would not only buy a used car from this man, you'd go to work for him. He had gray blue eyes, that he used to draw the viewer to him. His voice flowed out over us, telling us in its tone that there was no better place in the world to be right now than right here, listening to what he had to say. Its accent was exotic, but comforting, like a doctor who got his degree in miracles, and no, my friend, you don't have cancer. He was right up there with the best: Ronald Reagan, the host of Wheel of Fortune, my father in a nightclub.

He would look stern, then mournful, hope would creep across his face and then he would relax and smile at us. He used emotional effects like the diapason of an organ.

During his talk, the tape would occasionally cut to another scene. When it came time to use the map, he didn't use a pointer, but rather his long, expressive fingers forced our eyes to wherever he wanted them. During the time he spoke, he had us mesmerized, like children at a magic show. Moira didn't say a word.

"Tonight I want to talk about history and geography. Our species has been at its work for at least 30,000 years. Seven hundred lifetimes, as someone put it. Where is the history of that, eh? Who are these people that were our grandfathers? Who remembers them?" He paused. No one raised a hand. "Who wants to?" The silence was intense. Even I was tempted to talk to the TV and say, "I do," but I was always one for sitting in the back of the classroom and keeping quiet.

"I want all of us to remember them, and I want to create a series of memorials to them. On every continent to celebrate their coming. Look at the festivities and the hoopla surrounding the centennial of the Statue of Liberty. What is a hundred years? Nothing. What are these Europeans, the youngest spawn of these old ones?" He paused again. "Nothing." He let that sink in. Just in case you forgot, he said it again, this time with a sad shake of his head,

"Let us begin by building a memorial to the people who first came into this continent. Not *here*, in New York Harbor, on a ship," he sneered. Hey, wait a minute, home boy, those ships provided my grandfather, the tugboat captain, with a living. "But *here!*" He wheeled and pointed to the map. He seemed to be pointing to Alaska.

"In the time when the glaciers covered large parts of the world, our race, *Homo sapiens*, grew into its maturity and filled the Old World with their sculpture, carvings and cave drawings. Yes, we are an artistic species. I say 'we' because we cannot separate ourselves into races and nationalities. We all share this magnificent heritage." The music, Debussy of all people, welled up in the background.

"Look here." He pointed to western Alaska, north of the Aleutian Islands, and passed his hand over toward the Soviet land mass. "In that time, the Bering and the Chukchi seas were dry. Geographers call this land Beringia. We moved eastward across Asia into the Siberian dawn. Then we passed into Beringia." He stood erect and held his fists close to his breast. "We were a wandering people on our eternal Exodus, looking for a Canaan, led by an unnamed Moses. Who knows how quickly we passed into this continent. A valley or so every generation?" He chuckled. "Heading east, then south, looking for the musk ox, the caribou and the mammoth. Looking for peace." With that I could sympathize.

"There!" he shouted, "in the Seward Peninsula, you can see the route we took. Beringia! this darkened area, extended hundreds of miles across. This was our path.

"Once we crossed into this continent, we may have had a wall of ice in front of us, a hostile, forbidding barrier. There would be no herds on the glacier. We waited until the ice sheets parted, like the Red Sea before the Israelites, and we continued our walk into the dawn. Our Dawnwalk.

"Friends of Early America have obtained an option on a site of 500 acres overlooking the dazzling white caps of Norton Sound to the south and with a splendid view of the Kigluaik Mountains." He made it sound as attractive as Saratoga in August. Shots of the site began appearing. I don't know how long the season for wildflowers is in Alaska, probably just a day on either side of June 21st, but Kavanaugh's photographer was there for them.

"Now, how much money do we need? Let me be blunt. We will require fifteen million dollars to acquire the land. We will need five million more to build roads for the construction equipment, a small runway, and housing for the crew. Then there's the drawing up of plans, estimates, choosing contractors and purchasing building materials. All this before construction and labor costs. By contrast, maybe our ancestors had it a little easier, eh?" It was the "our ancestors" that did it. Somehow we were involved with this Indian exodus.

"What Bartholdi did with the Statue of Liberty is charming, but we aim for something on a heroic scale, a fitting memorial. I see it as an educational center, like the Smithsonian. The building, itself, will be both work of art and museum. We will have artifacts from all the peoples of pre-Columbian America. The work of their lineal descendants alive today will have an honored place. There will be a library, workspace for scholars, computers as needed, a media center, and a hotel adjacent. We may consider a theme park with trained artisans living out the daily life of the Beringians."

"This sounds like Nanook of the theme park," I said.

"Shh."

"Costs will be kept down to seventy-five million dollars. There will be an annual budget for operations of about seven to nine million.

"The Museum of the American Indian, the Smithsonian, the State of Alaska, the Bureau of Indian Affairs, the Department of the Interior, all express interest."

The camera zoomed in on his face. He looked out at us purposefully.

"We will need money, of course, but most of all we need the sense that we are not alone. If anything at all has touched you today, why, just send us a postcard. A little cheer can help a runner along. Just send us a card that says, 'Yes! Dawnwalk is one small candleflame in the darkness, it is a ray of light to guide us along our journey. We will not toss our heritage on the junkheap or bring it back for the deposit.' Just say to us, 'Yes! Yes to the First Americans!' If you'll include your telephone number, we'll even give you a ring to say, 'You're welcome.' "

The tape cut back to the wildflowers and another voice, India Barrett's, came on with the address which simultaneously appeared on the screen. Then fadeout and the hiss of a gray screen.

"What did you think?" I asked, stupefied.

"We found our Indians."

"That was Mrs. Barrett's voice on the tape at the end there."

"Oh, that bloke is a real salesman, ay?"

I rewound the tape, ejected it and put it back in its case.

Indians. Money. Mrs. Barrett. This was a nutty project, but so were Mt. Rushmore, Colonial Williamsburgh, and Disneyland. In any event, I was pretty sure I'd be talking to this anthropological snakeoil salesman before long.

"We can talk as we go," Moira said, interrupting my thoughts.

"Where are we going?" I asked.

"To see this man, Royal. I've gotten his address from the telephone directory. I'll read through this lot to find out if any of these beaks are experts and living, and can tell us something about the man who died. Got it, mate?"

"Got it."

"It's too warm for these jeans. I'll just throw on a skirt. I'll be packed in ten minutes."

She changed quickly, grabbed her bag, set the alarm, locked the locks and we were out of there. We found a cab moseying along Broadway at 112th and we drove through Central Park and over the 59th Street Bridge to the municipal lot where I had left the car.

As I pulled onto the Brooklyn-Queens Expressway and headed north for the Triborough Bridge, it was 11:30. I realized I should have called Sadie, but I decided I could check back with command central later. As I drove, I looked at the road almost as much as I looked at Moira's legs, which I was determined to move onto a bed again and then onto a canvas as soon as I could.

It's a great life if you don't weaken.

8

The town of Hudson sits on the eastern shore of the wide, blue river, a little more than a hundred miles north of New York City, awaiting, like my paintings, discovery and exploitation. It was, in the last century, as much a whaling port as Sag Harbor or New Bedford. Hardy men sailed from its wharves for two- and three-year voyages. Melville's father caught pneumonia here on his way back to Albany from New York. Then he died.

Warren, the town's principal street, rises eastward from the water's edge two miles to Route 9-H. Once you go past the recently built condos on the shore, you find houses built centuries ago by the Dutch who settled the area. Moving away from the water, you travel through time, eighteenth century giving way to nineteenth, each block featuring architectural details from yet a later era, though no block has entirely escaped the 1950's predations of the siding salesmen nor, for that matter, the restorative impulse of the 80's.

People with enough money or interest to restore the old houses to their original appearance had for half a century been as rare as whaling ships in Hudson. In the past ten years, new money had come into town. The hotel reopened, the paint stores were stocking colonial colors, and the antique shops were beginning to outnumber the bars.

It was 2:30 P.M. Moira and I found a small, noisy tavern, opposite an Off Track Betting Shop on the upper end of Warren, a few blocks east of Royal's place. The retired folks in the area who liked to chat and bet seemed to have made it their headquarters. Before I left the bar, I called Jack Giresse and made arrangements to stop by his place later in the day. I decided to leave Moira in the tavern and go see Cyril's friend alone. She wasn't happy about it. But I had to do some things on my own. Then, too, a vestigial chivalric impulse urged me to shelter the lady I had just spent the night with.

Val Royal's Antiques was in a restored, nineteenth-century, brick townhouse, incongruously enough a few doors up from the Tainted Lady Lounge. I didn't expect either had much overflow business from the other. The bright sun made the sidewalk in front shimmer. There was a small sign by the door inviting customers to step up, ring and walk in. So I did. The vestibule was dark and cool.

Before I could go further, I found myself knocked backwards by a squat, beefy, red-faced man who came hurtling through the inner door like a paratrooper launching himself into space. I fell into the door behind me, slamming it shut with a loud bang that reverberated in that tiny space like a firecracker in a submarine. He had been carrying a large wide mouthed jug or ewer in his girder-like arms. The ewer lay beside me, its handle neatly snapped off. He looked at me with little pig's eyes, squinting and angry. He came over and stood above me. Sweat poured down from him.

"Yuh broke it, asshole," he grunted.

"Look, pal," I started to say, leaning back against the door, trying to get on my feet.

"Yuh broke it."

"Look, chief, I didn't see . . . "

He kicked me hard on the side of the left thigh with a steel-tipped workboot. The pain was so horrible and intense I felt gored. He brought his foot back again.

"Asshole . . . " I threw the jug and caught him right under the nose. The jug clattered to the tile floor. He stepped back. Blood was streaming down from his potato-like nose across his lips onto his chin. I lifted myself onto my good leg.

He looked at me as if I were a car jack that he had tripped over and then quite naturally kicked. He looked puzzled. He scratched his dirty blond crewcut. "Oh well," he seemed to decide, "may as well kill it."

He rushed forward, bringing his knee up fast. I turned to my left and stuck my right elbow into his face. His head snapped back. I had caught him just under the cheekbone. He groaned and staggered backwards. I pushed off the door, grabbed him by the belt and T-shirt and spun him around, pushing his face into a corner of the vestibule. I sent a right hook as hard as I could into his right kidney. It stood him up with a moan. I hit him on the neck, driving down hard behind the right ear. He had a hump of muscle and gristle there like a bull. I hit him again and he slumped. I backed off. My leg was throbbing.

The light overhead came on. A slender, blond man, about thirty years old stood in the doorway, dressed in baggy white pants and a pink shirt with the sleeves rolled up.

"I don't suppose you're here to read the meter?" he drawled languidly. "Honest to God, Merkle, what *are* you doing?" He looked at me. "That thing's name is Ernest Merkle and he is as dumb as a busload of bingo players. Aren't you, Merkle?" Merkle turned around. One hand as big as a shovel over his cheek, the other behind his neck.

"He broke it," he croaked.

"No, Merkle, you stole it, and then you dropped it. I was going to pay you. Here, take a hundred and get the hell out. Please, dickhead?" Merkle snatched the bill and put the money in his grimy jeans as casually as if he had just rolled a drunk. He stepped gingerly over the basin and walked past me without a look or a word out into the street. Royal took in his sign, closed the door after him and slid the bolt. He knelt to pick up the fragments of the ewer. "Can I interest you in some crockery?" he asked. "Or would you rather I call an ambulance?"

"Oh, shit," I said. God, my leg hurt. "I mean, is there someplace I could sit down for a while?"

"Of course. Lie down too if you want. Move in. Do what you like. Are you going to sue me?"

"Talk. Never sued anyone. Never called a cop."

"Of course you didn't. Let's go inside."

After tottering through the doorway of Royal's antique shop, I steadied myself on a cherrywood chest with shells carved on the drawers. My leg was throbbing. As he walked ahead of me, skipping along the cluttered aisles, Royal gave the impression of being lithe and delicate, like a woodland bird which had just fluttered in the window. I moved slowly after him. He led me to an oak rolltop desk against the rear wall. Lying on top were scattered invoices, last week's *Vigilant* with an auction ad circled, canceled checks, two floral paper- weights, a notepad with phone numbers, a small bronze of an Irish setter, felt tipped pens in a tooth mug, catalogues, refer- ence books—the litter of the sloppy, pre-computer business- man. There were two Windsor chairs. We sat. I breathed heavily, trying to get control.

The shop smelled of varnish, wax and the odor of potpourri wafting from a yellow porcelain bowl set on a pedestal table with a malachite top. My eyes were darting around, trying to sort out, identify and appraise the stock, so as to get a line on the taste and avarice of the proprietor. There were quilts draped over a wooden rack, some good large pieces— wardrobes, commodes, desk secretaries—glass cabinets filled with smalls, as they call them; a collection of banjo clocks hung on one wall, and there were a few oils, too, including one very awful cows-in-the-Catskills genre painting. It was all artfully arranged, not so cluttered as to give the impression of a warehouse jumble, but filled with enough things so you didn't feel you had stumbled into the hunt master's drawing room. He looked at me, bemused.

"Want some scotch?"

"Yes," I said.

He opened a drawer of the desk and took out a liter bottle of Johnnie Walker Black. From a nearby shelf he took a glass, poured a couple of ounces into it and offered it to me. I took it, drank it, and handed it back to him. He refilled it and gave it to me once more. I held on to it. It was heavy, cut with flutes and bands of narrow prisms and decorated with an enam- elled plaque of a butterfly, a swallowtail.

"Well, sorry about that," he said. I shrugged.

"Um, who are you?" he asked. "Did Kavanaugh send you up here?"

"What do you mean?"

"You're not shouting for the police, an ambulance, a lawyer to sue me for my shop. What do you want?"

"Bulk said to look you up."

"Who?"

"Pal of mine. Cyril Hart. Said to look you up if I was ever this way. I can't find Cyril. Thought I'd stop by here."

"I'm sorry. I can't help you. I don't know where he is. The police are looking for Cyril, too. They believe he may shed some light on a particularly nasty murder hereabouts. Would your inquiry have anything to do with that?"

"Hardly."

"Why *are* you here?"

Since Mrs. Barrett had said Cyril had purchased some Americana from Royal, I decided to use that. "He said he had bought some antiques, Americana, local, eighteenth and nineteenth century."

"Really?"

"Yeah."

"Did you come here to buy?"

"Maybe."

"What's your interest?"

"New England folk art, portraits mainly. Ancestors, you know?"

"You're a dealer?"

"In a way."

"They go for the absolute earth now. *Terra-fucking-assoluta!* When I think of what I passed up as little as ten years ago. God,"

"Not really."

"What are you talking about?"

"When I paint them myself."

There it was. The conversation might chill out and he'd get rid of me. Not too fast, because I might decide to be nasty about the Merkle incident. I was betting on my man, though.

If that Newport chest I leaned on by the door was genuine, there would have been a velvet rope around it and a museum around the rope.

"You have any samples? Any slides?"

"Just some happy customers."

"Name one."

"India Barrett." Why not?

"She must have acres of real ones. What would she want with a fake ancestor?"

"Multiple houses and insurance. First she wanted copies of the ones in New York for up here. Now she's going abroad and the 'real ones' are going in a vault. I made two of everything."

"That how you met Hart?"

"Yes."

"Too bad about her husband," Royal said quietly. "The *atelier* to an *abattoir* transformed. Grisly." He shivered. "So you're a painter?"

"And a dealer."

"Been in the trade long?"

"Not really."

"I guess you worked here in the East? For anyone I'd know?"

"I don't deal with a lot of people and I don't know who you know. I don't work for anyone. I came here to get an idea about your stuff, so if I see something right for you I can bring it over if I'm coming this way and feel like going a few rounds with the help."

"Feel free," he said. "You look like somebody who can take care of himself."

"That's about all I can take care of."

"Cyril didn't mention you."

"Did you two talk about all the guys he knew?"

"Some," he said, "does that bother you?"

Peeve city. The mark had just turned to ice. I drank some whiskey. Christ, my side hurt, my leg felt like I had been hit with a lead weighted sap, Moira was out there alone and Royal seemed to want an introduction from a missing man. He looked at his watch, a Patek Phillippe. I was about to be ushered out, and why not? What must he have made of me? He meets me at the front door slamming away in a fight involving some purloined crockery with his employee. I drop broad hints at my own sleazy ways and cock a sneer at his relationship with the elusive Cyril. Not good. I had to try again.

"Look," I said, "you got me wrong. What you do and who you do it with is your business, okay? I take people like I find 'em."

He looked hard at me. "Bet you generally take 'em, eh bruiser?" he said finally.

I smiled, seraphically I hoped.

"Sometimes," he said, "we meet people in unexpected ways, don't we?" He was hooked again. There was still some play here, apparently.

"Sometimes," I said.

"Have you some time now?" he asked, looking at his slim gold watch again. He liked that watch very much.

"Sure."

"Come on next door then." He picked up the scotch bottle and carried it with him.

I followed him across the shop and through a door that led through the wall into the adjacent building, which was also filled with antiques, but of lesser quality.

"Mind the step. The floors of the two buildings don't match up."

I eased my leg down. We went along an aisle formed of oak bureaus with glass knobs, amber spotlights shining down on them to bring out the color. Wooden bowls gone oval with age sat on stripped and distressed pine kitchen tables. There were rewired floor lamps, mirror-fronted wardrobes, a rosewood pier glass, and more rolltops. On the walls were weather vanes, merchants' shop signs, faded doll dresses in shadow boxes, daguerreotypes, framed pieces of lace and some very dark pictures. It was second-line Americana, but it seemed profitable enough for him to start his workmen breaking through the shop walls of aptly named Warren Street.

I nearly walked into a tailor's dummy wearing a yellowing

linen suit, that had once been white, which looked right for a
turn-of-the-century dandy about my size to wear while stroll-
ing along the porches of Saratoga's hotels, the old Congress,
the Union, cigar in hand, nodding to the heiresses and their
chaperones.

Royal led me around a tall, folding screen with scenes of
cranes and temples on it into a back room, fitted out with a
sink, stove, refrigerator, table and chairs, and a window looking out on a garden in the rear, overrun by purslane and
plantain, dock and other weeds. He was a careless man
around the edges.

He opened the refrigerator door and took out two bottles of
sparkling water. "One can't be drinking all day to get the dust
out of one's mouth." I shook my head. He poured some more
scotch in my glass. He unscrewed the top of one of the green
bottles and poured himself a fizzy glass of water. He wasn't
the one who needed a painkiller.

"Speaking of dust in the mouth," he began airily, "poor
Cyril seems to have made quite an impression on Mrs. Barrett. Was he screwing the old bag, do you think? Huh? God,
she must be seventy. *Chacun à son frisson,* whatever turns
you on."

He was staring at me and grinning, his eyes seemed now to
have a watery glaze to them, maniacal. A rapid change from
the cool gaze of appraisal I had seen in the other store. The
relationship appeared to titillate him.

If I were to find out anything at all about what happened
the night Peter Barrett died, my journey would have to begin
here, in this shop. Royal was unsettling in a way that went
beyond his mannerisms. He was not strung out and he wasn't
going to pieces. He had the air of a man sliding around a
situation, trying to find an edge, looking hard at every angle.

Something in my fight with Merkle intrigued him. If I were
to make myself appear useful, or even entertaining, to him,
perhaps he might provide some hint that would let me see
into the puzzle of Barrett's last hours and Cyril's where-
abouts.

I would show him a side of my own disreputable nature. I
would be raffish. "When we think of Bosch, we think of

sensuality risible." This riff I had picked up from Giresse. "We'll take a print of the Garden of Delights, tip in a picture of them, of Cyril Hart, faunlike, and this old woman, India Barrett, sating their grosser appetites, with flowers, appropriate to the season, growing out of their asses." His eyes widened. "Photograph it, enlarge it. Scorn, mockery, and derision will follow upon its exhibition." I looked over at him. "Does that bother you?"

He clapped his hands in delight, "*I'd* buy it, but you might have some trouble with your wealthy client. I know, I know . . . ," he waved his hand frantically, "ask Mrs. Barrett what her favorite . . . ," he was gasping, "her favorite . . . *flower* is."

He laughed so hard, he had to stop to wipe the tears that were coming from the corners of his eyes. He came out of it, finally. "Can you draw as well as you talk? Huh, bruiser?"

Presto. Out came the pad, and on it I drew a quick caricature of Royal and Woody Woodpecker, complete with pileated topknot, pursuing indelicate interests. This might not have been up to the standard of my eighth grade comic book period, but it would do.

"What do you think?"

He took it from me. He stared at it, shaking his head from side to side. I had sensed he was a child, really, and this shop was his toy chest. His life was make believe. He would switch back and forth in his roles, I was sure of it, from Mr. Royal, cold, aloof, in control, to a little kid, little Val, who wants to play . . . nice.

"You'll do, I'd say. Can I keep this? Not for its erotic value, though, I . . . well, I may need to show it to someone. We've been looking for somebody. Somebody who can help us in, what can I say . . . ? A project. To the right person we'd pay, um, a lot for maybe three months work. But I have to get approval. You may have come along at the right time."

"Who would I have to kill?"

"Have you ever killed?" he asked instantly.

"If I did, chum, I wouldn't tell it to someone who partied with woodpeckers."

"No, of course you wouldn't," he said in all seriousness. The *louche* style, the thousand yard stare, even the totter-

ing swagger, had kept him talking to me. Now he thought I
was Trigger Mike. Time to get back to the main subject.

"Too bad about Cyril not being around," I said.

"He was fucking Rina, my sister." He pronounced the 'g'
carefully.

"So did you kill him?"

"If I killed all the guys who have dallied with my sister, I'd
be the plague."

"Hart was a good guy," I said. What was I going to say: he
was a sister fucking, psychotic slasher?

"Sometimes he was too, too . . . didgeroo-doo, you know,
chipper. I mean, with that Australian bonhomie of theirs and
calling everybody 'mite.' Too boring. Those people have no
past anyway. He really had no conception about what he was
buying. I think he just liked to hang around."

"Did you ever tell him that?"

"No." He stopped to reflect. "My sister might like something like this." He tapped his fingers on the drawing.

"Maybe I should talk to her." He looked worried, as if he
had made a mistake by bringing her up. "You should spray it
with fixative if you're going to show it around," I said.

"Will do," he said absently. He looked at the drawing. I
looked down at the butterfly on my now empty glass.

"You really know antiques?" he asked finally.

"A bit."

"Hold on. Let me get something to show you."

He left our little hideaway. I heard what sounded like a
closet creaking and the sound of a chain then some steps and
then the closet banged shut. He returned carrying an object
in each hand. An oval box about five inches in length and
three inches high. He handed it to me.

I saw the thin strip of elm, about an inch wide, encircling
the box, closed by a tab fitting into a vee-shaped slot. The box
was empty. I handed it back to him.

"Very nice."

"Do you know what it is?"

"Of course I do. A Shaker one-finger box. Maybe from up
the road in Mt. Lebanon. It's a nice one. Worth maybe five

hundred now." The Shaker craftsmen made thousands of boxes like that. They were used for storage and to package the goods they sold to the outside world. "It's a good piece."

"They made beautiful baskets, too. Merkle brought me this. I gave him three hundred for it." He carefully handed me a basket with a round bottom and a swing handle.

"Good workmanship," I said. I had one in my house. I kept letters and post cards in it, but it had been probably used by a local housewife for taking to market or gathering apples. Calvin Conklin had spotted it right away and told me about it. He had a collection. The man or woman who made this one knew what they were doing, and they had lived maybe fifteen miles from where we sat. Their country road was now a parkway and tourist cabins dotted the big hillside where they had pounded their precious brown ash trees till the wood separated from the growth rings and they could separate it into splints. "Not Shaker," I said, handing the basket back to Royal.

"It looks old."

Cluck. "It *is* old but it's not Shaker. They didn't make all the baskets in the world."

"Merkle lied to me."

"Maybe he did. It's still a good basket. One like this you could get five hundred for, easy."

"Who made it? Do you know?" he asked with a taunting note to the edge of his voice. "Tell me, if you can."

"Yo, back off."

"I'll pay you if you tell me."

"Okay."

"What?"

"Pay me and I'll tell you. Better yet, how about that linen suit?"

"Deal."

I took the basket from him. I examined it carefully.

"Brown ash and oak," I said, speaking aloud the way Giresse had taught me to speak to myself when I looked hard at something, to really see it and miss nothing. "See the double bottom, and how it's raised in the center." Royal leaned over and put his hand in the basket, and stroked the bottom with his slender, pink fingers. "That's from the basket maker's knee."

"One of the uprights, these flat pieces here, was always split down there to make sure there were an odd number of ribs so the weaving of the brown ash withes, these things, could proceed continuously around the basket. The Indians, the Mohicans, in this area, taught the early settlers to do that. There was interbreeding back then, too, I heard."

"Cold winters, up here," he commented.

"Look at the silhouette." I held the basket up. "See this braided piece coiled around the base of the basket. It's ash splint, to act like a bumper on the bottom. The handle is a simple curved piece of oak with a hole drilled at either end. The rims are thick, criss-crossed with lashings, and they're tight, really tight. The sheen on them tells me they're brown ash. This is a hundred years old or more," I tossed it in his lap. "Squeeze it." He did. "See how it's supple and strong. It's alive."

"Who made it, if not the Shakers?"

"Folks around here, actually. Years ago, they lived out where the Taconic crosses 82, up on the hill, where that state park is now. They kept to themselves, made baskets for generations."

"How do you know this?" he asked suspiciously.

"I know collectors, and I'm an observer. I'll take this one for three hundred, right now."

"No, I'll hold onto it for a while."

"You only paid a hundred."

"How did you know that?" He was genuinely surprised.

"That's the price you mentioned to my sparring partner. I listen as well as look."

"Yes, you do." He placed the basket on the floor. "Done time?" he asked.

"We've all done time, haven't we? That's what it's for."

"Federal?"

"Sort of."

"What do you mean 'sort of'?" I had been thinking of making up some story about being in the brig, but that would get too complicated. I decided to bristle a bit.

"What do you mean asking me these questions? Is this a

job interview or what? I figure I'd look you up, check out your action, peddle some wares, come back to you with some stuff as I'm making the rounds and now you come on like a parole officer. Hey, lighten up. What's doin'?"

"Yes, this is going along somewhat like a job interview, isn't it? No, I am not your parole officer. See the job I had in mind, it would require a certain kind of guy. One with talents like yours, a guy who can paint a little, a guy who can keep his mouth shut, who, 'sort of,' has been around."

"Guys like that, they don't come so cheap. It would take more than a suit for them."

"Recognizing that, and with a remarkably piquant figure in terms of remuneration awaiting your consideration, would you be interested?"

"Maybe."

"I find your sullen uncertainties refreshing. I am impressed with the way you handle yourself, if I may tell you, very impressed."

"Thank you."

"Would you like to work for me?"

"How much?"

"For a first quality portrait done in folk art style, five thousand, and there may be much, much more to come."

"Sounds good."

"What say you come up with some references, I check you out and maybe we'll make beautiful music together."

"Are you for real? References?"

"A name. I want a name of someone who knows you, who, let's say, in turn, friends of mine would know. Get it? These friends of mine, they'd tell me to go ahead. That kind of reference. If you've been inside, you know what I'm talking about."

"I never had anything to do with the mob or anything," I said.

"Hey. A name. You passed the audition. Now all you have to do is produce the union card."

"I'll think about it."

"Do. Please. We'd also like to see a sample of your work." A notion came to me of where I could pick that up.

"I'll call you soon," I said.

"Sure."

"I have to talk to a couple of people before I start handing their names out."

"I understand. I'll be here. And you might tell me your own name."

"Ventry."

"How curious." He looked at me quizzically. "Any relation to the gossip columnist?" he asked.

"None that I know of. Who is that?"

"Never mind. No need for a gossip columnist around here," he said sadly.

"Why here, if I may ask? Why is your shop here? Why not in the City?"

"Warren Street is ready to take off," he said with certainty. "Everybody knows that."

"Oh. Getting in on the ground floor, huh?"

"Oh, there's an absolutely cavernous basement below, *les caves du Royal,* perfect for wines, which I don't have yet, not so good for baskets, which I do. Yes, this is the coming place. Anything else?"

"The linen suit on the dummy?"

"Yours. I'll wrap it up."

I sat there while he took the Shaker box and the basket from up on the hill. I heard the closet swing open, the clang of metal, then it was shut again. In a few minutes he returned with a shopping bag. The suit was inside it.

"Get a good price for this."

"I think I'll wear it."

"Whatever."

He led me out through the door in the wall into the other, grander shop. He switched on the lights in the entryway where I had had my fight and opened the outer door. He clapped me on the shoulder. I winced.

"See you," he said. I waved and then limped up to the central square of the town where I sat on a bench opposite the St. George Hotel to see if I was being followed. When I decided I wasn't, though I wasn't sure how I could tell, I dragged myself into the hotel and found a phone. I looked up the number of the tavern where I left Moira, called her and got her on the line. I told her I was going to go get the car and drive around awhile to see if I was being followed, then come by and pick her up in front of the OTB parlor. I asked her to wait inside until she saw the car, then step in quickly.

In a quarter of an hour, she was beside me in the front seat of the Subaru.

9

"What happened to you, Ventry? Bloody hell, you've been in a punch up."

"Yup."

"These antique dealers a rough lot?" she asked with that singing Australian interrogative on "lo-ot?"

"Some guy I bumped into going in. Then Royal and I talked."

"Did you learn anything about Cyril?"

"Not where he is. Royal said he didn't know, but I'm sure they had something going."

"What did you talk about for so long? I've been in that bar for what seemed hours. The old fellas were starting to look good." It was just 4 p.m.

"He offered me a job," I said.

"A job? Doing what? Breaking heads?"

"Could be. I think Royal knows a lot, Moira. I'm sure he does. I told him I'd think about it."

"What's this then, in the parcel?" She pointed to the shopping bag in the rear seat.

"Old clothes, for when I'm feeling old."

"Right. Have it your own way. Where are we going? Dropping me off in another of these rustic taverns?" Moira asked.

"First to see a happy man, then sleep."

"What?"

"Every Frenchman I ever met, except Jack, was gloomy as hell. Their Celtic bloodlines . . . "

"Watch it!" she screamed. Going round a blind curve, I swerved to avoid hitting a flatbed trailerload of stacked hay-bales, pulled by an old tractor, a Ford 9 M.

"*Your* bloodlines are going to be all over the road, mate," Moira said, "if you don't slow the bloody car down."

"Their Celtic bloodlines," I continued after taking a deep breath, "and their politics incline them to melancholy. Even their word 'gaiety,' which we took from them, naturally attracts the word 'forced' to its side. But not Jack, though, not Jack."

"Tell me about him as we creep along, please, Ventry." I slowed to forty-five. The pick-up trucks and the K-Mart cowboys would be passing me soon. The reminiscences would take my mind off the pain.

"I first met him when I showed up at the West Side apartment of his mother, the formidable Rachel, for French lessons one August afternoon when I was thirteen. It was my aunt's idea. Madame was a seamstress at the time. She did designer knockoffs for people like my mother and aunt. That's how they met. One afternoon, during a lesson, as I was writing down a *dictée* she was giving me—Madame Halévy Giresse was a great believer in using the classical French writers to learn the language which would, believe me, someday knock the kepis off French-speaking customs officers in West Africa—Jack walked in with a life study of a nude in pastels he wanted to show his mother. Wow! After that the *passé simple* was passed over and I spent my time with Jack. He was about thirty then."

"Did he like little boys?"

"Jack?" I said shocked. "Bite your tongue! Jack had tons of girls. That nude was one of them. I got to draw her later on."

"That's why you took art lessons, to look at naked women?"

"You do when you're thirteen." A Bronco 4 x 4 pulled out behind me and roared by.

"Jack taught me everything: all about pastels and chalk, pencil, crayon, charcoal. How to hold them, where to buy them. He loves the materials. We spent months playing with different papers. There were so many I can't remember them all. Half I never even saw again: hot pressed smooth, rough,

Bristol board, ivory card, Ingres, good quality Schoellsham-
mer and light, Japanese papers, kozu shi, toshi. Some of them
were expensive, but he didn't care. It really was a kind of play.
He taught me watercolors, and a very little about oils, but
always, every day, back to drawing. 'See the line and draw it. It
is so easy, my little Yong-keee. The line, the line. *Toujours la
ligne.* Even in the caves of Lascaux, the same French Line, like
the poor *Normandie*, burning in your harbor.' Always laughing and joking. We never lost touch."

"He sounds a proper pal. What was he doing in the states?"

"He is a Jew. The formidable Rachel was an artist's model.
She was living in the La Ruche quarter, before the war, when
she took up with Jack's dad, an art dealer with a nice Catholic
family already. Jack didn't like to talk about it, but I pieced the
story together over the years. Daddy Giresse was alarmed by
the course of events. When Hitler started into Poland, he sent
his Jewish girlfriend and his boy, Jacob, packing. They went
to Portugal, then here. He managed to give them some paintings and drawings he thought they could sell. I saw one of
them years later, a Picasso drawing of his son, Paulo."

"What did they take them in, a truck?" Moira asked.

"They left the frames for Goering. They traveled light. When
they got over here they began selling everything, except that
Picasso. Madame set up shop with her needle and Jack went
to the Art Students League.

"By the time the cupboard was bare, Jack was pulling in
enough so Madame could lay down her thimble and spend
her days reading Colette. More to the point, he told me on the
phone back at the bar that during the hard times he was for a
while a 'go-fer' in Peter Barrett's studio, something I never
knew. He is going to tell us what Peter was like, I hope, and
who would try to harm him. Madame is still in Manhattan,
but Jack's up here, now, permanently."

Jack lived a few miles outside of the village of Kinderhook,
north of Hudson, in a house made from a barn whose stout
timbers and ample girth served two centuries ago to store the
winter hay for a Dutch farmer's herds of milk cows. It was
sited on a gentle rise above a five-acre apple orchard with a

view of the Catskill mountains across the Hudson to the southwest. Everytime Jack saw a bare spot, he dug a hole and stuck a shrub in it. The yard looked like a Disney World for house wrens.

By the goldfish pond where the koi drifted and slumbered, there was a corkscrew willow that writhed like the snake around Laocoon's shoulders. Further on, there were some boxes and wire mesh. Every now and then a Leghorn hen would go trotting by chased by a rooster.

Jack met us at the door. He was dressed in a checked flannel shirt, suspenders, old paint-stained jeans and scuffed work boots. He looked like Harpo Marx decked out for *A Night at the Lumbercamp*. He greeted me with a big hug and a "my boy, my boy" rumbling up from his chest. Then he made a fuss over Moira. He drank her in with his large, dark eyes and a big grin lit up his face. Somehow, he made patting a pretty girl's ass in the doorway a form of continental greeting. We followed him into the living room, large and colorful, filled with 19th-century farm furniture, including what he called his throne for the Columbia County *arriviste*: a Shaker chair with webbed seat and candle flame finials on the back.

We sat on sturdy Windsors at a large plank table which glowed with a self-satisfied buttery look from hundreds of hand rubbings. He had set out two glasses and a bottle of Bordeaux. The room was lined with cedar boards, given a very light coating of watery whitewash. Windows had been punched through the barn walls, some high above the old rough hewn rafters, to fill the house with sunlight. One wall had shelves filled with oversized art books, another wall held the components of a complex stereo system. In a corner, a small cast iron stove on a firebrick platform waited for winter, a mourner at the feast.

All of this was bought, he once told me, with the royalties from one drawing, an austere, very simple cityscape, just a few lines, for a town that hosted the Summer Olympics and needed a tasteful, but immediately recognizable and infinitely reproducible logo.

"Some wine?" he asked Moira. I told him I'd have some as

well. "Ah," he said, "abstinence is fatiguing," and went to get another glass. Then he poured, and we sniffed and sipped and murmured our appreciations.

"Moira's cousin is Cyril Hart, the guy who worked for the Barretts," I said, after a pause. His eyebrows arched up in polite interest, furrowing his brow into a half-dozen wrinkles.

"Did you know him?" Moira asked.

"No, I heard he is disappeared, but I'm sorry, we never met." He pursed his lips and shrugged.

"Ventry," he said, after a pause, "what are you working on?" With most of us this evokes a strangled response: if you are working well, you don't want to jinx yourself and talk about it, if you are not working, the last thing you want to talk about is paint. But Jack was special. So I told him I was fooling around with botanical studies, landscapes, " . . . lilacs and shit."

He looked at Moira and said, "Your friend has the soul of a poet: 'lilacs and shit.' How it fires the imagination. My protegé, my dear, wants his little pumpkin patch to be known to the world through his work. Oh yes, I see through this one. 'Lilacs and shit' Ah, yes! These are his dreams. Just as we say, 'Aix-en-Provence, that is Cézanne country,' this area here, this place from the Hudson to the Taconic Hills, he has the conceit that it will be known to generations of students passionately committed to his work as 'Ventry Country.' In French," he wagged his finger, "not so nice: *pays de vent*," he blew air through his lips contemptuously.

The old bull was trying to steal the young one's girl. It was his way of saying, "Hi! Glad you could make it."

"He is painting the lilacs, about which he knows nothing. *Serieux*, boy, be *serieux*. You have gifts. The human figure, eh?" Turning to Moira again, he said, "I give this one a lesson or two once. He was quite young. He can only do one or two things without making the mess, but for the figure, we are not so ashamed of him. For most beginners, the skin is a sack, for him a garment. *C'est vrai*. Bone, ligament, muscle, these he understands. The world lost a talented butcher when he decided he could paint. Perhaps, it is hopeless. Yes? Let him paint his flowers and you come over here and model, eh?"

"And you, Jack, what are you working on?"

"I show you!" He told us to take our glasses and follow him. We went through the kitchen to his studio, a separate building out back, connected by a short covered walkway. "*Mon atelier*," he said exuberantly. Royal had used that word earlier, talking about Barrett's murder. The *atelier* turned into an *abattoir*, a slaughterhouse. Had he been there?

"Wake up, Ventry, and look," Jack said, waving his palm in front of my eyes.

When he worked, Giresse was very fast, very intense. He never bothered with stretching his canvases. Sometimes he didn't bother with brushes but put the paint on with his fingers. The pictures were pinned one on top of another, like pages of a calendar. They had the floppy loose lines he had spoken to me about for hours in my teenage years, waving his arms in the air, gesturing like a dancer, lines which I had never quite given up aiming for in my own work. His colors in these canvases were rich and lush, almost edible in their exuberance, scenes of the tropics, of a garden beyond a verandah filled with white wicker furniture, green parrots with blue necks and dazzling flowers.

"Martinique," he said to Moira, "I rented. I may buy, for the winters." We walked back to the living room. We spoke about my show in New York. He had been there, of course. He said he had enjoyed himself. He would have enjoyed himself at Golgotha, entertaining the onlookers, consoling Mary with a cheerful word.

I asked him about Peter. He answered by concocting a theory about different kinds of painters. He was just showing off, really, to Moira, outshining the dolt she came in with. American painters are more *alert* than most people, I'll say that, even the crazy ones, but get very nervous with theories. We have fallen in love with our senses and want no cerebral distractions. Jack was European, so he ism-ized in a torrent for a while in his French way, a credit to his lycée.

"We are of two kinds . . . " he went on, "Stop rolling your eyes, Ventry."

He sipped some wine.

"Some of us are playful. Well, when I find a stone, or some gear off a tractor at the dump, I say, hmmn, This gear is not happy. It wants to be something else. 'What does this remind me of? How can I change this into something else.' The metier, chérie, is . . . mu-ta-bi-li-ty," he dragged out the last word, syllable by syllable, tee becoming tay. "Then there are those who look deep, very deep," he lowered the tone of his voice. "These are the artists who stare all day at a stone or a pinecone, no tractor gears for them, and say, 'what a pine-cone!' and count the rows and the petals, is that what those little nubs are called? They mystically enter into the pine-coneness of the pinecone or pineapple or whatever it is they are staring at that day. And they produce the most dreary pictures. Walking through galleries of their work is worse than the Stations of the Cross on an empty stomach."

"Not that bad, surely?" she asked mock seriously.

Jack nodded sorrowfully. "I regret, yes. So, anyway, if they have half a brain these dolts do the right thing."

"They kill themselves?" I asked.

"*Hélas*, not often enough. No. They steal. One looks around, sees what is selling, he cannot tell what is good. He imitates, then he sells. Successful? Of course, and therefore, by the standards of this charming country, they are the good artists, eh?"

"Everybody steals, Jack," I said. "If someone could create an absolutely original work of art, no one would be able to see it. We can only recognize art in terms of what we have seen before."

"Cabbagehead," he sneered. He smiled at Moira and said, "Don't pay any attention to this, *chérie*."

"What about Barrett?"

"Barrett had even fewer original ideas than you, boy. He was basically an illustrator, not bad really, who decided to become something he couldn't be, poor fellow."

"What's that?" I asked.

He didn't answer. He went over to a large pine cabinet, once meant to hold dishes, now filled with hundreds of LP's, CD's and tapes. He took a record from its dust jacket and placed it carefully on the turntable of the stereo system. In a moment the saxophone of Lester Young filled the sunlit room.

"You'll like this," he said to Moira, "this is *l'essence de l'Amerique.*"

He closed his eyes as he listened to the music.

"Don't pay any attention to him, Moira. He discovered jazz last year. When I first met him he thought Vic Damone was the spirit of the age." I had given him the Lester Young record for Christmas in 1964.

"*Crapaud!*" he shouted.

"*Salaud!*" I hollered back.

"Your boyfriend has no manners," he said to Moira with the goopy look that I knew preceded his mentioning to a healthy young woman in his Gallic, soulful way that, if she should wish to contribute to her own immortality and that of all women by allowing him to capture just this moment of her ripeness in a painting, why, all she had to do was merely remove her blouse . . .

I steered him back to Peter Barrett. "What was he like?"

"Ah, Ventry, Ventry. Why are you playing at this detection? I thought you had left that behind?"

"I promised India."

"Yes, of course. But you are on the wrong side, eh? 'One must commit a painting,' Degas said, 'as one commits a crime.' That is how you must think. Like a thief after the jewels, not a night watchman."

"And Barrett? How did he think?"

Jack threw up his arms. "About what you'd expect." Whatever that meant. "It is not easy to define a man like him in a word."

"Try."

"Ill advised?" The saxophone playing drifted through the sunbeams as we mulled that one over.

"Who gave him bad advice?"

"Everyone who paid him a compliment."

"How well did you know him?"

"Back in the fifties, before you were born, Moira, I was sitting in the old Cedar tavern, a hangout in the Village for artists and their girlfriends. I was broke, but hopeful, because a guy had told me I could get some work helping someone named Barrett with a big canvas. Barrett always liked big pictures.

"So, I am sitting there with the one glass of beer I could afford growing warm and flat, and this guy with a voice that brayed like a jackass walks up to me and starts reciting poetry, Baudelaire, in an awful accent and with several words missing. I thought he was a bum. I tell him, 'Pal, I am broke too. I can't give you anything. I am here to get work.'

"Of course, it was Peter and he liked it very much that I had no dough. He bought me another beer and started being wrong at the top of his voice."

"What do you mean?" Moira asked.

"He had lots of foolish opinions, which he asserted in a very loud voice."

"What did he look like then?" I asked.

"All Americans look alike to me."

"Come on."

"He affected an air, looking out of the corner of his eye to see who was watching him, you know. He wore shabby clothes, even though he had money. He talked about commitment, about how the style had to be right for the time. He seemed to be worried I wouldn't take him seriously. I was worried he wouldn't be able to pay me.

"As it turned out I agreed to work for him, so we celebrated. He got drunk and then there was an accident. Some men have no luck. As I was steering him back to his place, he fell on the ice and hurt his hip, broke it, in fact. I carried him up to his studio. I may have damaged the hip even worse, but I couldn't leave him on the street. Come to think of it, if I had left him there to freeze to death in the gutter it would have saved you all this trouble."

"But you didn't?"

"Well, I called an ambulance from the studio. It came and took him away. He was sober by then from the pain. He offered me a job when he was released from the hospital. I was supposed to help him as he painted, but we didn't get much done. His hip wouldn't let him get around and one can't really move the brushes for somebody else, eh? What a fiasco. We only spent a short time attempting that. We just listened to jazz records and talked, really. Had some wine."

"He had a show round about then, didn't he, Jack?"

"Oh, yes. That was the high spot of his career. After that," Jack lifted his hand and brought it gliding down, "pfft. He never did anything that came close to what was in that show."

Recalling what Schreier said, I turned to Moira and said, "There's one in the Whitney from that show."

Jack shrugged and went on, "You know, too, that man was so loud." He frowned in distaste. "He talked so loudly about crap: politics."

"What did he say?"

"Not much. You know he sort of pretended he was a red? But let me tell you about Peter the Red: he had no real ideological substance. He never read anything. All he knew were slogans."

Jack fell silent and then he slowly waved his forefinger in the air, back and forth, along with one of the jazzman's solos. "I can try to tell you how the poor schlub saw himself," he said. "Peter was a romantic. He had a view of himself as a worker, a skilled craftsman, one of a band of artist brothers. He thought he was some kind of *meister* painter. What a load of crap. Don't you think so?"

"Yeah. I guess." I said.

"I remember the pain in his voice when he said to me, 'Jack, in the Roman Empire, painters were . . . *slaves*.' God knows who first told him that, but he was upset. I can still hear the concern in his voice . . . 'slaves.' Moira, a black man couldn't buy an ice cream cone in a white drugstore in Mississippi in those days and he was crying over working conditions in the Roman Empire."

"Which artists did he admire?"

"In the sense I just attempted to convey: all of the successful ones."

"When he broke into abstraction, well, that early stuff of his looked pretty good."

"That's what they were doing then, Rothko, Barnett Newman, Bill de Kooning, Pollock. They were something." He sat meditatively. "In their way. It's not my style." He drained his glass. "You want some more wine, Moira? Yes? Let me pour it for you." He refilled our glasses. The sun, shining through one of the small windows set high in the wall over the stereo, let in a sunbeam right on the plank table. He set the wine bottle in it. "See, Moira. The glass radiates, like an emerald on the neck of one of Velazquez' *infantas*. Sparkling and effulgent: this wine bottle in the sunlight."

"You talk like a poet," Moira said. Jack beamed.

"Viridian," I said, "with chrome yellow."

"Maybe," he nodded.

"Can you tell me more about Barrett?"

"Since you ask, let me see what else I remember. You who have not listened to Barrett's monologue on the role of the artist in society have not known how far the limits of tedium can be stretched. His point being, and that not a difficult one to grasp I thought, and not one that I'd have to hear a dozen times before I understood it as he must have thought because he would go on and on about it when he was in his cups, his point being that it's *different*. Now is that difficult?"

"Different? What's different?"

"Peter said we were priests. Artist priests. The tribe came to us and said, 'Give us a picture of a bison, and we'll go kill the damn thing with our spears or hatchets or whatever and we'll give you a nice steak, well marbled, for your trouble.' Up on the wall goes the bison, maybe not such a big one, maybe these hunters are a little bit chicken, and then *boom*, the bison god sends a herd galloping in front of our clients and their spears. We get the food and we are important. The cave paintings had a purpose: they provided the images of the peoples' myths and they provided dinner. My distant cousin, Lévi-Strauss, would not agree."

He looked at Moira. "Peter loved that stuff. How special the artist was."

The music ended. Jack got up to turn the record over.

"I don't know if I'm making this clear," he said when he had taken his seat again, "but Peter claimed he had these bonds with all artists in every culture. And to the past. Men and women, about thirty thousand years ago. All contemporaries of his. The artistic community of this three hundred centuries is within our reach. A thousand generations. The ancient stones spoke to him, he said, which was a lie because he never let anyone speak." Jack waved dismissively. "I lost contact with him, didn't see him for years."

"Did you see him before he died?"

"Well, yes. I ran into him at the hardware store in Hudson. It would have been last summer."

"What did he say?"

"He asked me to come around and look at his latest work."

"Did you?"

"Yes. It was piffle. He did tell me he was going to take a trip. Why he should think I cared, I do not know."

"Where to?"

"Alaska."

"Why?"

"It was a hot day, I suppose."

"Mrs. Barrett is involved with some foundation that has to do with early man. Did Barrett's work have anything to do with that. His dealer and his wife said he was excited about something."

"I wouldn't know."

"What did you think of him, when all is said, *enfin*?" I asked.

He moved his chin slowly back and forth, ruminatively, and covered his mouth with his hand, a signature gesture of Degas, as Jack had pointed out to me, laying claim to an affinity with his "crime-committing" idol.

"I don't like knocking another guy's work."

"But go ahead," I said.

"Barrett, I thought, was very, very bad. Whenever I saw something Barrett had done, I had the sense I had just gotten a letter from an old friend who was . . . trying to sell me a life insurance policy. You see," Jack shifted forward in his chair, "because he had that one big show, he could raise expectations," he lifted his arm, "but there was nothing there." His fingers uncurled to show the emptiness he described. He picked up a toothpick from the table and chewed on it for a while, then put it down.

The subject depressed him. He hadn't even offered us dinner, and I was hungry.

"Anything else? Gambling debts? Mistresses? Drugs?" I asked.

"As you know, he married a rich wife. Types like Barrett generally do."

"Did he have any enemies?" He looked at me as if I had disappointed him.

"Who doesn't? I think, Ventry, it was a botched burglary. Some kid breaking in got scared."

"And took the time to truss him like that? No. Isn't there anyone he spent time with who might have had a motive?"

"He was a painter. I assume he spent most of his time in his studio. Alone. At least I do." He looked at Moira. He looked back at me. "He was just some guy I carried up five flights of stairs one winter long ago."

I stood up and took a turn around the room to stretch. My leg still ached. I could look beyond the kitchen to his work-place, at the chaotic assortment of canvases, coffee cans filled with brushes and turps, photos torn from magazines tacked to the wall. It made me itch to be back in my studio. What the hell was I doing here? Because a lady with good posture had bought one of my paintings, and her husband had painted a good picture of her when she was young and he was falling in love with her, and she had given me money to find out who had killed him and why, so then I could paint more pictures.

"Did the police talk to you?" I asked.

"Sure, one guy came by. I don't know anything. It was a burglary. Crack is up here, too, you know. I see the little glass bottles on the road when I take my walk. The kids go straight from beer to cocaine. They're bored. They do drugs, then they need money, so they break into houses. Peter had money, so they killed him. Maybe that's what happened. No one will ever know."

"Maybe not. Thanks, Jack."

"That's okay. How is your father?"

"As ever."

"He was good to us, mother and me," he said to Moira. "He helped us become citizens. Anyway, come by anytime, Moira. And here take this." He handed her an envelope.

"What's this?" she asked.

"The dirt on this boy you're with. It is a magazine with an article about his paintings. He did not show you, no?"

"No. Thank you, Jack." She smiled at him.

He walked us to the door. As we left, he took my hand in both of his and said, softly, so Moira, who was walking down the flagstone path to the car, couldn't hear, "Don't get involved with this, Ventry. Your work is going well, now. I see that. Keep to your paintbox. Work, that is what will be important to you. You don't need this. Paint, boy."

"You're probably right, Jack." He patted my shoulder with affection. "Don't worry. This won't go on too long. It was good seeing you." I turned and followed Moira down the path.

Once we were in the car and driving on the two-lane blacktop, I asked Moira what she thought of Jack.

"Your oldest friend? He's tops, Ventry. What did you expect me to say?"

"That he was a garrulous, dirty old man."

"Well, there's that, too, of course," she said sweetly. "A charming accent too. Paris overlaid with New York. Maybe a British teacher in there too, from Manchester, most likely."

"More like Amsterdam Avenue. This your linguistic parlor trick?"

"Too right. Where to now?"

"What time is it?"

"Six o'clock, near enough."

"Let's go talk to a newspaperman."

"Who would that be?" she inquired in the husky timbre and the languid aristo archness of the British actress, Joan Greenwood. "A gentleman from the *Globe*?"

"Definitely not my father. He's a gentleman, and not on the *Globe*. We'll be talking to the local media prince, Calvin Conklin. We'll drive into Chatham, and on the way I'll tell you how we came to be acquainted."

"Won't they be shut?"

"The *Vigilant* never sleeps."

10

Before I could tell her about Calvin, she opened the magazine and started reading the review of my show. While she read it silently, I said nothing.

She looked up. "I had you tabbed for a mawkish engenderer of propaganda from the first, mate," she said.

"Button it."

"I think it's the creamy sensuousness I'm attracted to, rather than the dagger-like strokes," she said putting the magazine aside at last.

"I can't read that stuff."

"But you have."

"Yes," I admitted, "but it has nothing really to do with me."

"What's it for then?"

"To reassure nervous buyers. To help them justify spending a lot of money on my paintings. I *hope* a lot of money."

"Well, that's all right then, inn't? Now, why don't you tell me about this Calvin fellow."

"His family has been important in the area for a long, long time. This means a lot to Calvin and he's got some great stories to tell. It's like getting a behind-the-scenes look at American history with all the fire and innocence and greed mixed in.

"Nestor Conklin, Calvin's great-grandfather, sells the farm, invests the proceeds in the China trade and whalers, makes a fortune and starts the paper in time to support Fremont's candidacy in 1856. Ever since, the paper has been Republican, prosperous and unopposed by any rival for over a century. Now, costs are up, advertising is down. It's not doing so well.

"The *Vigilant* backed Lincoln in '60, of course, because Nestor was a fervid abolitionist, but in the election of '64 all his rebel bashing couldn't stop Lincoln, a wartime president, mind you, from losing the county to General McClellan and the unenlightened voters of the Democratic party. Nestor and his paper couldn't even deliver the county to Lincoln. Lincoln! Grant's victories in the West had persuaded enough of the Northern electorate to keep the Emancipator in the White House, but Nestor went into a decline. Started shooting at Rebels he saw in the turnip patch and had to be confined to his room. They gave him a uniform and a flag and that quieted him down.

"Calvin told me all this the day I met him. He had shown up to do some background on a story he planned about landowners and hunters. He's a tall, lanky man, a little over fifty. He stepped out of his car, strode up to my porch, introduced himself with his lopsided life's-sure-a-son-of-a-gun-ain't-it grin and started asking questions. He didn't get far with me.

" 'My views on the subject,' I had to admit to him, 'are contradictory, unformed, and inarticulate.' "

"What a vocabulary the man has," Moira commented.

"Calvin felt like talking anyway," I went on. "I offered him a drink, and he stayed the rest of the afternoon. We just sat. He sipped his vodka, me my iced coffee and we watched the sugar maples along the dirt road in front of us. 'They are using,' he told me once, 'their carotene magic to transform their leaves into botanical fire: orange, gold and red.' "

"If he writes like that, no wonder the paper's in trouble," she said.

"He took to stopping by now and then, and he told me lots of stories about his father, Peary Conklin, who had represented this area in Congress in the Forties and Fifties. Calvin idolized him. He died about ten years ago. When Cal and I get together I try to pump him about local history, which isn't hard, and he loves to talk about art. He has a few very nice works, recent stuff. There's an Ellsworth Kelly I wouldn't mind having."

"Does the Conklin line end with him?"

"Looks that way. He never married, had no children. The paper might too. There are two new weeklies in the area. People seem to be making money with circulars that are just stuffed free in your mailbox. Not him, though. When he gets too infirm, he told me, he'll probably have to sell out to a chain. Guys come around from Gannet and Newhouse all the time. One day he'll just be too tired to shoo 'em off. Here we are."

The *Vigilant*'s offices are housed on Main Street in a three-story brick building, called The Conklin Block. The name was inscribed according to the custom of the last century in lettering a foot high on a plaque beneath the inevitable acanthus leaf scrollwork of the roof's overhanging pediment.

We must have arrived just before the deadline for the submission of classified ads because there was a short line headed by a woman filling out a form at the counter, and behind it a clerk with a phone at his ear. She was a no-nonsense, hunt country woman, decked out in khaki shirt, jodhpurs and riding boots. She was carefully pencilling block letters onto a grid for a classified. She had been less careful about what she tracked in with her boots. I looked over her shoulder. She had stall space to rent, lessons to give and tack for sale.

"Calvin around?" I asked the young guy behind the counter, writing on a pad with a pencil stub. He was new. He looked up. He looked back down.

"1978, Ford Currier Pick-up, Ernest? 'Runs Good,' you say. 'New Rubber.' Yeah. 'Body Good,' glad to hear it. Uh-huh. 'Tonneau cover.' You spell that, Ern? No, I'll get it from one of our old ads. '$1100. Will Dicker.' You goin' to bring the money in? Before five is fine. Eight dollars for fifteen words. Yup, fourteen, fifteen, that's what we got. One time. Right. What. You're buyin' a Bronco, well, I am pleased for you, Ernest. See you." He cradled the phone with a subvocal "Asshole," and turned to the equestrienne.

While he took care of her, I noticed he looked a lot like a younger version of the farmer down on County Route 13 who sold me a used tractor with a three-point hitch I could use to drag logs off the hillside for firewood. Calvin once told me it didn't do in small towns to indulge in idle speculations based on perceived physical similarities. All the old families are related, but some not publicly so, especially if they were of different religions.

"Many a Mason working in a bank looked like a Catholic farmer of a previous generation," he said, "Yes-sir-ree, but best not remark upon it."

In a break in the word count, I tried again, "Calvin?"

"Who're you?" He gave Moira a cool, assessing stare.

"*Newsweek.*"

He beckoned me around the counter and pointed to a door in the back. We went through, knocked smartly and walked in to find Calvin, sitting at his grandfather's desk in seersucker suit and red bowtie.

On the wall behind him were dozens of old photographs, groups of men, bewhiskered Republicans I gathered, all wearing hats and squinting into the camera. They'd have the sun just behind the camera in those days. In the center, in pride of place, was a painting done of his father, Peary, the congressman, who Calvin revered and whose memory my father recalled with considerably less piety.

"Ventry, you paint-stained wretch, you spawn of the tabloids' leading purveyor of the innuendo sublime, what brings you to my lair? And with such a lovely young woman. A thirst for employment?"

"I thought if you had the time we could sort of pick your brains a bit? We need some information?"

"On whom?"

"A fellow named Val Royal, owns an antique shop in Hudson, and a thug who works for him named Merkle, and anything you could tell me about the Peter Barrett case or Cyril Hart."

"Well, well, well, and what are we up to now, eh? The last time I spoke to you, you were too busy with your painting to sit on the porch and watch me drink your vodka. Now, you come on like a paint-smeared Colombo. Why, Ventry? Tell Uncle Calvin, who needs some good scoops and all that wire service income they generate."

"The last time you saw me, you were recalling the glory days of the Stork with my father."

"So you are looking into the Barrett case for him? I hope you know what you're doing."

"Moira here is Cyril Hart's cousin. Moira: Calvin Conklin, Calvin: Moira."

"Howdja do?"

"Howdy."

"Cyril Hart, she tells me, was spending some time with Val Royal. I went to see him and ran into this Merkle guy."

"Have you spoken to the police?" he asked.

"No. All I know is that you said a detective named Van Deusen, who is now dead, was in charge of the case."

"Sergeant Frank Van Deusen. You bought that tractor from his brother last fall."

"I did?"

"That's his kid, out front."

"Thought there was a resemblance."

"Yup." A pause. Then Calvin began tentatively, "If I were to fill you in with what I know . . . "

"I would, Calvin, do right by you."

"I expect so."

"An exclusive."

"You'd keep me up to date on what you're finding out."

"As much as I can."

"It's a deal. About Barrett, first, then. I'll get you photocopies of the stories, but this is basically it. On a foggy morning last October, he was found by the caretaker, a well regarded local man. Peter had been trussed up and tied to a bulky easel, used for holding and swiveling the very largest works, to turn them so he could paint on them without using a ladder. The killer had spun the frame, splattering the studio with Barrett's blood.

"The caretaker fled for help. The police arrived and went through their routine. The medical examiner later confirmed that Barrett's eyes had been sprayed. Had he survived, he would have been blinded permanently. The police found a can of oven cleaner on the floor but unfortunately there were no fingerprints on it.

"The weapon used to stab him had disappeared. What fingerprints the cops could lift in the house and studio belonged to Barrett or his wife or the caretaker, and some of Cyril Hart's in the room he used when he was there." He turned, as if suddenly remembering Moira. "I'm sorry," he said. She nodded. The tears started coursing down her face. Calvin pulled the red silk handkerchief from the front pocket of his seersucker jacket and handed it to her. She started to shake. I put my arm around her.

"Go on," she said to Calvin.

"None of the neighbors had noticed anything. The estate was surrounded on all sides by twelve-foot hedges. The studio had been equipped with alarms installed in the late seventies. They had been turned off. Maya and Aztec, the Barrett's watchdogs, were in the run made of hurricane fencing where they were penned when the Barretts were expecting visitors and didn't want them terrorized by the Dobermans.

"This is one of the few tangible clues in the case. It's pretty clear they might have been expecting the murderer. Someone else may have come before, but the police have never found anyone willing to admit that they were going over to the Barretts' place that night in October to see either Barrett or Hart.

"Barrett often worked at night. The caretaker left at four-thirty in the afternoon to go to a rehearsal of a choral group he performs with in Valatie. After practice, his wife met him there and they went off to a volleyball game, then to their house. His alibi was perfect.

"How can I get in touch with him?"

"Oh, Koopman's still looking after the place. Just go on over. Anyway he found Barrett at eight-thirty the next morning. He had been dead for a few hours. The place had been ransacked and several valuable paintings from his personal collection had been taken according to Mrs. Barrett: a Fair-

field Porter, a de Kooning, a Franz Kline, two by Roy Lichtenstein, a painting of Porter by John MacWhinnie and a Lee
Krasner." Calvin had a good reporter's memory for detail.

"And a drawing by Lou Darmstadt. I got the photos from
Mrs. Barrett."

"They're nice, aren't they? Dealers were alerted and Inter-
pol was contacted. Warrants were issued against Cyril Hart."

"Poor Bulk," Moira said softly.

"The Australian, Canadian and British police were alerted.
The County police assumed robbery was the motive. They
weren't talking about the mutilation of the body. That information hadn't been released.

"Barrett's funeral was a quiet and private affair. He was
buried in a plain pine coffin and brought to the cemetery, as
he requested in his will, in a station wagon. A wreath of
wildflowers was put on his grave by his wife. There was no
service. The event was videotaped by the police. There were
close-ups of most of the people on the fringes of the small
crowd. There didn't seem to be any known assassins among
them. There were some of his colleagues. Your friend Giresse
was there; some collectors and dealers, people who would
make the three hour trip up from the city.

"And there weren't that many," Conklin continued. "The
murder had gotten some coverage by the newsweeklies who
noted Barrett's connection with the Abstract Expressionist
movement and the theft. Interest dwindled when no arrests
were forthcoming. The paintings were never found."

"They're not likely to be, either," I said, "since possession
would mean an instant charge of accessory to murder.
They're gone."

"No doubt," he said, "important pieces, though."

"Calvin . . . " I began tentatively.

"Ventry . . . "

"I've been sitting here, and I've been thinking . . . "

"Yes?"

"Van Deusen was a good cop, would you say? Thorough?"

"The best. If he couldn't get anywhere, well, to be frank,
Ventry, I don't see how you're going to improve on him. Give
it a shot, if you want, but the trail's pretty cold."

"Can you get me Van Deusen's notes?"

He sat musing, for a moment. "Oh, I don't see why I can't get them from the Sheriff. It's an elective office," he explained to Moira.

"Right. Van Deusen was a thorough kind of guy? Followed all the leads?" I asked.

"Oh, yes."

"And didn't find anything?"

"He tried, Ventry, tried like hell. He hounded the neighbors. He gave the caretaker and his wife, Vera, lie detector tests and she's Van Deusen's wife's cousin. Matter of fact, Vera's related to that guy you asked about, Merkle. He interviewed just about everybody in town who knew Barrett, though there weren't many. Kept to himself, you know."

"And what about you, Calvin?"

"Me?" he asked, puzzled, "he never interviewed me. Why would he?"

"No, listen. You told me you want a scoop. You want a story all the wire services will pick up. Features. Interviews. A book. Maybe a Pulitzer Prize. Huh, that's what you think might happen if you break the story of who killed Peter Barrett?"

"I don't know about any Pulitzer."

"It can be yours, my man, it'll come some bright morning, that lovely little yellow telegram from the trustees of Columbia University. I think so. I really do."

"But . . . ?"

"But we have to have an understanding. If you tell the police, or hint in your paper, that Hart was connected with Royal in something shady, what will they do?"

"Go to Royal. Immediately. Question him."

"Right, and what happens? The lead dries up. Maybe what we have is nothing. Maybe Royal is just playing head games with me, but why don't we take a shot?"

"What are you going to do?"

"Get him to trust me. I'll work with him and see if anything is there. You get the story, I go back up on the mountain and paint for the rest of my life."

"And we'll find Cyril," Moira said suddenly. We both looked

at her. Calvin said nothing for a while. Then he said, "I repeat, it's a deal, amigo."

"Now tell me about Royal and Merkle," I asked.

"I don't know that much. Royal owns the antique shop you were in and another one next to it. He comes from out west somewhere. He has a sister who just married a very rich man, Richard Lovatt Hadley. He owns one of the biggest estates up here. He's old money. Very respectable, a tad eccentric, about sixty, collects art. I've known him for years. Her name is Rina, and she's a dish."

"Mrs. Barrett's lawyer cousin is named Hadley and she was going to have dinner with him and his young wife just after . . . You know it just occurred to me that Val Royal is related to Mrs. Barrett."

"I don't think they call each other 'coz'."

"No. Tell me if you can about this guy, Merkle."

"Some arrests. Bar fights. You know that basket of yours?"

"Yeah."

"It was his family used to make them. Years ago."

"Hard to believe."

"Well, it's so What else do you need?"

"Either of them into drugs?"

"Not that I know of."

From his vantage point on the wall, a Hudson River businessman of a century ago looked down at me. The figure was stiff, as if the artist had copied it from a daguerreotype for which the sitter had to hold a pose rigidly. The painting had a kind of awkward charm. It was not large, about 14 inches by 20 in a simple frame. "Tell you what, Calvin. Let me borrow that painting. It will give me an excuse to talk to Royal."

"Jeremiah Osterhoudt? One of my grandfather's backers. Went bankrupt in the Panic of '93."

"Lord Chalmers was having a hard time back then, too." I said idly. Both Moira and Calvin looked at me with blank looks of incomprehension on their faces.

"Pay no mind to him," Moira said, "he had a late night last night."

"Yes," I said. "Forget it. I'll return it before the next Panic, Calvin."

"I don't know how we ended up with . . . no wait, his daughter married a Conklin cousin, I think, over in Valatie or was it Stuyvesant Falls? . . . " not pausing in his ramble around the tangled foliage of the family tree, he took it down from the wall, wrapped it in last week's edition of the paper and tied it with a piece of string.

"That's about it then, partner. Now all I need to know is how to get to the Barrett place."

Taking out a sheet of paper he drew me a map. "Keep in touch, Ventry. Right up to date, so I can write the story if something happens. But most of all, be careful. This can blow up in your face." Though he tried to force a laugh, when we left, Calvin looked genuinely worried, a look that I would have thought hadn't crossed his face in years.

11

I wished I was clever. I was aching and tired and I didn't
know who killed anybody. At this point I had as much confidence in myself as the French General Staff had in Dreyfus.
Maybe less. I had a clue, I thought, in Cyril's connection with
Royal, but it looked like I'd have to become someone else to
go down that path. The irony was that I would have to turn to
my *father* for help in creating the person I was going to be. In
a proper Oedipal drama I would have offed him long ago and
be looking for myself. And, I would be found, happy as sunlight, up in my hillside studio painting away like the post-
post-modernist I am. If he didn't make a good enough mask
for me I might find myself with a date with a slasher, and
there would go painting career, notices and all.

If it hadn't been for this tawny linguist looking pensive by
my side, I would have found some way to weasel out of my
agreements. I can always manage that.

"Where to?" the t.l. inquired.

"It's been a long day."

"It has, yes."

"Let's head for the farm."

"Good idea. Is Barrett's studio near here?"

"Not far."

"Can we get in?"

"If the caretaker is around, yes. India said she'd tell him to
let me in if I came by. She herself has not entered it since she
had learned of the murder."

"It won't be dark for another hour. Let's go there first. Then we can talk at your place." I was pretty beat, but I didn't look forward to calling my father either, so I pulled over, checked the route to the Barrett place on Calvin's map, and found some dirt roads that would get us there.

Fifteen minutes later, we interrupted the caretaker, Jan Koopman, as he was spraying roses. He took off his protective mask and one of his gloves. He was a blond, freckled young man of about twenty-five with alert blue eyes and a carefully trimmed beard. He looked unnervingly like the man who inspected my cars. I was becoming fixated on the submerged bloodlines of the county. He said that Mrs. Barrett had called to tell him to expect me. He smiled, like all the men we had bothered today, at Moira.

"Mr. Koopman, were you the man who found the body?"

"Yes, that's me." He drew himself erect, as if he had been singled out on parade. "It's 'Kope-' as in 'hope' by the way."

"I'm sorry. Umm, there were some things that Mrs. Barrett wanted us to look at for the estate. Has anybody been in the studio since the murder, except for the police?"

"Sure."

"Who?"

"Me. I go in there all the time. Airing out the rooms. Putting down traps for mice after it gets cold. Testing the alarms. Checking the heat and the water pipes. Cleaning. Place gets dusty, you know, even if no one uses it. Think Mrs. Barrett'll try to sell it now? Sure lonely now. There's no one to talk to all day except Queen Elizabeth and John F. Kennedy here," he nodded toward the roses.

"But the house is still more or less the same as that night?"

"Pretty much. You wouldn't be here to make a docudrama for TV about the murder, would you? True crime, like?"

"No."

"Oh. Be a good subject, don't you think?"

"Ms. Hart here is related to Cyril Hart, the young guy who's missing."

"Yeah? Well, Ms. Hart, if you do sell the rights to your relative's story, I think I could play the role of the fella who finds the body, or maybe act as a consultant."

"I'll be sure to make a note of it," she said with profound insincerity.

"Tell me," I said, "you asked if Mrs. Barrett might be selling. Anybody around here looking at the place?"

"Realtors calling all the time. I let them walk around but they can't go inside. With all those windows, there's no need to, really."

"What's the place worth? They ever say?"

"This place?" He ticked off the assets on the fingers of his gloved hand. "Federal-style house with barn converted to studio, original beams, house has living and dining rooms, huge country kitchen, with separate driveway round back for deliveries, three fireplaces, family room, four bedrooms, each with bath, library, pool, greenhouse, gardens, 120 acres, a million six maybe. Be a lot more, closer to the city."

"You a real estate agent, yourself?" I asked. He smiled.

"Studying to be. My wife is one now." He looked around. "It's a damned fine place," he said, "just too bad about what happened. I really don't understand what your interest is but I can tell you this, mister, it ain't haunted. There are places they say, 'yes, it's haunted, right enough,' but not this one. Nothin' funny going on. You know someone wants to buy it, they'll be happy here as anywhere."

It occurred to me, in my own Sherlockian way, that I had heard no barking.

"Dogs still around?" I asked.

"Nah. Mrs. Barrett said to get rid of 'em. Useless creatures. Sent 'em to the pound. We're all wired up now. Much better than before. Sheriff's office, my house, alarms'll go off all over the county. Still some good furniture in there, paintings too. Come on, I'll let you in."

Barrett's studio, once a barn, was now an island of milky light surrounded by gardens. Koopman let us in and then left us. The studio had been sealed first by the police, then by the probate court, finally by Mrs. Barrett's order. Something of Peter should still be here for me.

I wanted to go over the room carefully and sensitively, not in any expectation of finding new evidence, but because that was how I was trained to observe, and, feeling tired, I needed to be methodical. Also, if I was bringing anything to this investigation besides comfort to a widow, it was an occupational sympathy, like one carpenter looking through another's toolbox, or a priest fingering another's missal.

I'm not a believer in auras or crystals. I never had an out of species experience. I just wanted to give the objects in that room, so close to the center of Peter's life, a little time to speak to me, so I would know him a little. Talk to me, room.

The studio was about fifty feet long by thirty wide. It rose maybe twenty-five feet to a beamed roof where five skylights let the light in from the north. From the stains around them, it appeared the skylights also let in the rain. The flooring was made up of ten-inch boards painted white, overlaid with dribbles, smears and spots of different colors. The walls, too, were white. An industrial-sized heater hung suspended from the ceiling in a corner.

On the east wall hung the original barn door which remained from the renovation. When opened, it would have allowed Barrett to move his billboard-sized paintings in and out. It would also let the breeze come in and dissipate the odors of mildew, turps and wet dog.

I walked slowly around the perimeter of the room. Against the north wall was the stereo equipment: a turntable, AM-FM receiver, cassette tape player, amp and equalizer. The speakers were the size of refrigerators. On top of one of them was a cassette case: *Dionne Warwick's Greatest Hits*. The last music he ever heard may have been "Do You Know the Way to San Jose?"

Next to the rough pine cabinet holding the stereo components was the artist's friend: a long, low couch and on it lay an orderly pile of pencil drawings which now had dust on them. I'd look at them later. The police would not have overlooked sketches of his killer. A few feet from the couch was a broad, low, gray metal filing cabinet meant to hold drawings, prints or lithographs. It, too, bore stacks of drawings and some books: *Pottery of the Southwest, Pre-Columbian Sculpture, Black Elk Speaks,* and Feder's *American Indian Art.*

"What's this for, Ventry?" Moira was standing over in the

northwest corner, under the large heater, by a solid bench on casters, about eight feet long, two feet wide and waist high.

"That's his palette," I said.

"I thought that was a jiggery-bob with a hole for your thumb."

"It's that too. This is just bigger. You get one after your first big show."

"Oh." The surface was encrusted with blobs of dried oils and squeezed tubes of Winsor and Newton colors: alizarin crimson, indian red, cadmium yellow, cerulean blue. Old pals. Beneath, there was space for cans and jars of colors, thinners, junk of all sorts. Behind the palette, next to the wall, there was a hot plate. He'd use that to heat wax when he was using the encaustic process. And when it got too gunky, he'd need to clean it. With oven cleaner.

In the center of the room, between two slender pillars which rose to support the old roof, was a twelve-foot stepladder. Against one of the timbers were some t-squares, long metal rulers and a pantograph for transferring images. Low plastic buckets, jammed with dozens of brushes, handles down, of many sizes and shapes, sat on the floor, like hedgehogs.

Next to the other pillar, tubes of titanium white were stacked in boxes a foot high. Near them were two metal bowls, probably to hold water for the dogs to slurp when they visited.

The south wall of the studio was the principal painting area. Down its fifty-foot length bolted to the wall there were paired wooden risers, fifteen feet high, every three feet, with adjustable clamps to hold large canvases. There were two large canvases hanging there now. They were both about ten feet high and fifteen feet wide. The sight of the two of them set off a spark in my brain. I decided to spend more time looking at them after I went around the entire studio.

By the door, there was a tiled foyer leading out of the studio. When we had come in, I had asked Koopman if there had been any changes in the studio, and he had told us there had been several oversized tubs filled with ferns and large-leaved plants which he had moved to the greenhouse so he could tend to them. It was too much trouble to disconnect the new studio alarms every time he wanted to water the plants. He said he and Mr. Barrett used to chat about some of the ferns, which were delicate.

Resting on the ground in the foyer were stacks of museum quality stretchers. Lou had hers made by a carpenter in Long Island City out of three-by-one inch pine. These looked the same. Next to the stretchers was a five-foot high mirror mounted on a pyramidal rack on casters. The mirror and the couch were related.

Barrett must have used the couch at times to sit and stare at his work, letting the images he held in his mind project onto the canvas, flickering from one set of combinations, tints, volumes and contrasts to another, while the canvas in front of him, like an anchor in a sea of visual possibilities, periodically nudged his fantasies back to the problem of the moment.

I put myself in his place. Yes, then he could come over here. He would stand up and step over to the mirror, and peering into it, see his work in a different way and begin another series of optical permutations. Just as Jack had taught me.

To more practical ends, in my own studio, I use the flat glass of a full-length mirror to affix tape and then slice it with a razor. I looked closely: there were scratches on the surface. In a bookcase, I found boxed video tapes of *A Chorus Line, West Side Story, Sunday in the Park with George,* Flaherty's *Man of Aran, Nanook of the North,* John Ford's *Drums Along the Mohawk* and a tape with a hand lettered label: *Statue of Liberty Centennial, July 4, 1986,* all lined up in an orderly row.

"Take a look at this lot," Moira called from the other side of the studio.

In a cardboard box, the size a large television set might come in, behind a blank canvas leaning against the wall, she had found what at first looked to me like the kind of rubbish artists are always picking up at flea markets, but as we examined the contents we both gasped.

The top of the box was filled with layers of American Indian artifacts, all labeled, all exquisite. She started taking them out and laying them gently on the studio floor. There was a brightly colored Cheyenne beaded pipe bag, a delicately carved Osage cradle board, a Pueblo bowl, a Chiracahua Apache saddle bag, three Kachina dolls, a Brulé Sioux Cat-linite pipe bowl, a Cayuga false face mask, carved with a menacing, lopsided grin, an Assiniboin beaded moccasin, a Crow shield made of buckskin and painted with images of horses and men.

Wrapped in a piece of black velvet was a carved, elongated wedged-shaped piece of bone, an ornament of some kind, with other material tied to it. It had been extensively carved and polished and had been carefully punctured with a series of symmetrically arranged holes of differing sizes. The label read, "Elk antler hair spreader for a warrior's topknot. Feather socket ornamented with the beak and scalp of the Ivory-billed woodpecker. Tribe Unknown. Upper Missouri." Someone else, perhaps Peter, had added, laconically, "Way of life abandoned, tribe lost, culture forgotten, bird extinct."

In a folder at the bottom of the box, we found about a hundred prints of other Indian artifacts. All of different tribes, all carefully described.

"Did the Indians do him in, you thing?" Moira asked in an eerie, hushed tone.

"I don't see why they would. If anything, he'd be very sympathetic toward them. That type of mutilation doesn't remind me of anything I've read about the Indians. No, this wasn't a ritual murder. It was a madman, a sadist. Oven cleaner. God help us."

"Too bloody right."

"Please. Will you stop saying 'bloody'? At least until we get out of here!" I was shouting. She looked at me shocked. I put my arm around her.

"I'm sorry. This is getting to me."

"I understand," she said, and I think she did.

In the southwest corner of the room were four fairly sizable easels, probably made to order for him; one was especially heavy. They would be built to support very large canvases, weighted with the stretchers that would keep his canvases plumb and true for generations.

Each of the easels had a center pivot which enabled Barrett to maneuver a painting to any angle he wanted, even upside down, flipping the image, as with the mirror, to get a different perspective, to see a work you have been staring at for weeks . . . differently. Or, he could bring a portion of a large painting he was working on within range of his brush, as his killer had brought the bound artist within range of the knife. Then he had spun him, spun him as if he were a wheel of fortune at a parish fair.

I walked over to the couch, gathered up the drawings, turned and sat with them on my lap. I looked at the two big works on the walls. I looked from one to the other. Moira sat by my side.

"What do you see, Ventry?" she asked. "You're shaking."

"Some good work, Moira. From what Jack said, I didn't think he would have had it in him." In my mind I was saying it was the dawn of creation . . . a brave new world. For this last effort, he had become someone else. He had returned to something like the early powerful style of his famous show, and created something glorious. Colors hurtling at one another, clashing, complementing, balancing, intensifying. Held in check by a pattern of line that was the mark of a superb intelligence. The paints lived on the surface of the canvas, like lichens on a rock, preying on one another. The lines were fractures in the earth, teasing us.

"Ventry, are you all right? You look as if you're in a daze."

"A today that is just so good it's . . . tomorrow. And then the aftermath. Thud. Those two paintings up there on that wall, Moira, were painted by a man who decided to live forever."

"I don't know, Ventry, it's all shapes and squiggles to me, like what the posh stores in Sydney buy from the Abos in the Territory to sell to Yanks."

"The aborigines?"

"Yes."

"Look at the colors, Moira, what do you see? The left one first."

"Greens and golds, yellows, oranges. Like a child with a box

of paints trying to paint a sunrise and mucking it up?" I
thought of young stars, rolling through space, filled with
promise.

"And on the right, what do you see?"

"Browns and faded reds, purples, some ashy blacks, I don't
know, it gives me a feeling like the inside of my eyelids when I
rub my eyes with my fists tight."

"Anything else?" She thought for a long moment.

"It's sad. It gives me such a feeling. I remember once on the
day of the Hobart Cup, after the party when all the guests had
gone, and I was alone and tired and a bit drunk, putting
things away. I came across a trophy for Shield Football, my
da's, who was dead by then. 'The Best and Fairest' it read.
Makes him real and makes him gone at the same time. Then
all the jollity seems so futile. It's all so sad, really. Weepy." She
wiped her eyes with Calvin's handkerchief.

To me, sadness like a mist. Smoke and somber hues. A
hushed battlefield.

"We're both tired," I said, "and projecting. We'll go." She
leaned against me.

"What do you see, Ventry?"

How could I put it? "It's what I remember my life was like
before I came to my farm."

"Oh."

"We should go now."

"A good idea. Are you taking those, too?" she nodded
toward the sketches.

"Yes. I can't look at anything more today. Tomorrow." I
handed the drawings over. She put them in her purse. To be
secretive about taking papers from the site of a murder, even
one where police interest had grown stale, was probably
wise.

Koopman met us outside, mulching his queens and presi-
dents with shovelfuls of cocoa bean husks. We told him that it
was too late to look at the rest of the house, and Ms. Hart
wasn't up to it anyway. He walked us to the car and waved as
we drove off.

12

"I am not an easy lay, Ventry. And I'm not a dewy-eyed fuckwit."

I had told her she had been brave.

We were on my porch, that evening, drinking the tea she had made, claiming it would be good for us. The tree frogs were churring up a raucous melody and the bullfrogs and green frogs by the pond added bass notes.

We were talking things over, as moths fluttered around us in the cone of light cast by the lamp mounted beside the door.

"You were the one who was shaken up in that studio."

"That was powerful work up on that wall."

"Granted, but don't come on the patronizing male."

"I don't mean to."

"Right off. I'm more than a pair of tits and a root after a booze-up, Ventry."

I kept quiet. I've learned something over the years.

"I have a well trained mind."

"I know you do."

"Well, let's use it."

"Fine." A rosy maple moth crawled onto my hand, looking like a fluttery piece of chunky butterscotch candy dipped in blackcurrant juice, a delectable morsel for the pipistrels, bats from my barn, darting and swooping around us in the darkness.

"Are you there, Ventry?"

129

"Hmm . . . yes."

"Do you know how to solve a problem?"

"Sure."

"How?"

"Find the answer."

"You define the problem," she began with all the patience only the truly angry possess. "Set out the limits of the search. Describe the features of an acceptable solution. Scribble down possible answers. Test the alternatives against reality. List the values used to weigh solutions . . ."

"Can't we just, you know, smack someone around?"

"Ventry," she growled with that upswing on the final syllable.

"Go on. I just never thought about things so analytically, that's all."

"We have to." The frogs croaked sympathetically. Churrr, ribbit and twa-ang.

"Okay," I said, "show me how it works."

"What do you mean?"

"Do it. What you just said. Weighing. Listing. You know, scribbling."

"Free association," she explained, "creative thinking. Right. Just give me some time." She had changed into a flowered peasant blouse and a yellow summer skirt that had a splash of sunflowers across it.

"Here we go. Are you ready?"

"Yes."

"Right then. One, Mrs. Barrett killed him because he was going to leave her. Two, your father killed him because of something that happened forty years ago. Three, the caretaker killed him in anger because he was going to be fired. Four, Royal killed him because he refused to sell him an antique. Five, Merkle killed him on Royal's orders. Six, the mafia killed him because they're taking over the art racket. Seven, the CIA killed him for practice. Eight, Conklin killed him to boost circulation. Nine, his gallery killed him to jack up his price. Ten, you killed him because this is *Trent's Last Case.* Eleven, local kids killed him because they were playing Dungeons and Dragons and he was a troll."

"He wasn't a troll. He was an abstract expressionist."

"Button it. Twelve, I killed him because he killed Cyril. . . . Thirteen, this Kavanaugh, who Royal thought sent you and made that creepy tape, killed him. Fourteen, he committed suicide. Fifteen, a secret society, an offshoot of the Rosicrucians, dedicated to the suppression of abstract expressionism, is killing off all that generation of artists. Sixteen, it was a burglary gone wrong, and the killer didn't even know Cyril or Barrett. Seventeen, Royal's sister was having an affair with Barrett and her husband killed him. Eighteen, the police killed him and covered it up. Nineteen, we don't know enough yet. Twenty, we'll never know enough."

"You are amazing," I said.

"You just have to let all the crazy stuff out onto the table. Ninety-nine percent of it is going to be useless, I know that, you know that, but, even so, just the act of thinking up possibilities stimulates the juices, like you making sketches."

She slapped at a mosquito.

"Yeah, but I draw one line at a time, not twenty," I said.

"Shoo, mozzie!" she waved at the space in front of her. "You have a repertoire of flip answers that in someone else would lead to bodily harm. Let's go inside and you can show me your etchings over the vintage port."

We moved into the living room and sat before the empty fireplace. I didn't have any port so we poured the tea over ice and added lemon and sugar. There had been too many studios that day, so I didn't take her out back, instead I hauled out my oversized carrying case and showed her some drawings. In some respects it was a family album. I showed her my mother, my aunt, Lou, pop's secretary, Sadie.

"I don't see any pictures of your father."

"You won't," I said.

"Why?" she asked.

"I could never draw my father's face."

"No one will buy tickets to a play with that godawful title."

"I erased and erased. It was hard for me to see him. I could never be objective."

"I understand."

"No, the boy I had been kept getting in the way: the one he

ignored and who turned to fighting in the streets, parks and classrooms, the eighty-pound Tony Galento. Anyone could see, anyone who watched *Leave It to Beaver* could see I just wanted him to ruffle my hair and call me 'Sport.' What I accomplished instead was to earn a rep in the eighth grade as a screwball to avoid."

"You were a loathsome toad?"

"Yes. His clothes were no problem," I continued. "At twelve I filled notebooks, I still have them, they're filled with line drawings of men and women's fashions. You want the roll of the collar, the knot of the silk tie, the drape of his jacket, the fall of the cuffs over the cordovans? A snap. Just like the ads in *Esquire* and *Harper's Bazaar*. But I always botched the face.

"Women don't think he's bad looking. He certainly had more than enough physical grace for my mother, but the vacant smudges between hairline and jaw made me feel inadequate, you know, even though I knew I shouldn't. I couldn't pin him down, and I wanted to.

"He acted the big shot to us on Riverside Drive and maybe to Sadie and a few cronies in the newsroom and the poker game, but I learned soon enough that he listened respectfully to an endless line of self-involved bores. Anyway, I just couldn't settle my feelings about him enough to draw him."

"You sound objective about him now. Did you have therapy?" she asked.

"It was Jack Giresse straightened me out. He didn't talk about Oedipus or Freud, though he loves theories. He talked about geometry, shapes, interior structures, bones and muscles, how aging bodies sag, the force of diagonals, the color of shadows, how one color changes when placed next to another. The whole program.

"But, one afternoon he said, 'I *cannot* show you how to see when one hand holds the pencil and your other hand squee-eezes your windpipe.' I can feel his fingers on my neck now."

"Lucky fingers," she teased.

"He told me, 'That's what your anger does, young Ventry, it suffocates you,' I had had the idea of drawing a Hogarthian Progress featuring my father going from one nightclub to the next. It wasn't going well. 'When you are working right, you *create* what you see, like Cézanne and like Picasso, *but* you must be at peace totally with your subject and yourself, *enfin tout à fait tranquil.*' Easy to say, hard to do. Hate will shrivel your talent, boy. You have no gift for caricature, yes? No. I think, perhaps,' he added with Gallic malice, 'you are not another Daumier? When you are stirred up, Ventry, you become once again that unhappy, tough Irish kid, garbling the language of Corneille in my mother's salon. No, some things you, Ventry, will never do decently because looking at them stirs up the desire to revenge yourself, eh? You want to slash with the pencil. There is nothing else for it. Go on to something else.' "

"Just walk away, Renée?"

"His constant advice. It worked, though. That's pretty much it. I thought about this a lot. When it came to an artist's dealing with the complexities of living in a three-dimensional world with other human beings, Jack counseled seclusion and non-involvement. *Sauve qui peut.* I think he's right."

"Am I an interruption?"

"Of course not. Drawing well is everything to him. He is a very singleminded man. He has no interest in sorting through the emotions or rousing the monsters that swim beneath the surface, not his own or anyone else's. If the old man was screwing up my art, forget about him. For Jack, like some Zen monk on a mountain, wielding a brush on a scroll, there was only *this* moment," I raised my hand, "which had light of just *this* quality, falling on *this* object," I touched her shoulder, ". . . so."

She took off her blouse. "Why not fall on these? And we'll talk more later?"

So.

I woke in the night. Or, perhaps, I lay dreaming. I was alone. Moira must have gone from my side quietly. I called her name, softly, then more loudly. I got up and walked to the windows which overlooked the pond. In the moonlight so bright it was like a second day, Moira glided naked through the meadow on her way to the water. The tall grass pulsed from the glow of ten thousand fireflies. It seemed to me that

she passed along the edge of the hickory grove as proudly as
if she were escorted by panthers. Were we awake? She was
like a priestess of the night, walking in our dreams unsum-
moned. The waist-high flowers—the black-eyed susans, the
oxeyed daisies, the Queen Anne's lace—nodded and bowed
as she stepped through them. The reflection of the moon in
the water did a jig as she dove in. The frogs grew silent. The
barred owls called to one another in the pines. They recognized one of their own.

I was up before my nature sprite the next morning and got
on the phone to my father's office about my cover for Royal.
"Can you help me out or not? I'm doing this for you."
"Sure. I'll get back to you. Better answer the phone this
time, now that you're back in the real world." As I hung up
the phone, Moira entered the kitchen rubbing her eyes. She
had put on one of my chambray shirts and nothing else.
"You looked beautiful in the meadow last night. Like a
Rousseau. I'd like very much to paint you."
"Give me some of that coffee, hmm?"
I poured us each a cup. "Who were you calling," she asked.
"My father. Here let's go out back with this."
We sat down at the white iron table on the small brick
terrace overlooking the pond. "He may be able to give me a
cover to convince Royal to open up about his relationship
with your cousin. Maybe it has something to do with this guy
Kavanaugh. Anyway he'll call back in a couple of hours."
"Tell me about this father of yours."
"Why?"
"This is why. You show up at my apartment prattling about
my lost cousin, you take me out, fill me with beer and fuck
me. What's a girl to think? Next thing I know we are investigating a murder, you're beaten up but decide it's a good idea
to set yourself up as an itinerant hoodlum painter. Why?
Because your da, who has ignored you all your life, comes up
here, trembling with the sweats and begs you to save him.
Then his posh old lady friend pays you in yankee dollars and
leaves the country. You tell me about this father of yours,
right now, Ventry. Something's not right."

"Where should I begin?"

"Where the bleedin' hell does he come from?"

"Pop grew up in Denver where his widowed mother, a very sour woman from County Kerry, ran a boarding house with a broomhandle and a tongue that could make miners blush. Pop said she would light a fire on cold mornings by yelling at the stove.

"My father once told me he and my mother flew out to Colorado when I was a baby to show me to her just before she died. The old biddy said I looked sickly and went back to reading her pamphlet on the life of St. Vincent de Paul. She had this thing about saints.

"It was in her house, anyway, that he met the roomers, the newspapermen and printers, who first gave him the idea he might take to journalism. The bastards.

"Pop was born on April 26, 1912, the same night the *Titanic* went down in the North Atlantic. According to my grand-mother, it had the words 'To hell with the Pope' riveted to its steel hull below the waterline by workmen in the Belfast shipyard where she was built. She believed in retribution."

"Me too."

"Right. I understand."

"Your grandmother?"

"She ran the boarding house during the long, angry, novena-going years of her bereavement. Her husband, Pierce Ferriter Ventry, a skull busting railway cop, died from step-ping off a moving train, dead drunk, and rolling a thousand feet down an embankment. Maybe a miner or a hobo push-ed him. No one seemed to care. At the wake the coffin was closed, no drink was served and, after she signed a waiver, an officer of the railway handed her a check for two thou-sand dollars. Then she bought her little hotel and took her son to church where he pledged never to drink. She didn't have to bother. It turned out he had a dyspeptic stomach, but the pledge makes him feel virtuous. Hell, he feels conse-crated.

"In the twenties, as he was listening to the lies of the boarders, he was reading the syndicated columns of Ring Lardner, Westbrook Pegler, Bill Corum, Walter Winchell, and

Fowler and Runyon. They were famous, easy to read and lived in New York City.

"This is the family legend. Pop as a boy dreamed of Gotham and the Great White Way. Other kids talked about gold strikes, rodeo, movies. Pop's daydreams featured 'dapper pols and femmes fatales,' Jimmy Walker and Texas Guinan, and that's from one of his songs. Oh yes, he writes songs. After Pop graduated from High School in 1929, he worked on the Denver *Post* for three years and in '32 he headed for New York."

"One has to see how good one really is, Ventry. It's too easy in Hobart and it was probably too easy in Denver."

"You and he'll get along."

"When do I meet him?"

"First hear the rest. He started out as a sort of piecework agent for various small time vaudevillians. He would go around with clippings and beg for jobs for the acts. If they were hired and he found them again, he got a couple of dollars. As I said he tried writing songs. He still does. They are dreadful. Anyway, on pretty short order, he used his Denver connection with Runyon to get some mentions in the column for his acts. Runyon took a shine to him and introduced him to Winchell who also gave his clients a mention or two.

"By ceaseless toadying, he managed to get a job on the *Tattler*, a short-lived tabloid in competition with Hearst's *Mirror* and Cissie Patterson's *Daily News*. Once he established enough contacts, he did pretty well. He ended up at the *Globe* and there he remains. He was certain the best and most glamorous job in the country had fallen in his lap.

"He was starstruck with the idea of working on a paper. You see, Moira, to my old man gossip was important and notoriety significant. He provided his readers with a snappy report on the doings along Broadway.

"Broadway was the Twenties fantasy of itself: city life, gangsters, showgirls, and newspapermen like Runyon with a talent for mythmaking. In the fifties, people with money moved to the suburbs and turned on television. Pop and his crowd went through the motions, handing in their three dot col-

umns every day but that world was going. The number of
newspapers in New York dwindled. Nightclubs were closing.
His world was changing.

"The *ancien regime* lingered on at the Stork, El Morocco
and the Persian Room. Pop made his rounds, along with
Leonard Lyons, Louis Sobol, Bob Sylvester, Winchell, chroni-
cling faithfully ephemeral sayings and doings of those who
had, for whatever reason, a name his readers would recognize. Pop never listened to anybody on the way up. Just
afterwards, once they made it."

"It doesn't sound glamorous," Moira said.

"No joke," I said.

"Go on."

"He never saw the Babe hit a home run to right and trot
around the bases on his spindly legs. He just saw him later,
putting on his cashmere overcoat and staggering out into the
night in search of a cab."

"Who's the Babe?"

"A baseball legend. Pop knew a certain kind of everybody."

"People like your father work in every city. I don't see why
you're upset. They're very common in London. Ferocious,
too."

"Pop saw himself providing a service to the community."

"Oh?"

"He thought he was a three-dot Proust. He wasn't shy and
almost never offended. He cultivated sources relentlessly. He
hired Sadie, a proto-databank who kept his files. He is all set
to roll on forever.

"Along the way, he made a few friends, and, I guess, he
made at least one enemy. But in a milieu where the feud was
a constant theme for this level of reporter, low, Pop tread
pretty warily. During Prohibition, if the columnists wanted a
cordial reception, they had to treat the owners with respect.
A lot of these guys were just a few months removed from
hijacking beer trucks. He never leaked secrets to any of the
scandal mags, no matter how much they offered. I don't
remember anybody threatening him with bodily harm or
lawsuits. He *liked* the people he wrote about."

"Even the gangsters."

"Especially the gangsters. One night he might be sitting in the Stork club with a mob boss like Frank Costello and the next night he might be talking to J. Edgar Hoover at the same table, number 50 in the Cub room."

"How do you know all this?"

"There was a poker game in the apartment every week, all the time I was growing up. He and his cronies nattered into the night about the old days. I just absorbed all this stuff.

"To deny himself something is to disturb the universe. When he got some money he put it on his back. He had lovely suits. The maid's room in the apartment was converted to a closet for him. And Wednesdays at four he had the nails on the ends of his soft, pink hands manicured by one of his old chorus line girlfriends in a midtown hotel barbershop."

"What did he do all day?"

"Christ, I remember every detail, from days I was sick or something, you know. Kids who sketch are quiet, I guess. He liked that. He would wake up around noon and have a break-fast of cereal and tea, oatmeal in the winters, while reading the morning papers, all of them, including the *Morning Tele-graph*, that's the, uh, *Racing Form*. I don't think he ever made a bet in his life, but he kept up with the social notes. Then he would spend an hour in the bath, reading and listening to the radio. After he got out, he would make a few phone calls and then spend a half hour or more dressing. About three thirty, the time I generally returned home from school, I'd see him step out jauntily onto Riverside Drive after the doorman made a fuss over him. He was on his way to talk things over with Sadie. Then he'd probably take in a show and about 11 p.m. begin his circuit of the clubs. After he wrote his column, he generally walked home. That was all the exercise he ever got and he'll live to be a hundred. Vince Ventry ain't gonna fall off no train."

"So, he ignored his family, did he?"

"We could have been in Denver." The phone rang. I took it inside. It was my father.

"I talked to Sonny," he said.

"The cop?"

"No, the hero of San Juan Hill. Wake up, kid."

"What did Detective Ehrlich say."

"He said what he said. Someone vouches for you, and you turn out to be a cop and a guy does time. Then he's pissed and the fella who set him up is going to have to kiss the third rail."

"We'll try something else."

"We're not going to try *bupkis*. I don't know how much time I've got left and I don't want to end up like Barrett or in the wind like that Australian kid. We go ahead."

"So what should I do?" I asked.

"Tell me more."

"I can get a line on these people if I can get closer. The way I see it Val Royal got Hart into some kind of scam. Someone, I don't know who, maybe Royal, got burnt. Maybe Hart was standing in the way of a score."

"Maybe scared."

"Scared?"

"Maybe this Royal, or this other one who we don't know, was scared. I remember going up to Ossining for the Shea execution."

"Pop, let's focus on the present."

"Shut up. Listen. You'll learn something. You there?"

"Go ahead," I said.

"In those days, John Q. Public felt it had a right to know how killers acted at the end. You've seen *Front Page*? In fact they were all beaten up before in their cells by the guards, so when they were carried to the chair they were too stunned to cause any trouble. Anyway we'd all go up on the train for the big event and file our stories, of the 'Kid feisty to the end!' sort, and then come on back to the City the next day.

"I talked to the Warden up there in Sing Sing, and we were talking back and forth about how guys ended up there. I asked him about love triangles and such nonsense. Well, of course, with a question like that, you could expect a smart aleck answer, but he played it straight. He told me to sit in this little room there, near his office, with a guard, and he'd send some guys in there to talk to me."

"Maybe you could come to the point?"

"Geez, I never heard of anything like it. This parade of cons, killers, all of them, come in like I'm the priest hearing confession and there they are, telling me their stories. I guess he told them I was a newspaperman. Anyway, the problem wasn't getting them to talk. Nope. They had their stories down and they came right out with all the details. Well, this one guy, from East New York, his partner was cheating him, so he blew him away. Another one of them robbed a gas station with a tire iron, bashed in the head of the pump jockey, got fifty dollars. Another fella, he thought his partner was going to kill *him*, so, when they were at a movie together, he shoves an icepick into his pal's ear. One guy took a bad beating in a park after a football game, I don't remember why, so he goes and gets a gun and next Saturday finds the toughie who did it and puts one in his head.

"At first it was scary, talking to them, and then it got even scarier when it came to me that murder was, you know, no big deal. These guys kill for money, because they're afraid or because they want to get back at someone. That's pretty much it. Money, fear or revenge. Those are your motives, son. Wiseguys don't kill for love."

"I'll remember that."

"Do."

"What about my bona fides?"

"Sonny came up with a gem. If we get a dead man to vouch for you, then he's not going to complain if someone comes looking for him with retribution in mind. Tell Royal you used to deal with Hershey Mintoff. He was as crooked as a suitcase full of burglar's tools and best of all he has been reposing in the bosom of Abraham for the last two weeks, so you can use his name and say you didn't know he died."

"Who was he?"

"Actually, one of the last of the city's licensed pawnbrokers but for all that, a goniff. He used to hang around the heavy hitters from the rag trade at the track and the crap tables. His brother, Solly, is a bookie who handled their action. Hersh used to move goods for people who wanted to collect twice on their paintings or jewelry, whatever, once from the insurance when they reported the theft and once in a private sale to Hersh before he boosted the stuff. It was not entirely unknown, what he did, and lots of people would figure he'd deal with a guy like you, antiques, fakes, you know, and be quiet about it, not tell anyone else."

"If he was so famous, why would no one turn him in to get themselves out of a jam?"

"His brother has a bad name on the street, so Sonny tells me, for the violence. One of his boys eats client's fingers. Yuch. You tell this Royal you worked exclusively for Hershey Mintoff. That'll get you by."

"What did he look like?"

"Good question, son. He was a skinny little runt with pop eyes, like Eddie Cantor, but he was bald."

"Where'd I meet him?"

"That's none of their business. They want a name, you give them a name. They want a biography, tell them to go to the library."

"Pop, is there something about this business you haven't told me?"

"Why would I do that? I got to go. Call me." He hung up. His reluctance to answer a question of mine while spending twenty minutes narrating a dusty anecdote with him at the center didn't tell me whether he was concealing something or not. I went back to Moira.

13

I had just gotten to the table on the terrace, where Moira was making friends with a dragonfly, when the front door bell chimed. I went through the house and opened the door. A policeman was standing there, in crisp, starched suntans and mirrored aviator glasses. His cruiser sat in the driveway.

"Mr. Ventry?"

"Yes?" I said in as neutral a tone as I could muster. Looking at convex mirrored lenses always irked me and gave me the sense I was either talking to myself or preparing for a self-portrait.

"John Berry, here. Got somethin' for you." He grinned. He handed me two packages. "You an agent?" he asked.

"Sorry, can't say." He grinned again, turned smartly and went back to his vehicle. I shut the door and brought the packages out back.

"Who was that, and what are those parcels?" Moira asked.

"It was Officer Berry and let me see . . ." I said, opening the first package. It was filled with photos of the Barrett studio. Peter Barrett's remains were featured in most of them. I opened the other one. There was a sheaf of typewritten documents with some handwritten notations. The grinning policeman had delivered the late Detective Van Deusen's notes on the murders.

"Calvin came through. These are some of the detective's files. I guess I have some homework. Listen. I'm going to call

Royal with my cover story, and then I have to read through these things. Uh . . ."

"Why don't I make myself useful?" she asked archly.

"No, that's not what I mean."

"I thought I'd sit out here and read through those articles on Barrett I brought up from the city."

"That would be good."

"Then I can go through what's in those packages after you."

"They're ugly."

"Oh," she said. "Ventry, I forget every now and then I'm only a woman. I want to tell you how grateful I am for you reminding me."

"No, Moira . . ."

"Let's just make it, 'Yes, Moira.' "

"Okay."

"Right." Silence. Catbirds were mewing in the bushes.

"It is a murder, you know." I said finally. "What's in that envelope ain't the June *Vogue*."

"So I'll find out. Now you have work to do, and so do I. Go make your call. I'm going to get the articles and read them out here." She went into the house and, after picking up the envelopes, I followed as far as the kitchen. I dialed Royal's shop. He answered on the third ring.

"You still interested in doing business," I asked.

"Sure, with the right guy."

"Look, I used to do business with Hershey Mintoff." Was that the right name? Or Mindy Hershoff? Too late now.

"Uh-huh. I heard of him. I also heard the little weasel is dead."

"I didn't do it, Val."

"Okay. You have a name. Do you have a sample?"

"What's the current deficit, Val? Muralists? You going to bury someone behind a wall and want the plaster to look good?"

"Very funny. We can do business. Just bring one of those folk pieces you carried on so blithely about, eh bruiser. The man I want you to meet is having a kind of a party."

"What kind of party is that? Do I bring a date?"

"You can bring Hershey Mintoff's fucking corpse if you want. Be livelier than some of the numbers likely to show their pallid faces."

"What's it all about?"

"My partner, Mr. Kavanaugh, is anxious for the cultural cachet, such as it is, implicit in the conception and production of a major musical. A series of backer's auditions, as they're termed, I believe, will be put on for the potential contributors. It's in a loft in Soho, tomorrow night. This is not the 'A' list, mind. Indeed, 'B minus' is probably more accurate. You'll be there?"

"Sure." He gave me the address, politely inquired if I knew how to find the downtown center of the New York art world and hung up.

I took the envelopes into my studio and spread their contents out on a four-by-eight-foot sheet of 3/4" plywood I have set up on sawhorses. I pulled a paint-spattered chair over to it, turned on the overhead fluorescents and sat down to work.

The next two hours I read through the M.E.'s report (death due to loss of blood caused by damage to the arteries), the *Vigilant*'s clippings on the murder, and Van Deusen's own records. There would be a file cabinet at the Sheriff's filled with interview reports, lab tests, and crime scene logs, but this would have to do for us. It was plenty. Van Deusen had been dogged in pursuit, going down colder and colder trails for a killer whose identity, if it wasn't Cyril, he was no closer to knowing at the end of his investigation than at the beginning. One small detail stuck out in all that welter of neighbor interviews and blood types. The house man's wife: Vera Merkle Koopman. She had taken the polygraph and had passed it: she hadn't lied about where she had been that night, nor about her amiable relationship with Barrett and her non-relationship with Hart. But Calvin had said she was a cousin of the thug I tangled with in Royal's vestibule.

It was a tenuous thread to pursue, especially in a county where so many people were related and you met with the same names over and over: Goodermote, Van Planck, Conklin, Van Deusen and here was Merkle. She might just be worth talking to. Maybe Van Deusen had been asking her the wrong

questions. My leg throbbed. I turned to study the photographs taken by the police at the murder scene. After shuf-
fling through them all once—there were thirty-six—I came
back to the photo marked #2, a shot of Barrett tied to the
easel.

I looked at it and looked at it. I tried to drive from my mind
that this was a murder and attempted to look at it as a photo,
just an arrangement in white, gray and black. I turned it
sidewise and then upside down. I looked at it close up and
then from arm's length. I covered parts of it with my hands,
cropping it in various ways. Time went by and the photo
didn't yield any insights. Needing a break, I put it on the table
and went out to Moira.

I found her in the brilliant sunshine on the grass overlooking the pond, holding a xeroxed article in one hand.

"Well, what have you found out about Barrett?" I asked.

"Hoelscher."

I looked blank. "He's the author of this monograph on
Barrett. He's sure of everything," she said patiently. "You
should read it. It's dismissive. Unlike poor India, he doesn't
say the Fifties were the Age of Barrett."

"What's he say?"

"Overworked themes," he says, "foggy, derivative, an un-
digested farrago of styles, one good show thirty years ago.
That sort of thing."

"Do you think Cyril knew of this view or did he accept the
family assessment?"

"It would be like him to try to find out as much as he could
about the Barretts . . . " she mused.

". . . and to be skeptical about India Barrett's adulation?"

"Could be."

"Try this on. Cyril gets into an argument with Barrett. They
fight."

"Barrett was old," she objected.

"He was strong and could have surprised him," I said.

"Fine, then Barrett bludgeons Cyril or shoots him, disposes
of the body and then, *then*, hangs upside down, burns out his
corneas with that spray, and stabs himself? That's not on,
Ventry."

A red-tailed hawk was being mobbed by crows, taking turns diving at it from above, forcing it away from their nesting territory.

"Barrett was sensitive about his status," I tried again. "That's why he was a recluse. On the Kinderhook estate he was Picasso's equal. Cyril shows up, not in the mood to tolerate what we have learned about this man's oversized ego, gives him a blast of 'stuff it, mate' and Barrett smashes him, Cyril reels, picks up a knife lying about the studio, and stabs him. Aghast at what he's done, he flees."

"It's farfetched, Ventry."

"It's a scenario which I got from Van Deusen's notes, except he didn't speculate the argument would have sprung from ego."

"Who'd go near any of you artists," she asked, "if you acted so ferociously?"

"Moira, I know you loved your cousin."

"He was not a lunatic."

"Straight out: could Cyril have killed Barrett? And then have been killed afterwards by someone else?"

She shook her head emphatically, "Cyril was not a cruel person. I simply *cannot* imagine him inflicting that kind of torture on Barrett. What would be his reason, for Godsake?"

"You think he's alive?"

"I . . . I don't know, Ventry."

"You see . . ." I began to explain.

"Yes," she interrupted, "if he's alive, where is he? Why is he hiding?"

"He may be dead, Moira." She nodded, tearfully. "It's tough," I said, "not knowing."

"I'm reconciled to that, to him being . . . dead. He wasn't a killer, Ventry."

The crows swooped back over the meadow. "Let's go ahead on that premise." Frankly it would be easier on us, I thought. I had made up my mind to act on the basis that Moira wasn't involved. I couldn't keep looking over my shoulder. Also, if she didn't know where Cyril was, and Van Deusen couldn't find him, then we wouldn't be likely to either. We'd have to turn our attention elsewhere. To Barrett, to Royal, to the

Merkles, to whatever leads Calvin or my father could generate from their hosts of contacts.

"We've reduced the number of suspects by one."

"No, by half. Someone who is not Cyril, kills Barrett. Who?"

We stood up. Bits of grass looked as if they were entwined in her hair. She brushed them off. We went back inside to the studio. She took another chair and sat beside me.

I picked up the photo marked #2. I looked at it again. Moira gasped. Her fingers dug into my arm. It was an ugly scene. How could I look at the ravaged body of a painter who had his sight taken away from him? Even a shallow, arrogant and manipulative one. Was that it? Some monstrous verdict on his seeing ability? My stomach knotted. I swallowed the bile that rose. I kept looking. Forcing the form in the photo into a shape and not a man. I thought of Jack telling me, 'When you look, look to paint.' Find your perspective. Look for the color. So, how would I paint this terrifying scene? I asked myself and started to tremble because, yes, I might paint this. His death agony could be put on my canvas with my hands holding the brushes. And then I knew with utter certainty that it would be good for my career. What an awful thought. But true. I knew it.

I felt guilty, excited and fearful sitting there, sweating, with a photo of a dead man in my hand, a man bound and stabbed. Looking at his torment as if it were a study for a painting. A modern day crucifixion, except he was . . . and then I knew. Not everything, but something. I had my own epiphany, a lurching, jolting face-pushed-up-against-it look into the mind of the killer.

"Ventry, you look peaked. Maybe we should stop."

"Too late."

"What do you mean?"

"I'll show you." I went to a bookcase that holds the books I like to flip through in the studio, in my hunts for ideas, and took out an old book with a cracked spine, a volume of Caravaggio's paintings that I'd had since I was fifteen. Jack had given it to me. He had given all of them to me. I found what I was looking for and walked back to her, handed her the book, open to the painting and she looked down at it.

"Oh, that's too horrible. That's bloody sick." We were look-ing at the Martyrdom of St. Peter, who, unlike his Lord, but very much like Barrett, had been crucified with his head facing downward.

"Do you really think, Ventry, that someone killed Peter Barrett to mimic this painting intentionally?"

"Not necessarily this painting. St. Peter's upside-down cru-cifixion was done over and over again, in church after church."

"I can't believe the motive for this murder was to recreate an image. It must be coincidental."

"Barrett's name is Peter," I said.

"A cult?"

"Perhaps. It's not one I'm familiar with. The kids up here who lean in that direction are pretty unimaginative. Heavy metal, Ozzy Osbourne, Satan worship."

"What about that other rubbish? Prisons and moats, is it?"

"Dungeons and Dragons. Attractive to lonely teenagers. God knows there are plenty of *them* up here, but this murder doesn't seem to fit that culture."

"Maybe we should check out other unsolved murders in the area?"

"See if anyone was fried like St. Lawrence? or stoned like St. Stephen?"

She turned the pages of the book. "Look! Here's a bloke upside down, like Barrett, but here he's thrown from a horse." It was the Conversion of St. Paul. Saul struck down on his way to persecute the Christians."

"Oh, damn."

"Ventry, what is it?"

"Paul lost his sight too. He was blinded. Is that what this is all about?"

"But he got it back, didn't he?"

"Yes, after he was baptized, I think."

"Where's your Bible?"

"Same place yours is: somewhere else. Fact is, I don't think I've ever actually owned a complete, unedited, begat-laden good book."

"Pity."

"Back to terror." She closed the book and looked up at me. "It's even more horrible," I went on, "thinking you might know what was in the killer's mind. Insane violence mixed in a weird way with Caravaggio. That is too clammy, damn much!"

"Clammy?"

"Cold, hard, utterly alien, disgusting!" I was shouting now.

"Hmm. Come here." I rested my head on her lap. "You've broken into a sweat. Just rest for a minute. We're letting our imaginations run riot, Ventry. It's from looking at the photos. As for the Caravaggio business, the easel was on a swivel, he could just as easily have been tilted up. Forget about your Renaissance painters. When we find the killer, we'll find out why he tied Barrett to the easel. Not before."

As she spoke to me, I held her, I could feel the muscles in her haunches as she shifted her position. After a few moments, I sat up. "So, what do you think?" I asked.

"I think you look at the world as if it were a painting, Ventry, but it's not."

"Where do we go from here?" I wondered aloud.

"Come on, squire, pretend you're an Aussie. Wrap me in your sunburnt arms again and say something clever and manly."

"Too right?"

"Not bad. Try again. Good on the arms though."

"Well, a fair start. I've agreed to go down to New York tomorrow. I can take you down or you can stay here. I don't think I'll be that long. Maybe we should pursue something else too. Van Deusen interviewed the wife of Barrett's groundskeeper. Remember her name is Merkle, related to the man who belted me around in Royal's shop. That intrigues me. One of us should talk to her."

"I'll do it. I'll need a car."

"You can drop me at the train in Rensselaer. Just one thing."

"Yes?"

"Don't vanish out of my life, please."

It seemed strange for someone else to be on the farm and me to be leaving, but less so with Moira than any one else I could imagine. The next day, with the Smith and Wesson, Conklin's painting and some of India Barrett's money in my bag, we headed for the train that would take me down to New York. Moira was going to visit Vera Merkle Koopman. Their number and address were in the telephone directory. I told her magazine writer was a good, all-purpose cover. I had bought drinks for enough of them. Me, I was an outlaw painter or some damn thing, but her I was giving advice to.

It was noon. Moira kissed me, patted my behind and strode off back to the car. On the train, I settled down for a hard think, fell asleep and dreamed of taking a train ride with Jack's mother.

14

I spent the afternoon haunting Handasyde and Beaky, looking at my own work. Finally, they put me out on the street. It
was time to go to the party. The address Royal had given me
turned out to be off Prince Street in Soho, on a block once
made up of small manufacturers. The buildings down here
were converted over the last fifteen years in complex, bitter,
typically New York ways, involving desperation, threats, suits,
intimidation, payoffs and politics, first into outright illegal
living space, then tolerated semi-legal, and at last, with a
Certificate of Occupancy, legal.

From the outside these old buildings had the charm of a
mail truck, but inside, creative people who knew materials,
design, the history of taste, and who had antennae that
caught the least flutter of a vibration of an oncoming trend,
people like Lou, in other words, made themselves at home
here.

I'd begun to hang out in Soho in the early Seventies when I
was spending more time in the States, working out of New
York. I went to all the downtown openings back then. It's kind
of hazy now, all the talk, the girls, the jug wine, the good
French whites, the Moët. I drank them all in.

A green thimble-sized bottle lay on the sidewalk before me.
I kicked it under a car. Those bottles are the seeds of the city's
death. They hold crack, the cooked, smokable, low-cost, and
unbelievably addictive form of cocaine that has brought
packs of desperate, paranoid users into the streets and sub-

ways, looking for the price of some coke to sizzle in their glass pipes in doorways or squatters' apartments. It's given us a generation of purse grabbers and chain snatchers, flooding the emergency rooms with wounded berserkers. They'll drink bleach to get high. That's the New York City crack scene. A crazed giant biting off gobbets of his child's flesh, like Goya's "Saturn Devouring His Children." Crack is not a drug for openings.

Drugs have always been down here, of course. You could trace the fads like the twists and eddies of the pop charts. When I first showed up, no one was using acid anymore, and only a few of the oldtimers used heroin. Bikers started selling meth crystals in the East Village, and they're still at it, but good downers were thought almost as wholesome as strawberries and cream. I took a good friend once to the emergency ward at St. Vincent's when she tried to drift off to the afterlife behind white wine and street reds. I watched the doctor put two pencils interlaced between her toes and squeeze. I'll never forget that scream. That was a real agonized sinner's note. They pumped her stomach, and now she has tenure, teaching art history in some state without trees.

Now cocaine. I saw it spread out and cover us quietly: thick, white, sudden and strange, like winter, God help us, in a children's book illustrated by Ezra Jack Keats. The innocent, insouciant, sung-about-in-blues-song, stylish high. I've never used cocaine. Generally, at parties, I sipped wine or vodka and took a hit on the smoldering paper and passed it on, listened to the music, danced a bit. A little flake? Want to be paranoid, impotent and broke? I'm old fashioned. I'll pass.

I was near the entrance to Kavanaugh's building, where a couple of gray, stretch limousines with tinted windows, built to lodge befuddled strivers in New York's traffic, were pulled up on the narrow sidewalk. The black-capped chauffeurs, leaning on the fenders, smoking, ignored me as I edged by. It was 8 P.M.

Near the doorway, a very large man confronted me. He was slope shouldered and dressed in a black suit and a black silk shirt. No tie, only a gold chain stretched round that monumental neck. He looked like a plowman's ox, decked out for the blessing of the animals. He stepped over to the door, grasped the handle with one hamlike hand and suspended the other over the buzzer of the intercom. Above him, the small red light of a closed circuit TV camera peered at us.

"Name?" he asked curtly.

"Ventry."

"Ventry!" he hollered into the small microphone.

"Okay," came the quick response.

He shoved the door open and I squeezed by him. I stepped into an open elevator that rose without me pressing any buttons. When the doors opened, two men eyed me as I stepped off. One was standing in front of me holding a clipboard and a pen. Redhaired and pasty-faced, he was wearing a size fifty-long cream-colored sports coat over a green shirt. Redheads are told only one thing about color and they never forget it. The man behind him was Val Royal.

"Name?"

"He's okay," Val interrupted, "I'll take him in."

The room we entered was essentially factory space, maybe seventy by a hundred, done over with track lighting and white paint. Cast iron columns, the bones, really the soul of the building, rose up from the dark, pegged oak floor. There was a baby grand piano in one corner and a bar set up in another.

There were some large contemporary pieces on the wall, a Jasper Johns, one by Jack Giresse—Orange Surprise Sunrise, a peppy, dayglo sun seen through scraped beachgrass that he'd done with his fingers and a palette knife—an Elaine de Kooning and a Lichtenstein dotted comic book panel of a teenage girl, weeping and scorned.

There was a long, butcher block counter covered with plates of finger food which separated the party area from a kitchen toward the rear, where shiny copper utensils hanging from racks were suspended from the twelve-foot, pressed-tin ceilings. Another counter served as the bar.

The loft was crowded with good-looking young people, talking animatedly with one another over the music coming from the tape deck by the bar. They were a trendily dressed lot, blousy shirts, billowy trousers, high-top pink-laced sneakers, a lot of thought had gone into their hair cuts. Most were whites, some Hispanics, a few blacks. A couple of the black girls had the posed languid look of the top-dollar model. Sprinkled about the room were some older men, paunchy and tanned, ties folded, not knotted across their shirts. They looked like gin rummy players from the garment center. Most were short and talking to young women who were tall. The music was hard-edged and insistent, percussive and unfamiliar: what they might play on Mars in the next century at get-togethers for the robot groundcrew. I liked it. Usually with a young crowd, it's the Talking Heads or someone's boyfriend.

"So let's get a drink," Val said and led me over to the bar. A young Asian woman poured the drinks: principally diet colas and Saratoga water. Chilling in a large metal bowl of ice were a bottle of white wine, blanc des blancs, and next to it a bottle of Absolut. Except for the help at the doors, fat was out. I said I'd have some of the vodka, Val took a Saratoga.

"Well, Val, are these the fakes?" I gestured toward the party.

"Be more generous. And quieter, too. Kavanaugh is over there." He nodded toward the center of the room where a bunch of people were sitting about a glass-topped coffee table, laughing at the jokes of a gray-haired man who was sitting on a couch with his back to me.

"Who's your good-looking friend?" asked a blond girl-child who appeared at our side.

"A business associate. His name is Ventry." Turning to me, with punctillious courtesy, he said, "Ventry, my sister, Rina Hadley."

"Is he straight?" she asked appraisingly.

"Ask him," he said in a bored tone of voice and walked off.

She looked up at me. Her eyes were gray like Val's and like him, she was small-boned and delicate looking, comely as a marigold. She wore a sapphire ring on one hand and a wedding band on the other. "Buy me a drink, mister," she pleaded in a girlish voice. She seemed half-drunk.

I picked up a bottle of Saratoga water from the bar and handed it to her. She reached instead for my vodka, took it and sipped it. I drank the water. She put her hand under my arm. She squeezed. I looked down. She smiled impishly.

"You a hood or an antique dealer?"

"What's it to you?"

"You're a hood. Those are the only kinds of people my brother hangs around with these days."

"What are you?"

"I don't hang around with my brother much any more." She took another sip of my vodka.

"Who are all these people?" I asked. The room looked like the kick-off for an ad campaign.

"People," she said wearily, "just people. Show people, business people, like that."

"Are you an actress?"

"No, I am a wife," she said very slowly and softly, looking down at the polished oak floor, enunciating each word, "the wife of Richard Lovatt Hadley. Do you know him?"

"No."

"You should. He's a nice guy."

"Right."

"So, what *are* you here for? You an investor?"

"No, to meet a friend of your brother's, Mrs. Hadley."

"Call me Rina."

"We might have a friend in common, Rina."

"Oh, who?"

"Mrs. Peter Barrett."

"She's a cousin of my husband," she said without much enthusiasm. "I don't really know her."

"Do you know Cyril Hart?"

"Cyril, oh." She opened her eyes wide and nodded, like a schoolgirl whose best friend just told her the test answer she had forgotten. "I got to go now. Call me." She hadn't given me her number, but assumed I could get it easily enough. She had gone over to the crowd by the coffee table and squeezed in next to the man telling the stories. I moved over toward a small group, who seemed to be talking about different open calls they had gone to lately looking for work and what work they had found. The talk was animated and reassuring to the eavesdropper because the talk hadn't changed much over the years. I circled through the buzz.

". . . I've a shot at the road company *Les Mis*. . . ."

". . . Yeah he flew me down in his own plane. I met him at Williamstown in stock way before *Superman* . . ."

". . . I was right for the part in *Hannah*, but I'm glad for . . ."

". . . No one takes class with him any more. He's got . . ."

". . . voiceovers . . ."

". . . my agent says LA might be right for me now . . ."

". . . Pacino . . ."

". . . stress fracture. I can still . . ."

". . . only a showcase, but . . ."

". . . it's all there in those Donald O'Connor . . ."

". . . New York face . . ."

". . . yeah, him too. He's got . . ."

". . . writer for Letterman . . ."

". . . *The Story of O*. Sondheim says . . ."

The career oriented narcissism of New York actors is like a figure painted on the ground of their lack of interest in ideas. Self-absorption held against the void. My one and only relationship with a New York actress ended because of her anorexic intellect. She fed her mind with these rumors and poses. As you can see, I'm well on my way to becoming a cranky old man, but she did have an interesting face.

I could now see the man, Kavanaugh, next to Rina. Even across the room the gray-blue eyes that shone out of the Dawnwalk video rested on me. His face in repose had the heavy sadness that Roualt put in his portrait of the dying king. You could almost see harsh, dark lines in his features. But he wasn't dying, and he looked dangerous.

Val disengaged himself from the group and came over.

"Kavanaugh backs plays, off-Broadway up to now. Anybody asks, you're a backer too."

"Right. These all actors?" He laughed.

"They're the props. We're the actors."

The party really revolved around the table in the center. I saw the eyes of the other guests, even while talking to someone else, flick over toward the dying king, sitting on the couch, telling a story to his retainers with broad gestures of his arms. It has to do with status gravity: if you don't have weight, your partner's eyeballs roll elsewhere. I bet the guests lying on Nero's couches acted the same.

Suddenly I was aware I was being summoned. I'd missed some cue. A tanned, powerful looking hand reached up in greeting. I took it and he guided me next to him.

"Hello, the name is Kavanaugh. Make a little room here. So you're a friend of Val's. Push over." The others on the eight foot, brown leather couch pushed over, as dutifully as first graders on a schoolbus on the first day.

I saw Kavanaugh look behind me at a commotion in the corner, by the bar. A garment center guy I never saw before was arguing with one of the girls. I couldn't make out too much over the music, though everyone else fell silent. Just a word here or there. ". . . answering machine . . . owe me . . ." He grabbed her arm, the girl twisted away. It looked like a dance step, a violent lindy. I felt Kavanaugh rise next to me. He motioned with his arm. Immediately, the red-haired bouncer hurried in short steps over to the bar. He took hold of the man's arm, one hand on the bicep, the other on the wrist. The man turned in surprise and irritation. Red squeezed. The other's face grew white and his eyes closed tight in pain. They shuffled toward the door that way, a small smile on the large man's freckled face. Val stood aside and closed the door behind them. It had been a quick demonstration of Kavanaugh's power. He started to sit down, then, instead, left the table to go over to Rina, who had watched the little imbroglio impassively. He put his arm around her shoulders. Nodding to Val, he and Rina went into another room.

My tablemates and I stared at one another. No one said anything. Val came over. He was laughing. "It's nothing. Forget the bum. I know him. He wouldn't put dough into *A Chorus Line*. This party just officially started." The kids brightened up. "Why doesn't one of you play the piano? Let's hear some songs. 'Send in the Clowns'." They all groaned in unison. "C'mon, showtime!" He tapped me on the shoulder. "We are to talk."

"Okay," he said, once we were out on the balcony, he spoke low and fast, with an insistent urgency, like a quarterback in a huddle. "When my sister leaves, Kavanaugh wants to talk to you. This could mean a good suck on the money tit. Don't screw up. I think he's a genius. The script calls for me to tell you about it later."

"What script?"

"We don't have time." He paused, opened his eyes wide, moved them close to mine and whispered, "he is the greatest man of the century." Then he drew back and just as softly said, "You really knew this guy Hershoff?"

"Mintoff." I said, surprised at Val's abrupt change in tone.

"You'd better. Red and his pal downstairs can do a piece of work for Kavanaugh. Know what I mean?"

"Yes." A piece of work is a murder.

"Not that I would know anything about it, of course."

"What was that all about with the girl?"

"Some old geek who doesn't understand how Kavanaugh likes people to behave. Now he does. Hey, you do coke?"

"No."

"Kavanaugh does but hates to admit it. Here they come now."

"Val, that man's insufferable," Kavanaugh said. "Keep him out from now on, would you? And Val, Rina's leaving." He gave her a kiss. "Would you see her down to the car, and then bring Mr. Ventry to my study? *Ciao, carissima*." It sounded like 'chrismé'.

Kavanaugh went back through the party, where a group was gathered round the piano, singing. He waved at them indulgently and pausing to whisper something to one of the older men, who laughed and nodded, he patted him on the shoulder, then continued to move through the room like a ward boss at a wedding. He walked through the kitchen and stepped through a door in the rear. I was left alone.

As I waited, I drifted over to the bar, where the Chinese girl gave me another glass of vodka. As far as I could see, Kavanaugh, this blarney-tongued Barnum, was a scene setter and plotter, a director of small interludes for profit and amusement. Obviously, he was using the prospect of work in a show to lure the ever desperate young actors and singers.

I was not getting the picture. What in all of this was worth killing someone over? Or perhaps two someones. A painter of faded reputation and an upwardly mobile Australian whose cousin's face had become part of my midday fantasies.

Who was getting anything out of all this? The actors, parts maybe, but they were just props, Val said. I didn't see how they could be part of the murders. The worlds didn't overlap that much. As India Barrett remarked,there were walls between them.

Kavanaugh was apparently involved somehow with the lovely Rina. And she was married to India's cousin. Was there a thread of some kind that ran from India Barrett to her cousin, Hadley, to his wife, Rina, and then to her brother and Kavanaugh? Was Rina at the center of this? She said I should call her. I bet she didn't have to invite many guys twice. And she had made the offer when I mentioned Cyril's name.

Val came back, "Let us go then, you and I," he said, and we went through the kitchen into Kavanaugh's office. The change from the modernist decor of the large room outside was as startling as going from the output of 100 watt speakers to the quiet of a sound-proofed study. His retreat was dominated by a gold leaf and ebony desk, at which he sat. The top was covered with silver-framed color photographs, of himself, in a bathing suit and sunglasses, with Onassis on his yacht, in a tuxedo with Nancy Reagan, again in a tux with Andy Warhol. But my eye went to a black and white photo of a young and ruggedly handsome Kavanaugh, standing between the imposing, fleshy presence of Alfred Hitchcock and his star Ingrid Bergman. This was a man with a past. I wondered if I could get him to talk about *Notorious*, or was it *Spellbound*?

The rest of the room was chockablock with ornate rococo, gilded candelabra, gesso statues of saints in lively colors, even reliquaries of colored glass or precious stones in gold frames; there was a chest painted to look like onyx and marble, a glass-fronted rosewood bookcase ten feet high, filled with leather bound volumes with gilt lettering. The walls were red damask, the drapes a subdued maroon. On the floor stretched a medallion design carpet, a Sarouk, in shades of rust, ivory and blue-black. The effect was of the private cabinet of an aging rich man of nineteenth-century tastes, a worldly prelate perhaps who liked soft lines and soft living and a spot of mortal sin. You wouldn't be surprised to find him in the boxes watching Degas' ballerinas.

We sat in leather covered armchairs, the leather was as soft and supple as a sable brush.

"Mr. Ventry," Kavanaugh began, "I *am* pleased to make your acquaintance. Let's get to know one another. Mr. Royal tells me you are an accomplished painter." He rolled the 'r' in painter as if it were a cherished word, that he let go reluctantly. His voice was rich, controlled, charming and persuasive, like an Irish tout.

"I try."

"Have you slides of your work?"

Val interrupted. "Mr. K, remember I told you this was the guy who likes to hide his light under a bushel basket, as it were."

"You knew Hershey Mintoff." Kavanaugh said. "What a sweet tempered lad, eh?"

"Very sweet. If he crushed the knuckles of one hand with pliers, well, he might very well leave you the other hand."

"But handsome. The ladies adored him."

"Only the blind."

"Ah, Hersh. Well, I never met the rascal, myself, but what you say is consistent with the memory he has left behind among some of my associates. Your clientele includes some wealthy people, Val says."

"Yes."

"India Barrett?"

"Yes."

"I've known Mrs. Barrett. We're on some boards together. I knew her husband, too, poor man. I called her, but she's away."

"A girl can sit by the phone waiting for a call only so long."

"And what do you paint? The fire raging within?"

"Whatever pays."

"I see. Well, why not?" He grimaced. He seemed suddenly bored, as if he were coming down from the coke. My actress friend said it was like having to watch black and white TV.

"There is a need right now, perhaps, perhaps not, for

someone with your skills and background." He went on. "I do not have the talent to pick up the brushes and the tubes of paint myself but I love beautiful things. I do, yes. I want there to be more of them." He smiled.

"Tell me," he continued, "how much money do you need?"

"How much is there?"

"I have many businesses, Mr. Ventry. Here, in Europe, in the Pacific. Do you know anything about any of my businesses?"

"No."

"Good," he smiled at Royal, as if the pupil had at last learned a difficult lesson, "that is the way it should be. Let me explain just one of my businesses. People in one country want objects from another. I'm the middleman, that's all. When there are not enough objects, I arrange for more to be made. When there are too many, I look for sales people. You, I think, might become one of these sales people."

"Maybe."

"Hear me out. Val can support the statement that one can make large profits working with me."

"What's the merchandise?"

"Electronics, fine art, antiques, children, ivory or rhino horn, medical supplies."

"Children?"

"For the childless rich here in the States. Believe me, you would envy the homes these infants go to."

"Drugs?"

He shrugged. "I leave them to government agencies and the lads in the mafia. They resent competition, don't you know. No guns or explosives. No military. No political intelligence."

"What kind of art do you handle?"

"The odd trinket, temple carvings from Laos and Cambodia, Chinese ceramics, tribal masks from New Guinea, crèche figures from Napoli, wedding shawls from South Africa, orthodox icons, Etruscan tomb figures, whatever you want."

"Mr. Kavanaugh makes the market."

"Thank you, Val," he said.

"Paintings?"

He looked heavenward. "Of course, and mosaics, illuminated manuscripts, prints, terra cotta, ivories, netsukes, bronzes, glass, porcelain, and for the literate, book bindings."

"Genuine?"

"Almost all have genuine antecedents, Lord. In Firenze, they can make anything."

"Why don't you open a shop on Madison Avenue?"

"Perhaps I have." He smiled thinly. "Did you know Nelson Rockefeller, of all people, opened a shop on Fifty-seventh Street where he sold copies of works in his collection? Red worked for him. He has very interesting stories to tell."

"I'm sure." I could just imagine the Gov and the burly giant at the door cruising the galleries together. He raised an eyebrow at the lack of interest in my tone. Maybe Red would chat with Pop in Purgatory.

"Do you know what people really want, Mr. Ventry?"

"No, but you do."

Startled, he looked at Val, then he turned to me and smiled. Very softly, he brought his hands together in silent applause.

"Yes, I know. Immortality."

"That's, uh, terrific?" Honest to God, I might as well be talking to a burnout on Riker's Island eating dirt. Sounded like the coke had frozen the synapses in Kavanaugh's brain.

"No one but our Holy Mother Church offers it directly, but in some forms a businessman, one perhaps with more vision than that shopkeeper Rockefeller, can sell it. In fact, I am already in the immortality business in a small way. Val? You tell the story so well. Mr. Ventry, some chartreuse?"

"Yes, please." He poured some of the monkish green stuff into three small glasses. We sniffed and swallowed. He nodded at Val, "My chronicler." We settled back, and Val began.

"One fine day, and a very fine day it would turn out to be, as Mr. Kavanaugh was going through his mail, he chanced to find a prospectus from a realtor. Since he buys and sells quite a bit of property, this is not surprising. What was offered was an inaccessible four-acre island off the New England coast, with lighthouse, serviced once a year by our boys in the Coast Guard, oh lucky lighthouse, and thereafter flashing from dusk to dawn and on foggy days, automatically. The circular explained the previous owners were accustomed, stout-hearted souls, to go out there by helicopter once a year for a picnic. Some fun. Wicker hampers and Sikorskys. There was a small house on the island, and, if you liked solitude, here you'd have only the seals and the gulls for company."

"The pounding surf, the planets moving across the night sky, the pulsing signal light, the passing freighters, the sun and mist," put in Kavanaugh.

"Exactly," Val went on. "The place was on the market for years. It was rockbound, the cliffs were sheer, you needed a helicopter to get on the damn thing. Once out there you could be fogbound for a week. Mr. Kavanaugh bought it for practically nothing. And I'm sure the realtor thought his direct mailing had found sucker one. But Mr. Kavanaugh had vision. And now he's made a killing."

"How?" I asked.

"You'll chortle when you hear."

"Well?"

"He turned it into a repository for people's ashes."

"Urn burial?" I asked. Val nodded. Kavanaugh beamed, then dabbed at his nose with a handkerchief.

"It was a perfect solution. No care, one-way trip, keep them in an office in New York until it's time to ferry them out a few cases at a time. Think of it. Our customers spend their working lives sharing cubicles in windowless offices, adjudicating claims or getting really ticked off because they were left off the distribution list *again* for the new policy memo. Someone like that will spring for a grand or two to end up listening to the surf pound against the rocks. Maybe get some sun."

"How can you listen if you're dead?" I asked.

"When Mr. Kavanaugh gets finished, the customers think you can."

"So it was a hit?"

"He made something, but wait, the real money isn't in retail, it's in stock."

"He stocked up on jars?"

"Ha ha," he said mirthlessly, "that too. No, he formed a corporation and sold shares. Mists of Avalon, Inc. Very attractive offering. Rina's husband helped us out with the SEC.

Equity in the island, booming business, good cash flow, fine
growth prospects, not much downside risk, very little liability
exposure and all those potential customers up there in the
comptroller's office on the 23rd floor, who do not want to be
buried alongside the Long Island Expressway. The issue sold
out and you want to know who our biggest buyers were?"

"Institutions?"

"No, no. We only had about two percent institutional in-
vestment. No, I'll tell you who: the clucks who signed up for
the jars! They wanted a piece of the company."

"The guys who bought the urns also bought shares in the
company?"

"Sure. Women too."

"What for? Did they think they could take it with them?"

"Doesn't matter. Mr. Kavanaugh has their proxies. You'd be
amazed at how many people left their shares to him."

"Why?" I was genuinely puzzled. "How did he get them to
do that?"

"This brings us to where he got the idea. This will amuse."
Kavanaugh lifted an eyebrow and nodded in modest ac-
knowledgement.

"On yet another fateful day, this insurance agent was trying
to sell him a policy, whole life or something. Mr. Kavanaugh
always likes to hear someone else's pitch. Then, when the guy
thinks he's got a fish, Mr. Kavanaugh starts pumping him. Of
course, the guy talks up because he doesn't want to lose a
sale. Casual, Mr. Kavanaugh is, as if he's just about to reach
for his Mont Blanc and sign up for a ten million dollar policy,
but first, well, he'd like to get a sense of the *soundness* of the
company he's dealing with. The salesman spends two hours
telling him everything he knows about the company. Eventually, the salesman tells him about the one percent of the
policy holders who make the insurance company their beneficiaries."

"The company?"

"Yes. Now what does that mean to you?"

"People are lonely."

"Right, lonelier 'n hell, lonelier than I hope we ever know,
but to Mr. Kavanaugh? He thinks he knows more about them

than that. They don't know what to do with their dough, which he is beginning to think is rightfully his, and that they made their money over to the company because they like the fresh faced salesman. He came and talked to them. Spent time with them when no one else did."

"It's sad."

"It's not *sad*. Virgin prairie isn't *sad*. Mr. Kavanaugh asks the guy if he could acquire the names of policy holders who made the company their beneficiary."

"What happened?"

"The guy reacted like Mr. Kavanaugh asked him if his mother wouldn't be interested in some bondage games. But he coaxed the guy, played with him, asked him what his goals were. Believe me, all these guys, they've got goals. This one wanted to make the chairman's circle. How bleak, Ventry, life really is."

"The leading salesman?" I put in.

"Right. Well, when *il grand signor* here was through with him, his horizons had broadened considerably."

"What happened?"

"The guy signed on and took a few lessons with us." He smiled at the memory. "Then he found his man in computer operations to run a sort for beneficiaries with the company code."

"How'd he get him to do that?"

"Took him to the West Indies three weekends running in February for coke and whores."

"Oh. Those were the lessons?"

"Hey, the guy had a gift."

"Then?"

"Our salesman has the list; he leaves the company and starts pitching not whole life but shelf life."

"And they became your clients?"

"And shareholders. Mr. Kavanaugh gave him a piece of the company."

"Where is he now?"

"Out there pitchin'. It was a long list. And when it comes to an end, it's a good bet he'll find a horny programmer in another company who could use a tan."

"You're probably right."

"So, this is your man. Mr. Kavanaugh opens his mail, reads a real estate brochure for an uninhabitable island, a guy tries to sell him insurance, and just out of that envelope and that conversation he makes millions." My father would like Kavanaugh. I'd have to ask him if they ever met.

"Some men are born with big ding-a-lings, thank God," Val said, "and some men are born with other gifts. Mr. Kavanaugh sees people the way others can't."

"What are all these people at the party here for? Picking out a spot facing west on the island?" I asked.

"Oh no, no." Kavanaugh said, "I'll explain them in a moment. Another liqueur? A cigar?" He held up a box of Uppmann's.

"No, thank you." I said.

I wondered what my role was expected to be in all of this, and if and when they'd get to the tape and the Dawnwalk foundation. If Kavanaugh saw through me I'd have some explaining to do. It was time to get down to our business.

"I'm hurt by the lack of a proper memorial for the first Indians who crossed into North America," he began, in a swirl of blue cigar smoke. "I am raising funds for a museum and teaching facility in Alaska, dedicated to the memory of those first immigrants, who came across from Asia twelve thousand years ago. My target date is 1992. I will succeed." He paused, as if he was gauging how far he could go. "The numinous power of their shamans," he continued, "leads me along the path, and I will not falter." Val was nodding away. "Some people of great wealth, like our mutual friend, India Barrett, are supporters. I seek now the participation of the masses. I have hopes of putting on a musical, on Broadway. The groundlings will flock to it. This will be an important step in publicizing our goal and raising money. The old men outside are angels. Earlier, the young people were performing some of the songs and dances for them."

"Why don't you get some Indians?"

"To hop? Be serious. I need Broadway level dancers, singers and actors, Mr. Ventry. I'm working on it. We'll hire some Indians later."

"Or paint the whites in red face?"

"Please. This is serious. No more wisecracks. I'm seeking breakthrough recognition here. I need the right participants." He mentioned some names, all recently successful on Broadway. "I have methods to approach them. Pressures I can put on some of them to attract the others. It can be done." He drew confidently on the cigar.

"I can't dance, Mr. Kavanaugh. I can't even hop."

"Of course not. You are a painter of some expertise, Val tells me. A strong man, perhaps a bold one." He leaned back in his chair and blew smoke toward the ceiling in the attitude of someone reminiscing. "Such a one was Cellini. Perhaps you, like me," his speech took on a soft incantatory rhythm, he was off again, "were born in the wrong century and yearn to live in another age, but failing that, you seek, don't you, to recreate the spirit of that time that was denied you, making its memory live. Cellini himself stood on the shore of the Mediterranean and watched Triton surge through the waves and then he drew Triton's very soul out of the allegorical gold his workmen brought him . . . the salt cellar of the French court . . . such power."

'Salt cellars?' I asked myself.

"It's Cellini's monument. Dawnwalk will be mine, alive forever." In the silence that followed he puffed meditatively. He really could get worked up, like a bullfrog on a lilypad. He turned to me. I hoped he couldn't read my mind. "And you," he said, "I must see *your* work. Deny us no longer."

I handed him the likeness of Jeremiah Osterhoudt, bankrupt.

He nodded over it and held it delicately in his white hands, casually, with an air of professional acquisitiveness. He passed it over to Val, who whistled.

"If the payoff," I said firmly, "is going to be big enough, I'll do what I have to."

"We would expect no more from the painter of this exquisite piece, who is a friend of the late Hershey Mintoff." His words had a tinge of irony to them. What part of my story did he not believe? Val handed it back to me. I returned it to my bag.

"What do I do and what's my cut?" I asked.

"We need the cooperation of Richard Lovatt Hadley," Kavanaugh said, "to sew up the corporate angles and to present to the world a guarantee in that astringent style of his that we are, more or less, honest."

"Why shouldn't he do that?" I asked disingenuously.

"Bless you, Ventry. Just the right question. I thought things were moving along very well. His cousin, India, after her husband's tragic accident, took a keen interest in our foundation. Then after she brought him in, he took an even keener interest in Val's sister who had been delivering some crockery from Val's shop and never quite found her way back."

"They are even married," Val interrupted, "a turn of events which fluttered my jaded heart and delighted all those who hold the frail emotions of shop girls sacred."

"We were pleased," Kavanaugh continued, "but things are not . . . progressing as rapidly as we'd like. Rina, dear girl, has no head for strategy. No, Val, not a word. I didn't even want her here tonight with the coke. To go on. Hadley needs to be coaxed."

"How?" I asked.

"We think his ego needs to be stroked," Kavanaugh replied.

"Not exactly my line."

"Ah, but it is. To show our great admiration for him, we will tell him that we would like to have his portrait painted, and since this is a historically oriented venture, in, let's say, early nineteenth-century folk style?"

"How does this . . ."

"Listen," he hissed. "Just wait. He is modest, really, but he is over fond of his young wife. He will urge us to have her portrait done, so he can . . ."

". . . stick it in the back of his limousine and moon over it on his way to the opera."

"Val, Val. No, he would have found a place for it . . ."

"Would have?"

"No, the painting will never be completed."

"Why not?" I asked.

"He will discover evidence that suggests his wife is fooling around with you . . ."

"Not good for the ego."

"No, but in a scene I will prepare for her, a scene worthy of Verdi, she will force him to confront her with his suspicions, prove them wrong, demonstrate a fierce love for him and . . ."

" . . . fuck his brains out," Val finished for him.

"The virile Hadley, beating his chest with his foot on your neck, figuratively speaking, will doubt no more and be even more inclined to grant his wife's wishes which will be . . ." He looked at me over the long ash of his cigar.

"To back a play, sell a foundation, build a Dawnwalk memorial." He nodded and flicked the ash off.

"If you do us this service, you will be rewarded."

"How much?"

"Hmm. I must be getting old, I hadn't actually settled on a figure."

"Ten thousand, or cut me in for a percentage," I said. "This sounds like the big time."

They liked the sound of that non-cash outlay percentage, so much they offered me another drink of that ghastly green stuff. I declined, promising myself a nice astringent cold beer when I got out of there. Two.

"Here is Mrs. Hadley's telephone number. Why don't you give her a call tomorrow." I took the slip of paper from Kavanaugh's fleshy fingers. "Now I have been away from my guests long enough. Let's rejoin them." He carefully stubbed out the cigar and rose. That smoke was going to lodge in the room's precious hangings and stay there stinking for a long time. Following Val back to the party, I wondered if his shop in Hudson represented some effort to reproduce the master's baroque decadence? They seemed comfortable in their roles: Kavanaugh playing Fagin to Val's Artful Dodger. I wondered, touching my sore leg gingerly, stiff from sitting so long, if Val required his own acolyte. Was Merkle to Val, what Val was to Kavanaugh? Was Val looking for Daddy? If I understood their connections, would I be any closer to finding Cyril Hart or learning who had killed Peter Barrett and why?

The party was still cooking along with all the glee and real emotion of a 16mm porn film. I said goodbye to Kavanaugh. I told Val I'd be in touch and that I'd call his sister.

15

The following day, I walked across Central Park South to Rina's apartment in Lovatt house, one of the Hadley family holdings, I assumed. I had called Moira after leaving Prince Street and told her I'd be another day. She said she had called Vera Koopman and would be seeing her that night, after choral practice. They were doing Orff's *Carmina Catulli* and did we want tickets? I said to buy a pair for the good will. There was no answer at Lou and Cheech's; Lou is an early riser and will turn off the phone, so I'd checked into a hotel, the Wellington on Seventh Avenue. From there I'd called Rina, who asked me to drop by the next day. Here I was.

I gave her apartment number and my name to the doorman. He telephoned upstairs and then nodded. When I knocked on the door, Rina herself opened it. She was wearing a long T-shirt that came to the top of her thighs and had a faded picture of Ziggy Stardust across her breasts. I followed her inside. She had great legs.

She turned and whispered something I didn't quite catch. Bending over to hear her better, she slipped her tongue in my mouth and put her hand between my legs and rubbed slowly, firmly up and down. I think she must have done it before.

On the way over I had come up with every kind of opening gambit and stratagem to get her to confide in me about her brother's operation. My plans were equally matched in probable futility. In the end, I decided to go over and see what turned up. Some sleuth.

"Let's talk for awhile," I said when my mouth was my own again.

"Fuck first, Ventry. Rules of the house. We fuck first, and then we can talk all day long if you want. We're alone."

"I'd like to ask you . . ."

"Come on," she said. She pulled me by the hand into an enormous bathroom. One wall was glass and overlooked the park. There were mirrors on every other side. She touched a set of buttons inside a hanging cabinet, and music came flooding into the room from small speakers set high in the corners. Lots of strings and no sopranos. The marble Jacuzzi tub set in the floor was six feet across. It had more levels in it than a shopping mall. Stooping, she turned it on. Lights beamed in the water and the jets on the side walls of the tub set up a whirling commotion. From a small fridge in one corner, she took two chilled glasses and a bottle of Moët. She expertly twisted off the cork and poured us each a glass. Today I had to chill out and forget Moira.

"I love bubbles," she said after draining her glass quickly, "let's go play in them." She pulled off her tee shirt. Her slender, athletic body glistened in the steam rising from the tub. Her skin was a light gold from the sun. She had firm, globular breasts. I took off my clothes. You can rationalize anything.

"You're hurt," she cried. "Look at that terrible bruise on your leg." She put her fingers gently on the purple and yellow patch on my left thigh. "Does it hurt?"

"No," I lied. I put Moira out of my mind. I had to. Hand in hand we stepped down into the bath.

I took Rina and enveloped her in my arms. We kissed. I was sitting on a ledge in the tub and a jet of water was pushing hard on the muscles of my back.

We squirmed and rolled and licked. We fondled and stroked. We dove and straddled and rubbed.

There was a pad covered with a towel on the tiles next to the tub, probably to lie on while using a sun lamp. Standing up I took her wrist and led her out of the tub. I gently lay her down on the pad and knelt beside her. I bit into her, tasting the soft, wet hairs, and she moaned. I slid up her body and sucked like a child on those delicious breasts, kneading them with my fingers and feeling them fill up my mouth. I saw she had minute golden hairs curling up from the aureoles. Her nipples were rose-colored. I touched them with my tongue tip to feel them stir and rise. I slid into her. Her eyes rolled up in her head. We rocked softly. I could feel the water on the tiles beneath my toes. I held myself up on my forearm and she raised herself up to me. We slowly moved back and forth, side to side. Her internal muscles contracted rhythmically, leading me on. Her mouth was slack. She called out, "Honey, oh, hunh, hunh, hunh . . ." in ever increasing cries. Her fingers dug into my shoulders. I called out. Groaning and roaring, I put my hands on her firm ass, bouncing up and down on that pad. She grabbed me around the waist and locked onto me, quivering. My eyes were tightly shut. I imagined myself soaring and then I spurted into her in waves of fire. She held herself against me, rocking in quick spasms, as if there were a raging spirit inside her, desperate to be quieted. Finally, we lay still.

Her eyes looked dreamy. She sighed and gave me a soft kiss. I felt her muscles tighten on me. I lay my head on the mat. She ran her fingers through my hair. We parted slowly.

"That was nice," she said. "Let's go back in the tub." The music was still gliding along. She poured some more champagne which we took in the water with us.

"Hadley doesn't fuck much anymore," Rina announced.

"Gee, that's too bad." What could you say?

"Yeah," she said. She looked at me brightly, "You're nice."

"Thank you," and is your brother setting me up to kill me, I asked myself?

"Val thinks you're nice too. But I know someone maybe doesn't like you." She said it teasingly, pushing her foot between my legs and rubbing.

"Who's that, Kavanaugh?"

"That weirdo," she said, "No!"

"Then, who?"

"A guy. I was once in sort of trouble and well this guy who was sort of a cop helped me out. We used to talk. Then I introduced him to Val and Kavanaugh and he sort of works for us now."

"He knows me? This sort of cop who sort of works for you now?"

"Yeah, I guess so. I don't want to mention his name. Val and Kavanaugh asked lots of people about you. He thought I should be careful around you. I don't know. Made you kind of interesting." She looked up at me with a grin. "He didn't explain himself very clearly if you want to know the truth. Val thought we shouldn't have any more to do with him, a cop and all. Kavanaugh wanted him on board."

"What exactly did this sort of cop say?"

"He said you weren't to be trusted."

"Jesus Christ! Who is this guy?"

"Just a guy. A guy that Kavanaugh keeps on a string. I told Val what he told me. He said people like this guy who was talking about you just didn't understand sensitive types, like artists and stuff cause you're an artist and Val's sensitive. Blah, blah, blah. Val went on about it and got madder and madder."

"Should I be worried about this?"

"Nah."

"Rina, what's the big deal. Tell me who it is."

"Oh, forget it. Some old guy. I'm sorry I mentioned it."

"Do you see him often?"

"Now and again. Maybe I'll see him tomorrow, maybe I won't. I go along sometimes when Val pays him."

Obviously she had decided not to tell me who her informant was. While I was thankful that Val seemed ready to believe in me, this "sort of" guy frightened me. Maybe Cheech could follow Rina for me tomorrow.

"You know Cyril Hart?" I asked, getting to the real reason I was there.

"Sure. He's funny."

"How do you mean?"

"Well I don't understand him half the time but he gets me in stitches. I haven't seen him around in a while. Val knows him, too. I asked Val where he was, but he said it would be better to concentrate on Hadley and forget Cyril for awhile."

"When was the last time you saw him?"

"He used to come over now and then, for a little party. It's been months. Could you give him a message?"

"If I see him, sure."

"Could you tell him to give me a call?"

"Sure. Any special reason?"

"We had fun together. I hate losing track of people. It's happened to me all my life. Val doesn't always know what's best," she said petulantly, twining a strand of her honey colored hair around her finger.

"Rina, where do you come from?"

"Question time, huh? Why do you want to know?"

"I just do is all."

"You first. Where did you grow up? Do you have any brothers or sisters? What was your family doctor like?"

"My family doctor?"

"Yeah. Tell me."

"He was very nice. He had a large stuffed marlin on his wall, and his name was Mercuri and I thought he invented mercurochrome and now he lives in Florida and goes fishing everyday."

"What's mecure . . . chrome?"

"It's red stuff your mother, well, my mother used to put on cuts. Now you."

"I guess you could say Val and I come from California. He's a few years older than me. He was born in 1963 and I was born in 1967 in San Francisco. I remember living in a place called the Sunset, but I was born in the Haight, Val told me."

"Who was your father?"

"We don't know."

"And your mom?"

"She died when I was little."

"I'm sorry."

"Me too. I sort of remember her. Val has some of her pictures. She's all dressed in hippie-dippie clothes, like Janis Joplin on that album with feather boas and pearls? Yeah," Rina took a long deep breath, droplets of water ran between her breasts, "yeah, she died. She was into drugs. She really tried, Val said, but it was not to be. I just remember bits and pieces, here and there, like when I got up in the morning finding her passed out in front of the TV. A needle was hanging down from the inside of her thigh. The Flintstones were on."

"Was Royal her name?"

She shrugged. "Mom liked the sound. *Her* real name was Crofut, but she told Val there wasn't enough magic in a crow's foot. That's how they talked back then, I guess. She called me the Princess Royal. And Val was the Prince. She never talked about, like, who our real fathers were or anything. It was just her. There were guys around, but some of them were creepy."

"What happened then?"

"We got took into foster homes. Taken. There were a lot of them. The Stimolas had color TV. I got beat at the Longs. The Traynors had a smelly dog and I wouldn't go in the kitchen when it was there 'cause I was afraid. The Westres had a lot of stuff I couldn't touch. The Razneks had a garden I had to weed. I don't know. They were all weird. Mostly in San Francisco and Daly City. Val and I were never together, but he played hooky all the time. The agency would tell him where I was and he'd find me somehow. Then, *finally*, he met this guy who took him home to live with him in this big old house, a redone Victorian? There are lots of them out there, but I never saw any like it here in New York. They paint them these wild colors and they have turrets and all. Anyway, the guy was really nice to Val. He didn't have to go to school or anything. He owned an antiques shop, and Val worked there. He gave Val lots of money and great clothes. Val stayed with him for five years. Then when Val was eighteen, the guy died. Val took over the shop, and I went to live with him in the house. That was great. I was fifteen. I didn't go to school any more.

"It was about a year after that there was a lawsuit and the brother of the guy who took Val in claimed the house and all, but Val had a big sale real quick of all the antiques, it was like an auction but it was also like a party, y'understand, and we started traveling right then. We rented a car and drove to Mexico. Val had a credit card and we bought stuff and lived in Acapulco and then Puerto Vallarta. Val made friends with these guys from New York, so we decided to come here. The guys lived north of the city, so we moved in with them. They were restoring a house. All Val's friends do."

"How did you meet Hadley?"

"He bought a celadon vase from Val. It was really expensive, and Val had to deliver it. We drove over to the house in his powder blue MG. I sat in the passenger seat with my legs straight out in front, holding the vase all wrapped up in my lap.

"When we got there, it was like being in a theme park. I mean there was a large hot air balloon on the lawn in front of this guy's mansion. I'll invite you over. There's a curving gravel driveway with elm trees that Hadley has to take care of specially. We go up to this wooden door about ten feet high and ring. A guy with a silk ascot and velvet jacket opens the door. He looked kind of silly. I thought he was the butler. It was Hadley. We say we have the vase, and he asks us in.

"So we stay for lunch. Well, why not? We have some sort of cold dish, umm, hacked chicken and cold pasta with basil and tomatoes. Hadley eats it all the time. So Val and Hadley talk about the vase, collector's doubletalk, but I knew he was sending me messages, you know. I told him I had a dress just the color of that vase that I wore to my eighteenth birthday party which Val gave me. *Then* he asked me if I would like to take a ride in his balloon."

"Yeah?"

She giggled. "I thought he was bonkers, but he turns out to be really a very accomplished balloonist. They go up in the late afternoon or in the early morning. Val couldn't stay around. But I did, for both. I've been with Hadley ever since."

"Does he know about you and other guys?"

"I don't know. I never told him. Some guys are kinky, like you, and want to know all about what other stuff I've done and all, but I haven't done much. Really, I don't know all that much. Soap operas, especially the glitzy nighttime ones are a help, but they don't have anybody like Val, though Hadley could just walk onto any of them. He's elegant, Hadley. I learn a lot too by asking people special questions, like when I asked about your doctor. It tips me off to what kind of life you had."

"You'd make a great detective, Rina."

"I thought about it, like Cagney and Lacey. I'm more the Lacey type, I think. What do you think?"

"You're probably right."

"I could work as an undercover airhead. See, you're smiling."

"How'd you meet Kavanaugh?"

"Brother, you really ask a lot of questions. Wouldn't you rather just fuck?"

It was not a question to linger over. "In a bit."

"Okay. Val took me to one of Mr. Kavanaugh's parties. He's going to put on this Broadway show. It'll be like *Cats*, only about Indians. He said maybe there's a part in it for me. But I told him I didn't know anything about musicals, so he sent me tickets to a lot of them. Maybe I'll take lessons. There aren't too many blonde Indians."

"There are wigs."

"I don't know. You got to join Equity, see. It's a lot of trouble. Mr. Kavanaugh gives me coke. You want some?"

"No thanks."

"Well then, neither do I. Val says I've got to stop for reasons too obvious to mention. So I guess I will. You don't use needles, do you? I want you to know I've never used needles. Never ever." I believed her. I assured her I hadn't either.

"What does Hadley think of Kavanaugh?" I asked.

"Are you trying to pump me?"

"No, just trying to get to know you. What does Hadley think of Kavanaugh?"

"It's hard for me to figure Hadley out. Still, older guys are nice. They take care of you and then, you know, they want to play kids' games, like go up in balloons or swim between my legs in the big tub. But Mr. Kavanaugh? He likes giving me presents and stuff, but he doesn't play. He has a heavy load of responsibility, running the foundation and getting the show off the ground."

"Is that what Hadley says?"

"Yes."

I thought it was time to try another approach.

"Let's play a game. I name people and you tell me what you think they enjoy doing the most."

"Fucking doesn't count, right?"

"Right."

"It's got to be something else."

"Right. Here goes," I said.

"Just don't go too fast. Can I have a towel? Thanks. I love these, so fluffy and big as a blanket. See the H? For Hadley? Just let me wrap this around us. It's getting a little chilly in here, isn't it? Okay, go ahead."

"Val?"

"That's easy. Val likes to read. He's not happy unless he's got a book in his hand. He reads all the time. He'd even like to get plastic books, so he could read in the shower. He takes long, long showers. When I lived with him, I'd rub oil on his back to keep it moist. And the Y, he swims laps every day. Once his hair started to turn green from the chlorine. Now he wears a shower cap. I guess you could say we're both water sprites. But I don't read much. Not at all, actually, but I watch TV."

"How about you."

"Me? I like to sit naked by this window and let the sun warm me up and I imagine I'm in a forest, by a pool. The tall trees have these vines hanging down from them, and bright flowers, white and yellow and red and scarlet, are growing all around me, and some petals are drifting slowly around the top of the water, and this large orange butterfly comes and rests on my shoulder and I'm just glowing."

"That's very beautiful."

"It's my favorite daydream."

"Hadley?"

"Oh, like I said, he likes to fool around with me in the tub. He, uh, likes his collections. He spends hours just staring. Picking something up and putting it down. He loves horses. Upstate, he rides every morning. You're going to paint his picture, aren't you."

"If everything works out," I said. "That's why I want to know about him."

"I guess I'll be seeing more of you, then," she grinned.

"What about Val's friend, Merkle?" Her expression changed instantly, her lips pursed and she frowned.

"Oh, him. Creep city. He just picks his nose all day and waits for Val to tell him what to do. There's more smarts in a bowl of granola."

"Kavanaugh?"

"Mr. Kavanaugh. He likes to be in the center of things and boss people around. I tried to get him to dance once, you know, but he wouldn't. He said he was content to watch. He never lets go. He's always so controlled. He seemed to get off on just choosing the records."

"Not like you?"

"I have to get out there and do it. What I'd really like is to be a lead singer for a band, a real tough band, like Chrissie Hynde and the Pretenders, or Joanie Jett. I wouldn't have to wear a wig or take lessons then."

"You were talking about Kavanaugh."

"Yeah. He has a trick memory. He knows when everybody died. Not just famous people either like Jim Morrison or Kennedy. He gave Val this big dictionary with people's death dates in the back. He knew them all, just about."

"Who didn't he know?"

"I'm trying to remember. Some guy who wrote musicals. You'd think Mr. Kavanaugh would know about musicals. There was some baseball player, too, but I could understand that. I don't know anybody who goes to baseball games. Anyway, Val started teasing him about the ones he missed, and the game stopped. Mr. Kavanaugh put on a David Bowie album, which was sort of like a peace offering because everybody says Val looks like the thin white duke. He took out this jar of coke and offered it around but I was being good with Val there and didn't take any. Neither did Val, but Mr. Kavanaugh coked up and just talked about his plans. The Book. The Foundation. The Museum. The Musical. Is all this real, do you think, Ventry? Is it going to happen?"

"I don't know."

"Do you think the Indians want a big monument in Alaska?"

"We could ask them. What does Hadley think of all this?"

"Hadley loves American Indian art. He's on the board of the Museum of the American Indian. Hadley doesn't need to work. He told me he made three million dollars one year in the bull market. Aren't bull markets great? He told me he wants to be in charge of acquisitions for Dawnwalk."

The quality of the Indian work Moira and I found in Barrett's studio suggested a first-rate source, perhaps Hadley's collection.

"Did he ever talk about Peter Barrett?"

"Yeah. Barrett had married Hadley's cousin. Remember, you asked about her at the party? When Barrett was killed, Hadley hired more security men. We have a man with a guard dog twenty-four hours a day now."

"He didn't talk about the murder?"

"No. Not directly to me."

"To someone else?"

"Let me think. You know how conversations are. You don't really pay attention? I mean conversations other people are having.

"Just after it happened, we had a newspaperman over to dinner in the house upstate. He owns a paper up there that Hadley is thinking of investing in. He knew all about the murder." Sounded like Calvin paying for his dinner. "Brrr. I just didn't listen carefully. Hadley was fascinated. He had gone to the funeral and all. It got so gloomy I went into the kitchen and got some carrots and went to the stable and fed the horses. They love it when they see me coming. They toss their heads and whinny. Now that's it. Come on." She rose and led me into the bedroom.

After we made love, Rina fell asleep, her saucy smile lingering on her lips. I got dressed and walked out the door, wondering who was spreading the bad word about me.

16

I went back to the hotel and got my bag, then took a cab to TriBeCa because I wanted to spend the night with Lou and Cheech if they'd still have me. I needed to talk to Lou and I needed to ask Cheech to follow Rina. It was about 2:00 P.M. I stopped off on the way at a deli for two chilled six-packs of Beck's beer, some chips and some sandwiches.

I got out on Spring Street and walked over to their place. Cheech was just leaving when I arrived at the front door.

"Cheech!" I hollered.

He turned around, "Ventry!" He caught me in a hug. "Ventry!" he shouted again. I held tightly onto the brown bag. The manic, mischievous look shining out of his wideset, dark eyes suggested a full tilt carnival running in his brain.

"What's happening?" I gasped. He let go.

"Gee, I really can't talk now. Lou's upstairs. I have to run. Work in Progress. Ventry! Great to see you."

He started chugging down the street, a blue nylon tote bag slung over his shoulder, heading toward his latest creation with all the enthusiasm of a lonely minister hot footing it back to the rectory to discuss matters of conscience with a moist-eyed eighteen-year old girl.

"Is it safe to go up?" I shouted after him.

Without looking back, he waved and pointed upwards, toward the loft where Lou was to be found. The last time I had visited she had been taking photos. Then she painted the photos. Took photos of the paintings. Cut them up. Painted them. Glazed them. Shot at them with a .22 rifle. Photographed them again. Enlarged them and so on. It was one hell of a long march back to the original object. After my visit, she also agreed not to use the steel front door for a backstop. The bullet had sung past my head in the doorway and chipped the plaster in the wall behind me.

I rang the bell and waited. When Lou came down on the elevator to see who it was, her face lit up and one hundred and forty pounds of emotional Viennese pinned me to the wall. Lou had told me early on that every man should have a Viennese in his life, but we had never gotten together. I was the pal. Her lips pressed up to mine, and she gave me a hard, friendly kiss.

"*Schottsie!*" she cried, "You're late!"

"Late?"

"Cheech just left. He'd want to see you."

"I met him on the way in," I said, "I wanted to stay here tonight, if it's okay?"

"Of course, c'mon up."

We got on the old freight elevator and rode up to the fourth floor. She owned the building and used three of the lofts. When we arrived, she unlocked the Fox lock with its iron bar inside wedged against the door and the pick-resistant Maslow. I could hear the parrot shrieking within. When she turned over the Segal deadbolt, we were in.

If someone ever put a potato sack over your head when you were a kid, then you've seen Cheech and Lou's apartment. It was done up, completely, in light brown burlap fabric—walls, floors, ceiling, everything. They had rigged up burlap shades on the lamps and burlap curtains on the windows. She had a few pieces of art from her private collection, most by Black Americans, including a superb Romare Bearden collage, a naked, pensive Conjur Woman holding a bloody knife with another woman beside her in a bird-filled forest. It gave me the shivers every time I looked at it.

I put the beer in the refrigerator in what could be called the kitchen area. It took up about a third of the loft. The sandwiches and chips I left in the bag on a formica table on which they placed a burlap tablecloth when they were expecting company. "You're due for a redecoration, Lou," I said, "burlap was the fabric of the Eighties."

"I know. You're right. Cheech says that what we might want. . . . Hey, give me one of those beers, okay? Thanks. Cheech says maybe an effect like we were fish inside an aquarium. We'd have these giant faces with big, bulbous noses, you know? They'd be peering in through the walls. We'd have a giant cat's paw, with the claws extended, coming down from a blue ceiling."

"*Apropos* of claws in the ceiling, where's Marcel Duchamp?"

"He got a little hyper on some catnip Cheech gave him, so he's mellowing out under the bed," she nodded toward the platform raised in the center of their light show/entertainment/living space area where their large bed sat, covered with burlap. The far third of the loft held Lou's studio.

"There'd be white gravel on the floor, Cheech says. I don't know."

"Well, you have a waterbed to sleep on," I said.

"Yeah, but we'd probably have to sleep in the water."

"You could have a humidifier hooked up to look like an aerator."

"Hey, you've acquired a gift for whimsey. The hard edges aren't so hard. You'll have to tell Cheech that when he comes back. I don't think he'll be long."

"Where was he going?" I asked pulling on a beer.

"It's a tape job, I think. He had the Sony with him. He might be going over to the Bowery to record the bums telling him their astrological signs, or he was going up to Grand Central Station to talk to people waiting on the information line. Talking to people on lines has opened up a whole new world for him."

"I could really believe," I said, "that up to now Cheech has gone through his whole life and never even noticed the existence of lines. Never learned the concept."

"Living with him," she said, as she sat down on one of the kitchen chairs, "has not been boring."

We sat there drinking the beer. I opened up the chips and

we started alternating handfuls. We opened up a couple of more beers.

"So, Ventry, you're a cop again?"

"One job."

"Why?"

"I can live and paint for a year or more on what Mrs. Barrett's giving me."

"I can understand that."

"Have you ever heard of a man named Kavanaugh?"

"Morgan Kavanaugh? As a matter of fact I have. He's bad news. He buys occasionally. He could be just a coked up gyp artist, but he seems to have access to money. There's been talk of a musical. One of my models works for him, now and again."

"Any connection to Barrett?"

"Not that I know of."

"He knows India Barrett."

"Too bad for her." Then she said softly, "and, Ventry, too bad for you."

"Why?"

"He may not have killed anyone. He may have nothing to do with poor Barrett's murder, but don't get involved with his games or you'll never find your way home."

"That bad?"

"Ventry, you are not a reflective person by nature. You think you are but you aren't. Action attracts you. The energy I see in your paintings can distract you and lead you out of the studio. Men like Kavanaugh are drawn to that energy and they use it. Their stunts can have you spinning for years."

"I can't just walk away."

"You have before."

"I took her money."

"She has more."

"It's . . . complicated, Lou. There's more to it."

"Oh." We fell silent.

"Tape," I said. "We need some Electric Elegiac Environment."

She switched on the tape deck and the jaunty, dangerous chords of "Midnight Rambler" came through her 250 watt speakers. I had made the tape when we were at school together. She played it for me sometimes when I came over. Mick and the boys gave way to Otis Redding who had been loving too long to stop now, and then Jim Morrison asking the way to the next whiskey bar. Marcel came out and jumped onto my lap. He closed his eyes and started purring. Rod Stewart sang about Maggie May and playing pool. We finished one six pack and started another. Lou sat in her chair her eyes hooded, looking inward like a Nilotic priestess. The Lovin' Spoonful asked if we ever had to make up our mind. Janis begged us to give her a piece of her heart; James Brown's soulful, harsh voice clamored for attention, "Poppa's got a brand new bag," and then Cheech came bounding into the room and, standing in the center, raised his arm.

"This is a Nostalgia Free Zone!" he yelled in proclamation. He rushed over to me, "What's happenin', man?" He kissed the top of Lou's head and then took a swig of Lou's beer. "Hey, bird!" he shouted at the parrot, who screamed back at him, "Hey, Cheech!"

"I'd like to hire you, Cheech," I said.

"Ventry, start at the beginning and I mean the beginning," Lou said.

So I did. I told them everything I knew to date, all about Pop coming to see me, India, Moira, Val, Kavanaugh, Hadley and winding up with Rina and the guy she may be meeting with Val. "I can't be in more than one place at a time, Cheech, so I thought of you."

"Ventry," he said with a straight face, "I can't be in more than one place at a time either. Can I, Lou?"

"Did you ever try?" she asked.

"No, now that you mention it, no." He looked thoughtful. Cheech once walked to Montauk from Central Park after looking thoughtful.

"You can follow people, Cheech. You are, as you used to say, the Cézanne of shadowing. I'll pay you to do this, just like the people you used to follow paid you."

"Do you need pictures?" "Is Cheech going to get hurt?" They asked simultaneously.

"No videotapes, no recordings. Surreptitious snapshots, okay. This won't be dangerous for him. I just need to know where Rina Hadley goes, and especially who she sees. She'll probably spend all her time in Midtown, maybe come down here. I'll pay you a thousand for three days. Here it is." I put the ten hundreds on the table. Cheech looked at them the way you'd look at a raffle ticket you bought from a boy scout: polite interest. He stuffed the cash in his pocket.

"When do I start?"

"Tomorrow morning at six in front of her apartment building, Lovatt House on Central Park South," I said. "Start early. Maybe she gets up and jogs, though she doesn't look the type."

"Fine," Cheech said. "Well, with this windfall, let's get some Chinese delivered and maybe a tape or two for the VCR. Uncle Chiang's latest service, Ventry. The delivery person stops off at the video store. A Basil Rathbone *Sherlock Holmes*, I think, and, yes, either *The Man Who Knew Too Much* or *Strangers on a Train*, whatever Uncle recommends."

"How about *Notorious* or *Spellbound*?" I asked.

Later that evening, as Lou and Cheech finished the last of the cold sesame noodles, I called Moira at the farm. She had news.

"I spoke to Vera Merkle Koopman, Ventry. I was open with her and said that Cyril was my cousin. She said Koopman used to arrange for her to get a day's work cleaning the house every now and then. Her workdays sometimes coincided with Cyril's visits. She liked him. We cried together. She's quite maternal."

"Did anyone else visit him?"

"Not when she was around, though she would find a lot of glasses in the sink sometimes and liquor and wine bottles in the trash. She thought either Barrett was drinking heavily or he was entertaining."

"No sign of a girlfriend?"

"I asked. She said no. I asked about her cousin that beat you up . . ."

"He didn't beat me up," I objected, "I . . ."

"She said he was quite peaceful these days," Moira continued, ignoring my protest, "something you said must have set
him off."

"I said 'Hi, chief.' "

"Maybe he's not a chief. Anyway he works for Royal on a
regular basis. Did you know that?"

"No. Royal didn't indicate anything like that in the shop.
Quite the opposite, really."

"Vera spoke well of Royal. She thinks he's had a calming
influence on him. He used to get into a lot of bar fights. And
something else you should know."

"What's that?"

"Vera said at one time Merkle lived for hunting and always
brought her family some venison after killing a deer. She said
she asked for some last November, and he told her he didn't
think he'd go out after it anymore."

"Now, that's interesting."

"She also said Ernest had just bought a new truck. That's
how well he was doing."

"Ernest Merkle sounds like someone I should talk to."

"You were proper mates the first time," she said acidly.

"Maybe I'll think of something."

"And me?" she asked.

"And you what?"

"Should I think of something, too? Or do I just sit on my
duff?"

"You're the brains of the outfit, you know that," I told her. "I
just don't think it's a good idea for you to chat up Ernest
Merkle. He's violent and unpredictable, no matter what Vera
says."

"So are you," she shot back. What could I say? "You still
there, Ventry?"

"Yes."

"Right enough. Your pal, Jack, called up and then drove
over here to see me."

"Oh. Did he make a pass at you?"

"Yes, but his heart wasn't really in it. I gave him your
champagne. It was the only wine in the house. I hope you
don't mind."

"No." I thought of the Moët I had drunk with Rina, "you did the right thing."

"He brought a package for you."

"Open it up, please, Moira, and tell me what it is."

"He said you'd ask that, but you had to open it and see it for yourself."

"Okay. If he says so."

"When will you be back up here?"

"Tomorrow night, I hope. I'll call."

"Good. I remembered to open the garden fence so the woodchucks could get in. Good night, Ventry." She hung up, and I went inside. While Cheech and Lou cuddled up and fell asleep, I watched *Spellbound*. As the Salvador Dali dream sequence unfolded, the image of the enormous eye, threatened by the sharp point of a scissors, merged in my mind with the grisly memory of Barrett's tortured, blinded face.

In the morning, after a restless night, as I lay on the futon on the floor of Lou's studio, I could hear the quiet, happy noises of Cheech and Lou making love on the large bed in the loft's center room. A truck, grinding its gears, came coughing along the street below. I could hear the soft, self-satisfied cooing of the pigeons, perched on the broad, flat windowsill. The sky was growing light outside. I could just make out the ornamental ironwork on the building across the street. The sounds on the bed ceased, and I heard Cheech pad across the burlap to the shower, which soon started hissing. A few minutes later, he poked his wet head in through the door and spoke softly,

"Ven? You awake? It's five thirty and I'm on the case."

"If you need to reach me, call my father's office and leave a message with Sadie or the machine." I gave him the number. He was dressed in scuffed workboots, chinos and a red flannel shirt. He had a light tan raincoat over his arm. He looked like he was going to serve a summons on a lobster boat. I asked him if he had the camera with him. He took the Minolta SRT 200 with the 70/150 telephoto from beneath the coat.

"You got film, Cheech?"

"I got film, Ventry."

"Run away if things get weird, Cheech. Okay?"

"How do I tell?"

"Cheech, if people start hitting you, chasing you or taking out small arms and pointing them at you, leave. Leave everything and come home."

"It'll be fine, Ventry. See I got my release forms for people I photograph for a show. Anyone starts with me, I take their picture and stick a form at them. Chills 'em right out. No sweat."

Had I lost my mind sending this child of the ionosphere to chase after Rina?

"I just filled Mr. Coffee. Help yourself."

"Thanks, Cheech. You're all I got."

"I figured. Well, see ya, Ace."

Lou joined me at the kitchen table, dressed in a bleached white T-shirt and white overalls on which someone had painted a sinuous black python curled around a leafy branch.

"Working today, Lou?"

"I work every day," she said primly with a trace of her morning Austrian accent, "and if Cheech gets hurt I'll slice your balls off! You wouldn't be getting Cheech hurt, would you, Ventry?"

"Never." I swallowed hard, "Never. I think she's up to something, but Cheech isn't going to get involved. No way, Lou. Rina's probably going shopping or she'll just sit in a bar and get smashed. But if she meets a friend, I need to know who it is."

"You going to stay here tonight?"

"Yes," and then I said, "You'd like Moira."

We sipped coffee.

"Haven't liked the others."

"She's different."

"Since you can't, or won't, let go of this, I've thought about Barrett's murder and maybe I can give you some help."

"Thank you."

"It may be farfetched but Barrett's death scene seems to me to be a kind of drama, with characters and motivations, all taking place in the killer's mind. The murder scene, that hellish image of the poor man tied, stabbed and blinded, is what remains on the stage after the major player, the killer, has left."

"Where are you heading?" I asked.

"Maybe I can describe the killer."

"How?"

"By the manner of death: the artist bound to the easel, his eyes burned, his flesh repeatedly punctured by a knife. The act is heightened by the repetition within it. Tension grew within the killer."

"Yes."

"If so, he will do it again. It's a primal scene and it demands to be reenacted."

"Your classic serial killer?" I asked.

"I think so.

"My speculations on the easel are complex. Is it an altar upon which the victim is sacrificed? No, I don't think so. What is an easel? Something closely identified with a painter. A kind of a co-worker, a companion. The painter approaches the easel as if it were a partner, holding the canvas."

"Let me get this straight. You're saying Barrett might have been killed because he was a painter?"

"The easel is the sign of a verdict in the killer's mind. You are dying, Barrett, because of something you did, or represent, as a painter. Why then was Barrett bound to it, with his back to it and hung with his head down? Clearly a kind of denial of the sexual position, of the erotic relationship between Barrett and the other, not the killer, which perhaps was seen as a threat to the killer."

"The painter threatened the killer."

"The painter and the easel triggered the killer."

"So I need to know more about Barrett's professional life?"

"Not necessarily. I can't take you any further. The killer obviously killed someone named Peter Barrett, but in his mind, he could have been killing some other painter, perhaps one who injured him in some way."

"Who?"

"How many stab wounds were there?"

"More than twenty, as best they can tell."

"Hmm. That's at the core of the act, that repetition. The stab wounds are both a signature and an expression."

"Are you saying this is like a work of art?"

"No, nothing of this is art. He was in a frenzy, a prolonged moment in which to feel the guilts and pleasures of release as deeply as possible."

"What of," I asked quietly, "Barrett's eyes?"

"That makes us cringe, doesn't it. Either Barrett or the killer saw something that he should not have seen."

"So he puts out Barrett's eyes."

"Exactly."

"But not his own eyes."

"Symbolically, maybe," she said.

"And he is free to do it again."

"Not free. Oh no, this killer is the least free of men, but unblinded, yes, he may reenact the scene again."

"You think we can expect another murder?"

"Yes, I think so."

"Why?"

"If my hypotheses are correct, Barrett's murder would not resolve the conflicts in the killer's mind. The tensions screwing deeply into his brain remain. He will need to seek release. Something in his mind will set him in motion."

"Who's he likely to kill?"

"Who's chasing him?"

Oh. That slowed me down.

"How do you know you're right?" I asked.

"I don't."

"Could the killer have been Cyril Hart?"

"From what you said, probably not."

"Could the killer be a woman?"

"We can do anything, but we are unlikely to have the experiences or the drives that would lead us to do this. I know something very important about him."

"What's that?"

"He's invisible to you."

"What do you mean?"

"Don't ignore the possibility you've met him, even spoken to him, but you just can't see him doing this."

"You mean otherwise I would have already collared him?"

"Though it's just been a few days, think about it. Ask yourself, is there anything that might prevent me from seeing the killer for what he is."

"You mean love? Attraction for Moira Hart? But you said a woman couldn't have done it. And that Cyril Hart probably didn't do it."

"When you're not beating people up, Ventry, think of who you are and what you can't see."

"I'll try."

"Boldness won't get you through, Ventry, not with men like Kavanaugh. You have to think. Don't get lost in his world."

She switched on a tape, Schubert's Quintet in C. She was telling me to hit the road.

"You carrying a gun?" she asked.

I shrugged.

"Let me see it," she demanded.

I placed it on the table. It had a cotton rag still wrapped on it to protect my pocket. She took the bundle, and unwrapped it. She hefted it, spun the cylinder and then sighted down the barrel. I could smell the oil.

"Got a permit?"

"Not for the city."

"Gonna whip it out when the bad guys throw down on you?"

"I just brought it along."

"Shoulda left it to home." She loaded the pistol and placed it on the table. "Pray these bullets fire. If Cheech gets hurt, Ventry, shoot me when you see me. You got that? Cause I'll be coming to blow your head off. Finish your coffee. I must work, Ventry."

I put the small revolver in the side pocket of my jacket, got up and stood by the door until she came over to open the locks.

"Honest to God, Ventry, find out what you are supposed to do with what's left of your life and do it."

17

I took a short walk down Prince Street and thought of stopping by Handasyde and Beaky again, to try to answer Lou's
parting order. I should call Pop's office, now, though, to see if
there were any messages. If I called later he might be there.
He surprised me by answering himself.

"Where's Sadie?" I asked.

"Come over, Son, please," he said softly and hung up.

When I knocked on his door, hung with the large plaque
decorated with a copy of the treasured caricature of him
done years ago by Hirschfeld, he let me in. His hair was
sticking out at the sides and his red silk tie was askew. His
hand trembled as he reached out to pull me inside.

The office had been ransacked.

The file drawers had been pulled out, turned over and
emptied on the floor. The room was awash with paper:
folders, newspaper clippings, photographs, typescript, letters
and index cards, the archives of gossip, going back decades,
lay tumbled, looking like mulch waiting for the pitchfork. I
picked up a handwritten note on thick, peach notepaper; the
odor of perfume still clung to it. Dated 1951, signed Bobo. She
was filing for divorce and thought Pop should know. I let it
flutter back onto the pile.

"What happened?" I asked him.

"This . . ." he pointed unsteadily at the floor.

"Where's Sadie?"

"They took her to St. Luke's."

193

"Who?"

"The EMS, in an ambulance."

"Is she hurt bad?"

"I think she'll be okay."

"What happened?" I demanded again.

"She heard a knock, buzzed the door. Two men in ski masks rushed in and grabbed her." He stopped, looked around, bewildered.

"Get it together." I took his hand. "Robbery?"

"No . . . yes. They grabbed her bag and took her cash, and her subway tokens. Jesus. One guy backs her into a corner, tells her what he's going to do. Like rape her, you know? The other guy just trashes the files. And then they gag her and tie her to a chair, threaten her. I think they slapped her around a bit, her face was all red. Then they left."

"Let's get over there." Sadie, my poor Sadie.

"Soon, soon." he said.

"Any description?"

"One guy, white. She saw his hands. He shouted obscenities, and he hurt her. The other guy, she couldn't tell. He wore gloves. He stood around."

"What did the cops say?"

"Nothing."

"Nothing?"

"I didn't, well, tell them about the threats to me. I mean, what's the point? They were just patrol."

"So what did you do?"

"I found her. Untied her. She was completely hysterical. I called 911. Then I phoned in the story."

"To the paper?"

"Of course," he said, looking at me quizzically. "They're sending a photographer up."

"You're kidding?"

"I don't know what's keeping them."

"I don't either, Pop. You sit for a bit and keep your mind on those photographers." I trudged over to his desk by the window, pushing the litter ahead of me and to the side with my feet, as if I were making a path through freshly fallen snow. I sat down. There were no pictures of Mom or Aunt

Helen or me on the desk. No drawings of mine on the wall. He had gotten a lot of awards, though, from people who didn't know him. My father sat waiting patiently, expectantly.

"Look," I began, "these guys wanted something. What? Who are they?"

He shrugged his shoulders. "Sadie was distraught, really. She couldn't tell me much. She was terrorized."

"I don't mean Sadie!" I shouted. "You!" I pointed my finger at him. "You tell me who they were, damn it, and what they wanted."

"I'm not sure," he said hesitantly.

"Come on, talk to me. Have you had any other threats?"

"Just that business I told you about."

"Nothing else?"

He shook his head. He probably hadn't. People liked to see their names in the paper, it turned them on, magnified them. But, when dealing with anyone really powerful or dangerous, Pop was very cautious. That's why he had lasted all these years. He was not so much a muckraker as a muck sniffer. He never stirred anything up.

"What *did* Sadie say?"

"She said the creep with the bad mouth said they were going to take some tidbits or, God help us, tit bits. Son, she was badly frightened."

"What did they take?"

"Some files. Which? She wasn't sure."

"Do you keep sensitive . . . uh, I don't know . . . secret stuff here? What someone might think of as prime blackmail material?"

"Of course. Though, actually. . . . I mean, I don't think anybody really cares. Most of this stuff" he stooped down and picked up a handful, "is kind of stale." He let it drop. "You've got your rumors, gossip, and innuendo," he started to tick them off rhythmically on his fingers, an old routine, done over restaurant tables for his cronies:

"Your chatter about folks in the big dough.
    Your planted items
    and your deny'ems;

your backbiting and your speculations,
your contretemps and peculations . . ."

"Get a grip, Pop," I said softly. "Save the song for the press."
"You're right."
"Pop, can you find out what files those guys took?"
"Sure."
"You can?" I was surprised. The place looked hopeless to me.
"Here, take a look."
He walked over a mound of paper to a closet, bending over, he scooped some files in his arms and shoved them aside to make clearance for the closet door. He opened it and took out a massive rolodex circular card holder from within. He brought it over to the desk and set it down.
"This lists all the living people I have a folder on, or people who maybe died but still might be mentioned in the column. I keep those files here. These people," he waved at the mess on the floor, "are alive, or very important."
"What happens to the others?"
"They get sent to the morgue."
"What?"
"I've got storage space with Big Yellow. It's a good deal. That's where I keep the dead people."
"They on another rolodex, too?"
"Yup."
"Maybe someone should go over to the warehouse and see if anything's disturbed?"
"Okay. I drop by once in a while, anyway. But first I've got to sort out what's missing from here."
"How?"
"I match up the cards to the folders on the floor. The cards say what cabinet drawer the file is in, and on the back, sometimes, the date I started the file."
"I'm going over to the hospital," I said and got up and walked to the door.
"I'll stay here and start working." Now he had an excuse to stay with his files.

"You going to get some help? Office temps or something?" I figured Sadie wouldn't be back for a while.

"No, I have to do it myself. I have a cot in the closet. I'll bring it out and sleep here till I'm done. Should be only a couple of days," he said with confidence. I understood in a way. I'd stay that long at the job too if I had to sort out my drawings. But that wasn't it exactly. He *was* those files.

"I'll be in touch," I said and closed the door behind me.

Years as a news photographer taught me how to maneuver myself into emergency rooms. I found Sadie, holding hands with her husband, who looked dazed, sitting on plastic molded chairs in a crowded hallway beyond the emergency room. I rushed over to her.

"Sadie, I just left Pop. What happened?"

She looked up at me. Her eyes were red and the lids swollen. There were welts and bruises on her face. She clutched Max's hand.

"She'll be okay, kid. A nurse called me by Playwear, where I'm cutting." Max worked in the garment district in the East Thirties. "Ooh, was I scared? Sadie beaten up! 'Hurt bad?' I ask, 'Come over' she says. I came right over. Meine Sadele is pretty tough. We'll go home soon."

"She see a doctor, yet?"

"A doctor, yes, he says, 'take x-rays', so x-rays we took. Now we sit. Maybe is better we just go home, huh, Sadie?"

"Sadie, tell me, what happened. It's all right. You're safe now."

She looked at me. It wasn't right, her eyes seemed to say. Where had we been? I knelt on one knee in front of her and took her hand from Max and put it on my cheek.

"Dollink boy, *zuninkeh*," she put her other hand on my head and hugged me into her lap. "Those awful men, *paskudniks!*" She seemed to revive. I looked up at her. She was smiling at me. "I was so afraid your father was going to come back with his gun. Then they'd hurt him, too."

"Did they ask for anything? What did they take?"

"Files. '*Oy*,' I said, 'About them I don't know anything. Somebody else takes care of all that,' I lied. Files they took."

"Which ones?"

"I don't know."

A doctor came over, carrying a folder. A Sikh, he had a dark red turban and a black beard rolled and tucked neatly under his chin.

"Mrs. Epstein?" he asked.

Max answered warily, "Yes?" I stood up, but held on to Sadie's hand.

"Has there been any vomiting?"

"What?"

"Have you any upset in the stomach, any dizziness?"

"Sadie," Max suggested, "You have go-round, maybe, in your head?"

"To tell you the truth, Doctor, I don't. Maybe a little head-ache."

"The x-rays show no sign of a skull fracture. Should you experience excessive dizziness or nausea, come here or call a doctor immediately."

"That, I promise. I can go home?"

"Yes."

"Let's go home, Max," she said.

We walked outside together where I hailed a cab. We got in and told the driver to take us to Max and Sadie's neighbor-hood in Brooklyn. The cabbie told me I had to be kidding. I was in no mood to be jerked around and neither were Sadie and Max. I handed the cabbie one of India's hundred dollar bills and he started up without another word.

In the back of the cab, which was new and clean and without the gray plastic shield to protect the driver from getting his throat slashed, Sadie sat between Max and me. I still held one of her hands.

"Kid," she said as we started over the Williamsburgh Bridge.

"Yes?"

"You know it would be interesting to know what those *mamzers* wanted so bad they beat up an old lady."

"Anti-Semites," murmured Max.

"Pop's working on it," I said. "He's going to keep at compar-ing his list to the files until he's found it."

"He loves those files."

"It was a mess up there, total chaos. Even after he compares his list, though, we won't know what was in them."

"That's what you think?"

"What do you mean, Sadie?"

"The great artist never heard of the xerox machine? If there was a fire, God forbid, what would the *balebos* do without his files? So I copied."

"What did you do with them?"

"What else? I sent them to Big Yellow."

"Ah, Sadie, Sadie."

"Your *tante* Sadie's not so dumb, eh?"

"What can I say?"

"Say you'll stay for dinner?"

"I can't. I have to work. I just wanted to make sure you were home safe."

"Safe, the mayor says no one is safe. Oy, Max."

She spoke to Max in Yiddish so fast I couldn't follow it. He shrugged. Turning back to me she said, "The stars hinted something terrible was going to happen. But what can you do?"

I left them in their apartment and I took the subway into Manhattan. By the base of the cable station that sends commuters and tourists swinging out over the East River in gondolas to Roosevelt Island, I found a cab to take me to the storage warehouse Sadie had directed me to in Long Island City. The driver accelerated onto the 59th Street Bridge and the tires hummed on the metal grids that make up the roadway. We dodged through Queensboro Plaza, maneuvering around the El columns, went over the Sunnyside Railway yards, turned past a city prison and pulled up in front of a large building as yellow as a beach ball.

I paid off the driver. I wondered when New York cabbies stopped saying, "Have a nice day." I went into the building and found a reception desk with a sheet of plexiglass extending from the top of it up to the ceiling, like in a liquor store in the *Barrio*. A young, dark haired, Hispanic girl, about eighteen sat behind the counter reading a book. She had a retroussé nose and large, lovely brown eyes. Her full breasts strained against the bright yellow blouse she was wearing; a small plaque pinned to it said "Milagros." She looked up at my approach and smiled. I explained what I wanted and her eyes got larger and larger.

She shook her head. Now what?

"Louder," she said.

I shouted.

"Do you have a key?" she asked.

"Yes," I held up the key Sadie had given me.

"Oh, fine." She pressed a button and a buzzer sounded. A door to her left swung open and I went in. "Hi!" she said.

"Hi!"

"I can't leave the desk, but just go over to that stairway and walk up two flights. The doors are all numbered. It's real easy."

"Thank you, Milagros."

"Oh, you're welcome." She giggled.

I took the elevator upstairs and followed the signs in a small hallway to the door of Pop's storage space. I opened the door with the key and switched on the overhead light. It was dim, but serviceable. The room was dry and musty, filled with the odor of paper slowly crumbling. The cardboard file boxes were lined up neatly in rows. I had expected something more archival, like an infinite number of folios stretching down through the Tartarean gloom of a Piranesi drawing.

The files were organized by decades and alphabetically, by last name. Sadie told me that they tried to keep titles and subsequent marriages from gumming the works by keying on the family's name, at birth. The Duchess of Windsor, for example, who ranked right next to Emma Goldman in Sadie's pantheon, would be found under Warfield and, in her era, Mrs. Barrett, under Wentworth.

Starting at the thirties, and moving through the eighties, I pulled the files where I could find them, on Mrs. Wentworth, Peter Barrett, Hadley, Rina Royal, no mention of her brother, no Merkles, and surprise, surprise, a file from the fifties on Kavanaugh. Some stuff on Lou Darmstadt, nothing on Cheech. I looked up my own files and found them, starting in the seventies. I left them there.

I now had a stack in the center of the aisle. It would be difficult to read through them here. I was feeling sweaty and itchy, working in the close confines of the storeroom. The newsprint files from the thirties had started to dissolve and, as I moved them, flat yellow crumbs of paper started to spill out of them. I needed to find a secure place with a desk or work table and a two-hundred watt bulb overhead. I'd take them to Lou's studio. In what? Sadie would have brought a shopping bag with her. What did I have. I had a belt. I took it off and wrapped it around the pile and tugged it closed. My files were size 34. I put them under my arm, opened the door, turned off the light and locked up.

Downstairs I waved to Milagros and walked over to Queensboro Plaza where I grabbed a cab before it made its run over the bridge into Manhattan. Back to Soho. Where a surprise awaited me after the door was opened for me.

Standing naked in Lou Darmstadt's burlapped loft, holding a pose, as I staggered in with my files, was the young Chinese girl who had served me a drink at Kavanaugh's. She looked at me levelly.

"Good. You are here, Ventry." Lou said. "My friend Chen here called and asked me if I knew where you could be found. She has something for you."

"What's that?"

"Information on Kavanaugh," Lou said. "Get dressed, Chen. We are finished."

"How'd she get here?" I asked.

"Ah, Ventry, she works sometimes at Handasyde and Beaky. She recognized you from your tug boat self-portrait. Puzzled at the unseemly interaction between you and Kavanaugh, she mentioned it to me when we spoke. I told her to come over, that you'd turn up eventually. Cheech wants you to call him in an hour at the Foundry. Take Chen out somewhere and grill her kindly. I need to finish this." She turned back to the canvas and snapped back into concentration on her work, like the basilisk. I put the files next to her drafting table, said I'd be back, and left with Chen.

In the Canal Bar, we found a table and ordered drinks. It

was quiet. The rest of the downtown art world wouldn't show up for a few hours yet. The young Chinese girl sitting across from me was about five-six and weighed perhaps a hundred and ten pounds. Her straight black hair framing her oval face was left to hang freely over her shoulders. Her skin glowed with health, and her face was animated, as if after some restraint, she could let the interested glint in her eyes show through, lift her brows, purse her lips, tilt the angle of her jaw, all expressing her inner feelings. She was like a dancer, flexing constantly.

I listened to her run on about Lou while I sketched her even though I had to get back to the files, had to call Cheech, Moira, Sadie and Pop, or maybe Sonny Ehrlich, Dad's retired detective friend could be helpful, and Rina, too, before I ran into Merkle again or found myself sitting on one of Kavanaugh's shelves within sound of the surf.

Chen wasn't self-conscious. I filled the pages of my book with quick studies of her mercurial facial expressions.

"How," I asked her, "did you come to be pouring drinks in Kavanaugh's loft?"

"It's pick-up work, while I go to school."

"What can you tell me about Kavanaugh?"

"I have to tell story my own way."

"Okay."

"I study Art History," she said proudly.

I swallowed my impatience and asked where.

"I'm at Columbia."

"You don't find the language difficult?"

"Oh language hard. English very hard."

"Why not computers then, or mathematics?"

She rolled her sparkling brown eyes. "Oh, all Chinese are studying *computers*. Art very beautiful. I love medieval art especially." She stressed the syllables of all her words equally: mee-dee-vul. "I am writing a paper on comparison of 12th century Italian monastery fresco lion with 14th century German statuette of rider on horse. Both *very* beautiful. Work go slowly. You want to see it? Maybe you correct English? Tenses *very* hard."

She was beautiful, alert, had something to tell me, but was she for real? Shouldn't she be in a silk scroll painting in a mandarin's garden, playing the lute while her court lady companions sipped tea. Lute *very* hard.

Though I couldn't wire up my informants to a polygraph I could ask her about her background to get a sense of her motives in talking to me.

"What did you do in China, study art?"

"Oh no. Party not permit it."

"What did you do?"

She wagged her head back and forth, like a child debating with herself and trying to be cute. "I lived with my mother and father in Beijing until I graduate from high school. I wished to go to University then, but that was time of Cultural Revolution. I cannot go to university, I must go to farm in Inner Mongolia, Red Guards say so. I spend four years there. Very hard. My parents get me a job with railway. For six years I am electrician on state railway system in Mongolia. Repairing train signals. If they not working, very bad accident."

"My grandfather worked on the railroad in Colorado," I said remembering Pierce Ferriter's tumble down the scree.

"America different," she insisted.

"Could you at least draw while you were there? After your job was done for the day?"

"I could not draw there. I could not draw in Beijing. I cannot draw here." She looked at me wickedly. "I cannot draw at all. Look at art. Yes, I can do that. Not much art in Mongolia."

"How did you get from Mongolia to here?"

"Oh, my parents get me visa to leave China and study here."

"How did they arrange it, your parents?"

"Oh, I don't ask."

"No?"

"My father is night watchman. Before Cultural Revolution he was teacher in Fudan University. Maybe one of his students now in government, eh? Maybe he help me out because of past kindnesses my father showed him."

"Any family here?"

"All in China." She sipped at her Coke. "I need money," she said.

"What for?"

"To live in Italy for year. Write thesis. Need five thousand cash. Very soon."

"How do I fit in?"

"You have money to find out big secret. Lou tells me this. I help you find out. I tell you what I know. You give me money. That's all I want."

"Do you know what you're getting involved in? Do you know what people like Kavanaugh are like?"

"I tell you a story, eh? My boss one time on the state railway named Wu. He was very greedy, very cruel. He take bribes. Arrange for secret shipments of lamb to party cadres. Sell electrical supplies for gold. I know all this."

"How?"

"His girlfriend. She had gone to same high school as me in Beijing, eh, but much younger. She pretty, but very lazy. Understand?" I nodded. "She size Wu up pretty quick. Soon she not have to work any more. But she get lonely and we talk."

"I see."

"Not complicated. Wu the big boss. Anybody want anything in that sector must go to him. He is real capitalist roader." Her eyes lit up at her joke. "Pretty soon Wu is getting rich. He showed Lin Lin, my friend, his gold bars. They are flat, like poker cards. He has *many* gold bars. Lin Lin tell me he is making deal. He will steal a backup generator system and sell it to local people. Much gold."

"Where does the gold come from?"

"Oh, there is much gold in China. Many prospectors. Mongols go everywhere. They smuggle, bring it back to buy switching systems generator from Wu."

"So then what happened?"

"Greedy Wu tell girlfriend. Not so smart. Lin Lin tell me. That generator in my section. I say to myself, "Chen, greedy Wu get away with everything! No good. I make appropriate socialist response. My big red move. I go see local party head,

Huang. I inform on Wu. Trap is set and Wu is caught. Huang *very* happy. He ask what I want. No hesitation. Good report and ticket to Beijing. Goodbye smelly Mongolia."

"And here we are," I said. She looked around at our neighbors, two of the early downtown crowd hanging out, a pale young woman dressed in matte black and nun's shoes, sitting with her project of the moment, her self-consciously self-involved boyfriend, lounging behind his Ray Ban sunglasses. Chen nodded, "Yes, it's wonderful."

"Okay, Chen, it's a deal. Now, why did you tell Lou you had information about Kavanaugh and had to see me?"

"You are painter. Old painter dead. You find out who killed. Eh?" Her "Eh?" was a rising two-note query that would be heard down the tracks and across the Mongolian plains. People looked in our direction. "I see you at party with Val Royal and Mr. Kavanaugh. I say, 'Chen, this is wrong.' I know from gallery you friend of Lou's. She *very* good person. She know me and tell me what you doing. You very brave." I closed my notebook.

"Those two, Kavanaugh and Val, think I'm stupid or don't understand English. Talk in front of me at bar. Understand *very* well. Remember all."

"What do they say?"

"They plan to get much money from Royal's brother-in-law. You going to kill him I think they say. Then they kill you. Sister inherit estate." Well, that explained why they were so eager for me to see Rina. The doorman saw me, got my name. Looks like they were heading me for that shelf within sound of the waves.

"What happens to her?"

"Will obey elder brother. Big projects go on ahead."

"Do you know who killed Peter Barrett?"

"Not who. Why."

"Why?"

"Do you believe me, so far?"

"Yes."

"I tell you my story. I inform on smelly Wu to advance myself. Now I need Italy. Five thousand cash." She had a capacity for directness a syringe would envy.

"You can have it tomorrow."

"In writing please. Intention of giving Chen money. Date please."

I scribbled on my drawing pad 'I promise to give Chen . . .

"What's your full name?"

"Write Lin Lin Chen." Oh. I looked at her, and she stared back, unwaveringly.

' . . . five thousand dollars in cash on demand in return for services already rendered.' I signed and dated it.

"Peter Barrett was being blackmailed by Cyril Hart, with information Val Royal and Kavanaugh give him."

"Why?"

"Not sure. They say Big Gossip was sure to figure it out." Hence the threats against the Old Man?

"What happened to Cyril Hart?"

"They say this, when I am cleaning up after party. You were gone:

"Royal, 'Why not just put squeeze on cousin Hadley like we did on Barrett?'

"Kavanaugh, 'It's easier if we get both Hadley and Ventry out of the way. Don't forget the outcome the last time around, my coltish friend, when Cyril put the bite on Barrett on his own and events got out of control. Clumsy fool deserved what he got.'

"Royal, 'Who would have thought Barrett would take a hammer to him. I mean, really.'

"Kavanaugh, 'Be quiet. I'm still worried about Vince Ventry.'

"Royal: 'But that was so long ago.'

"That's all." She let out a long breath. "Am quick study. *Very* good memory."

"What did I say that evening?" I asked.

"You say, 'Well, Val, are these the fakes?' and then you talk lovey with Rina Hadley."

"You can pick up your money at Lou's."

"Thank you," Chen said, "Good luck." She got up and hurried out, her boot heels tapping on the floor. I signalled the waiter for the check. When it came, I dropped a twenty on the table and left.

18

Back on the street, I called Cheech at The Foundry, his name for the Crosby Street studio of a friend of his who took an assembly line approach to the making of art. He had an idea editor who screened suggestions for work, a planning group to come up with proposals on how to go about doing a piece, a cost estimator, and a variety of art students hired for a few months at a time to bring it into existence. The Foundry's output sold very well.

"What's up, Cheech?"

"Hey, your lady friend is some looker. She doesn't seem to have a lot of friends, but I'd say I wasn't the only person following her."

Oh, hell. "Who else?"

"Big guy. Had red hair."

Kavanaugh's man. "Was he following her like a bodyguard or like a tail?"

"I'd guess bodyguards'd take the same cab, wouldn't you think? Not the next one along."

"How'd you keep up?"

"She didn't come out of the house till eleven. 'When she did I grabbed a cab, gave him a hundred, and said 'do it, my man.' We all went down Seventh, across Fourteenth and down Broadway to a bar near Tower Records. Nice place. Has a big boat like a chili pepper hung from the ceiling. Large plate glass front. I could see everything."

"Come on, Cheech, who'd she meet?"

"This old guy. I didn't recognize him."

"What did he look like?"

"Sharp. Very sharp. Lightweight, tropical worsted."

"What do you know about wool suits?"

"My old man was a tailor for Robert Hall. Didn't you know that?"

"No, go on."

"Like I said, he was old, sort of. Had a hat on. Ruddy face. Big jaw. Not thin, muscular, seemed in good shape. Got a picture for you. Had the film developed and printed already down here. Can run it up to you."

"She see anybody else?"

"A little while later. Young guy goes in and sits with them. Very thin, blond. Looked like Bowie. Looked like her. They both look like Bowie."

"It was her brother, Val."

"The three of them talked. I got a picture of him, too, rushing out ahead of her."

"What about the redhead?" I asked.

"He sat in his cab, then beat it after he saw she met the old guy."

"Why?"

"You're asking me?"

"Did he see you?"

"Nah."

"That it?"

"Yup. Want the pictures?" Cheech asked.

"Christ, yes. I'll meet you outside in ten minutes. I'll just swing by in a cab."

"Why not walk?" he asked, puzzled.

"My leg hurts."

"Right, Ace."

"Can you do it again tomorrow?"

"You said three days. Three days you'll get."

"Thanks Cheech."

A little later, my cab turned onto Vesey Street and I saw Cheech standing against a building with all the solidity of the stone itself. He smiled as he saw me. I paid off the cab.

Cheech handed me an 8 x 11 envelope and said, "I could use a beer."

We walked up the street to a bar, settled on stools and ordered beers. I opened the envelope.

"Oh, no." I groaned. "Oh, no."

"You all right, Ventry?" asked Cheech.

"Bad news, Cheech. Real bad. This is tough to take."

"Tell me."

I had some beer. "A long, long time ago, in the Fifties," I began, "Pop's cronies from the newspaper business would get together, maybe once a month, for a poker game in our apartment on Riverside Drive. There'd be a lot of whiskey and beer, none for Pop, and they'd talk and say 'fuck' a lot, and get around to singing the same song, about Lydia the Tattooed Lady. They were writers, mainly, a cop or two, no civilians, they'd say, not in their Park Row Palimpsest and Poontang Society. They never shut up.

"They would talk all night of the old days. They gabbed on about Ben Hecht and Charlie MacArthur, Grantland Rice and Jimmy Walker and Babe Ruth. They talked about stunts, and capers and who was the toughest guy on Broadway and who went on the worst bender.

"They were a cast of characters, all right. They called themselves Short Arms and Dookie Do, Kid Iggie, Sonny the Cop, and Brilly from Philly, who used a pound of grease in his hair and had to sit hunched forward in armchairs because antimacassars went out with spittoons. Neither my mother nor my aunt liked these men very much and didn't like me hanging round them. But I did.

"They played on an old, beat up, scarred, burnt, sturdy, round mahogany table in our dining room under five bulbs burning in the plaster rose fixture on the ceiling. The table top had hundreds of rings on the varnish from drinks and beer cans. Rings on rings.

"Sometimes they would throw on an old green army blanket as a cover, which Mom would throw out the next day. They'd play on bare wood then until someone brought another blanket. My family never had any dinner parties or anything. I'd sketch or do my homework on the table during the week and leave it cluttered with junk, pieces of plywood from model kits, comics, waterguns and clay snakes. Then Pop would yell at me to clean it off and that's when I knew there'd be a game that night.

"Their rules were simple: no women, no wildcards. Since Pop never drank I suppose he won, but I was long gone to bed before they settled up. When someone called a hand, and won, they'd always say: "You're fresh out o' luck, fella."

"In the early part of the night, before I got sent off to bed, I'd sketch them for dough. If they liked what they saw or their pals liked the rough caricature of, say, Iggy's red veined, bulbous beezer or Sonny's bald pate, gleaming like a radar dome on the tundra, and his jaw like the prow of an ice breaker, somebody would give me a quarter or a half. Then I'd spray the sketch and sign it. I must have made twenty off Sonny the Cop alone."

Sonny hadn't changed much. Cheech's long lens through the plate glass had captured a good likeness. I was fresh out of luck.

Tears and anger rose up in me. My throat was tight, my stomach was churning. Sonny the Cop on the payroll of the man who I was pretty sure helped put Peter Barrett in the grave. It wasn't a lucky morning when Pop picked his old pal, Inspector Sonny Ehrlich, to give me a cover to convince them that I was on their side. I was lunchmeat. If Ehrlich told Rina that I was lying, and she told her brother, he and Kavanaugh would come after me. At best I couldn't penetrate any further into their operation. At worst, well, later for that.

I had to talk to Pop. Find out about Ehrlich. I had to know if he tipped me to Val and Kavanaugh.

Failing that, maybe I could get something from that air-head, Rina. Catch her alone. Be clever. I had to do something. Move. I paid up and we left. We stood outside.

"Ventry?" Cheech asked.

"Yeah?"

"A friend of yours?" He nodded behind me.

I don't know what I expected to see, but the sight of Merkle behind the wheel of a pickup truck in Soho wasn't it. He pointed at me, the engine of the truck roared, and he inched up beside us.

I pulled the .38 from my jacket pocket, dropped to one knee and pointed it at him. Merkle whipped the truck in a U-turn and sped away.

Cheech was still standing. "I saw that guy when we met yesterday," he said calmly. "I guess you were being followed."

I guess I was. Merkle meant Val. Where had he picked me up? Why the hell didn't *I* ever turn around?

"I'm going back to your place now, Cheech. I left some files there I have to go over."

"Let's do it."

19

Lou was still working when we let ourselves into the loft. Cheech went over to the perch to play with the parrot, who screeched out "Talk to me, handsome! Whaawk! Talk to me, handsome!" I turned on the lights in the room where Lou did her work in collage and photography. The drafting table was bare. I spread the files out under the brutal light of the 200 watt lamps and went through them. I tried to push the image of Sonny talking to Val and Rina out of my mind so I could concentrate on my hunt through the yellowed clippings and pencilled index cards. After two hours, I found an answer, or part of one.

I called my father.

"Vince Ventry, here."

From the file labeled Morgan Kavanaugh, I took a sheet of my father's note paper, personalized with his caricature.

"8500 to C for papers," I read aloud carefully. "Three and a half from Mrs. G for her and J. Five from W himself for K."

"Is that you, son?"

"What's this all about, Pop?"

"Where are you?"

"At a friend's studio in Soho."

"I better come over. What's the address?"

"The phone will do." I read the entry to him again.

"Frankly, son, the paper is a memorandum-for-the-file in code."

"Why in code?"

"The transaction was illegal. You don't know what it costs me to tell you this."

"That's right, I don't. Go ahead."

"I was involved in it with others. I had to protect them of course, hence the cypher. You know, son, I had forgotten about it. Gee, the years go . . ."

"Who are they?"

"There have been so many people, deals, stories."

"Who?" I demanded.

"Read it again."

"8500 to C for papers," I read aloud carefully. "Three and a half from Mrs. G for her and J. Five from W himself for K."

"C is a congressman. You know, I had an understanding with him. They all did me favors. I could help them out with, well, campaign funds, stories and so forth."

"Go on."

"The papers are citizenship papers. C would either get Immigration moving on somebody or else introduce a private bill."

"So someone came to you for these papers for three people. I found this in a file labeled Morgan Kavanaugh. He's the K?"

"Yes."

"And the numbers?"

"The basic price or contribution back then was five thousand. We called it a unit. I got the five straight for Kavanaugh and thirty-five hundred from Mrs. G and her kid. I made up the difference myself."

"Why the discount?"

"She was good looking. You got to take it where you can get it."

"Who was she?"

"You know her."

"Who was she?"

"She taught you French. What did you think of your lessons, kid?"

"Rachel? Mme. Halevy Giresse?"

"She was a firecracker in the sack, kid."

"Jack's mother?"

"Her kid got papers, too. You still see him?"

"Why didn't she go the normal route? Take lessons in night school or whatever?"

"The kid's old man was a thief and a collaborator. That didn't go down well after the war. Kavanaugh found that out. When Kavanaugh got here in the late Forties, he contacted her. He was blackmailing her. The old man, Giresse senior, was dead by then, she knew that, but Kavanaugh convinced her anyway that she and Jack would be deported if she didn't take care of him. Said he wanted to meet some nice young rich girls. Mme. Giresse pimped for him. She was making dresses for the whole Colony crowd. She arranged for him to meet India, who he promptly seduced. She told her family she was going to marry him. He's slick, but not what that family had in mind. They talked, her father and him. Included in his price to butt out was the citizenship."

"So the 5 from W himself for K is Wentworth anteing up for Kavanaugh."

"The Wentworths paid right up. They gave the money to me who gave it to the congressman. Clean and simple. I gave him a lot over the years."

"Were my French lessons included in the package?"

"No."

"I am glad you said that."

"Really, this brings back the old days."

"So India Barrett knew Kavanaugh all these years?"

"Yes."

"And this foundation? This Dawnwalk?"

"That's Kavanaugh's cash cow. He could always convince India of anything." I thought back to her expression when she gave me the video tape. Perhaps what I saw there was lust.

"Who was the congressman, Pop?"

"It doesn't matter now."

"Who?" I insisted.

"Peary Conklin, Calvin's father."

"Are you serious?"

"Hey, I get a machine Democrat from the city and all of a sudden there'd be a line of guys with their hands out. Peary

Conklin was greedy, but he was just one guy. And the price
was reasonable."

"You know Calvin thinks the world of his father."

"Unlike you." Well, there it was.

"He was corrupt, huh?" I asked naively.

"Son, elect Jesus Christ to Congress and in three days he'll
be taking bribes."

"And Calvin never knew?"

"Of course he knew. He must have."

"What do you mean?"

"In New York, in the Fifties, years after the Wentworth deal,
I was at the Stork and Peary and the kid come in. The boy's in
uniform, looked great. Peary had called, said he wanted accounts brought up to date. The congressman was a little
sozzled. We have a few drinks in the Cub Room at my table.
Sherm sits with us a while. The kid's dazzled. Then there are
just the three of us. Peary says, 'let's have it.' I see the mood
he's in, so I just fold it in a napkin in my lap and put it in front
of him with the edge showing." He stops.

"Then what happened?"

"Drunken Peary reaches for it but knocks his drink over.
The kid grabs the napkin to clean it up, before it drips on the
old man. The envelope falls out and the kid asks 'what's this?'
I just look away."

"What did the congressman do?"

"The kid opens the envelope and takes out the money. We
had thousand dollar bills back then. He looks at the congressman as if his old dad had just given Joe Stalin the plans to the
H-Bomb."

"What did the old man do?"

"Nothing, he was so out of it."

"And Calvin?"

"His head just keeps getting lower and lower, the hair
dropping in front of his eyes, so I can't see if he's crying or
what."

"Yeah?"

"Then he puts the envelope back in the napkin, brushes his
hair back, and asks me if Joe DiMaggio ever comes in. Can you
beat that? Just blows it right off. Does Joe ever come in?

Course, Joe did, you know. So I suppose Calvin knew well enough where some of the family money came from. He saw it. Just ignored it."

"Was Barrett involved in any of this?"

"No, but when Barrett came along and India fell for him, he looked pretty good to the Wentworths, after Kavanaugh."

"How did you meet India?"

"Let me see. Yeah, one night at the Copa, Kavanaugh is with India and starts messing with a couple of guys sitting at a table nearby. They were with a boss, you know, what we used to call a don. Kavanaugh made some threats. He was a tough kid in those days, now that I recall. But these are guys who haven't heard a threat in years. I mean anyone who wants to argue with them knows he has to take them out. Threats?

"I know who India is, see? So, while Kavanaugh is making more noises, I slip into a seat next to her. She's wide eyed. I tell her her boyfriend's in trouble. I give her my card. She asks me can I do anything. I know the boss. I go around to his table. He's enjoying this. He knows me. Anyway I smooth things over. India gets Kavanaugh out of there. Later, when they need the citizenship papers, she calls me in. I'm the honest broker." As always, he seemed to enjoy telling the story.

"Does Kavanaugh know who I am?"

"I haven't talked to him in thirty, no Christ, almost forty years."

"Was Sonny Ehrlich mixed up with this?"

"Nah, this was political."

"About Sonny, I think he ratted on me. He may have told Kavanaugh's pals I'm no friend of that loanshark."

"Sonny just wouldn't do that. He called. I didn't know where to reach you. He said he has to see you real bad. He's probably going to straighten everything out."

"Is he setting me up?"

"No. I'd say he just wants to talk. He always liked you, Sonny did. He said not to call. Just go up there right away. He said he was in a hurry and for you to get the lead out." He gave me the address. I hung up, and then called the farm. Moira answered on the first ring.

"Everything quiet?"

"Christ, Ventry, give a girl a call, now and then, why don't you?"

"I have to see one more person down here, I'm close to finding out . . ." What? That Cyril was a blackmailer? ". . . what this is all about. Then I'll take the train up. We have to talk to Jack again. He's been holding out on us."

"Hurry," she said. I told her I would and I hung up. I took five thousand dollars of Mrs. Barrett's money and put it in one of Lou's photo envelopes, sealed it, wrote "For Chen" on it, put it on the kitchen table, took my bag with Jeremiah's portrait, the gun and what was left of the money and let myself out. Lou was still working.

Sonny lived in upper Manhattan, in a 1920's period apartment building of dark red brick in Washington Heights, just north of the George Washington Bridge and just west of Broadway, on a quiet street lined with plane trees. It was peaceful, a cop's neighborhood. There, in the early evening, I saw girls skipping rope, young boys on bicycles, two old women, both with small dogs, talking together on a corner. In front of Sonny's house, two young mothers sat on the stone steps gently moving strollers back and forth. I had to step between them.

Upstairs, Sonny answered the door, looking disheveled, his eyes were bloodshot. He was dressed in a white tee shirt and black pants. His feet were bare. He stepped aside to let me in. As I passed I smelled oil. He had a rag in one hand and his service revolver in the other. He had obviously been cleaning it.

To the left was a bedroom with an unmade bed, the sheets tangled. Ahead was a small, windowless kitchen with the lights off. To the right the living room stretched twenty feet to the windows, overlooking the turn of the century Dutch Reformed Church across the street.

Running down both sides of the room, extending five feet high on either side, were boxes a foot and a half square, built to hold thousands of LP records, cassettes and reels of tape. Two large speakers stood sentry on either side of the window.

The turntables and amplifiers were set in among the cabinets.
There were two wooden chairs, a scarred coffee table and a
standing lamp. Near the cabinets, I could see tattered foam
padding sticking out from the stained, burgundy carpet covering the floor. The paint was peeling. Dust covered the cases.
The slats and tape on the venetian blinds on the windows
were grimy. There were no photographs and no paintings.
One drawing, by me of him.

"Would you like a beer?"

"No."

"Sit down, anyway." I did. He took the other chair. "Some
collection, huh?" He waved his hands at the walls. "My mother liked the music. She came from the old country. Galway.
Her father was a fiddler in Oughterard. She used to tell me
how he played for the young people dancing in the cross-
roads, in the street, like. Before she came over and married
her darlin' Jewman. So I started buying her records to listen
to. She sat here all day, a bad hip. Once a week I would take
her up the hill to church in a wheel chair, but, you know, she
hated to be seen like that. Mother just sat, looked out the
window. Why not? I just kept buying them. Then tapes, too.
All Irish. Some from Scotland, Brittany, Newfoundland, Australia, here, Japan even. Really. Wherever. You want to hear
something?"

"No."

"It's okay. I'll turn it down low." He reached behind him
and pushed a button on the reel to reel, then turned a knob
on the amplifier. A lament came on the speaker. A quiet,
sobbing screech. Some Irish woman was wailing: oooooo-
choooo-ooone. It sounded awful, like a subway car going
around a curve with a locked wheel. Then another one joined
her. Then another. He didn't seem to be paying any attention.
He took a book from next to the tape machine, opened it and
showed it to me. I was looking at an old photo of a man I had
never seen before.

"See, that's Chief O'Neill. He was a policeman in Chicago
around 1900, then he became chief. Whenever an Irish musi-
cian turned up and needed a job, the Chief would put them

on the force. No kidding. He really did. He grilled these guys, sweated them for the songs and tunes they were carrying around in their heads. He transcribed it all. Otherwise it would have been lost. What a guy, huh? A *policeman*. When I heard that, well it was fate or something that brought me to this music. For years I couldn't figure out what I was supposed to do. Couldn't see it. I just kept buying records."

Sonny was manic. I let him talk.

"I got talking to this professor who lives in the building. He was carrying a big package from Goody's and so was I. He looks at me and I look at him. He's puffing away at this big, old pipe of his. He's all in tweeds and stuff. 'A fellow collector?" he says. I say 'yeah, you know, I just buy all these records.' 'And what, may I ask, are your areas of interest?' 'Mainly Irish or Celtic related,' I say and then down there in the foyer he starts asking me all these questions and I tell him sometimes, most of the time really, I just play a record once to see if it's okay, then I put it away. He said him too. It was real nice. I go up to his apartment and he shows me his collection. He had these boxes made. I get them from the same place now. He tells me he collects mainly Bach. He had copies of the same piece, a dozen or more of the important stuff, "St. Matthew's Passion" and like that. He wanted to give me his doubles, but I've got my own stuff. We talk now and again. We're discophiles," he said proudly.

"Where's this going, Sonny?"

"Shut up, kid," he yelled at me. "I'm warning you. Shut the fuck up. I'm telling this story." He was half out of his chair, menacing, as if he was going to lose control soon.

"Sonny," I tried again, "I don't care about your mother. I don't care about the records. Where's the kid, Hart? Who killed Barrett? Do you know who? Come on, Sonny. I don't have much time."

"You don't got this gun either, so shut up." he snarled. I had the .38 but didn't know what I could do with it. Sonny continued.

"You see I met her in a record store. Tower on Broadway. She asked me if I knew where something was. Bon Jovi or some such. I walked her over to the rock section. So we got to talking, Rina and me. I made her for, like, a model, maybe a user. She told me later she made me for a cop." He rubbed the cotton rag, a strip of torn tee shirt, gently against the barrel of his revolver, moving his forefinger up and down its blue metal surface, dark as a hornet.

"Maintaining order," he mused, "so the public can go about its lawful business."

"Sonny?"

"Meeting her was like opening all the record covers in the world at once. That day in the record store something happened inside me. Just startled. She and I went to a bar, O'Neal's, by Lincoln Center. We talked. She kept talking about how she needed someone to protect her. 'From who?' I asked. She told me about Kavanaugh. I signed on, kid. I filled the bill. We had an affair. I'd meet her in Midtown, and we'd take a cab up here."

Rina? Here?

"She told me Barrett was killed."

"Who killed Barrett?"

He ignored the question. "She was worried her brother, Val, was mixed up in it. He and Kavanaugh had some big deal going with Barrett."

"What was the big deal?"

"A monument. They were going to raise a lot of money through Hadley and his friends for this fucking monument. Barrett was going to be the front. The plan was to divert most of the money to their accounts. Then she got wind of plans to put on a musical. Then an art show. It seemed like pretty rudderless thinking to me, but I never got really involved. I was just seeing Rina."

"What else?"

"Oh, about her. About how she needed to have a lot of sex. That she was looking for someone to take care of her."

"Hadley?"

"Yes. That's why she married him."

"You?"

"Me."

"So you were playing horny father-confessor to this hot-looking screwball who was wrapped up in a major league scam to defraud?"

"Sounds right."

"And you didn't do anything?"

"Oh, I did plenty. I'd stand outside of her place by the park. Then I'd follow her. Watch her back. See no one took her off in the street. Hey, I'm not on the job. I've got lots of time."

"What about me?"

"What about you, kid?"

"What did you tell Rina about me?"

"I told her you wouldn't hurt her."

"What did you tell her?"

"That you used to work for a magazine. These days, I heard, you seem to be a burnout, not doing much of anything."

"What about Hershy Mintoff, the story *you* gave me, Sonny."

"She didn't ask. I had reassured her, I guess. I didn't know it was her crowd, kid, that you were getting mixed up with when your father called me."

"No?"

He shook his head. "Then she asked me if I knew Vince Ventry."

"She had made the connection?"

"Yeah," he said, "I told her I knew him pretty good."

"What then?"

He shrugged. "She asked me to look in your father's files."

"What for?"

"Stuff about Hadley. I think she's going to leave him soon. She thought she could get more if she had something on him. She's nobody's fool, Rina. She had also heard Kavanaugh talking about how the Old Gossip could piece the business about Barrett together, so we were after the Barrett and Kavanaugh files too. She was looking for an edge. Rina really isn't secure in any kind of relationship, kid."

"So you broke into Pop's office. To reassure her? You beat up Sadie? Why, Sonny? Tell me."

"Yeah, I broke in. No, it wasn't actually me that was beating up on Sadie. You know I had never met her before, face to face? It was Val. As for why? I'm pitiful. All I got is a room full of records and nothin' else. I never stole. I never took, not really. Then I got old and I met Rina and she was young, and when I was with her I wasn't old and bored anymore." Silence. "Who cares?" he asked, not expecting an answer.

"That with Sadie, though, that was bad."

"Yes," he said, "yes, it was."

"What did you find?"

"Nothing. I couldn't figure the files out and I was supposed to look for stuff about Kavanaugh and Barrett and his wife, too, and Val had the old girl so terrified she was no help. I kept being distracted by them. He's sick. Finally, I had to hustle him out of there, or else he would've killed her."

"Do you listen to yourself?"

"Yes," he said again, "yes, I do." He said this with the finality of a man slamming a car door shut after a long, tiring trip. He rubbed his cotton cloth around the end of the barrel of the gun as if he were wiping the top of a bottle before drinking. He put the muzzle of the revolver in his mouth, pointing it upwards. He looked at me, then lowered his eyes. The shot still came as a shock, like a muffled explosion. He fell backwards. Blood and tissue spewed onto record cabinets. The groaning women on the tape kept up their keening. I clutched at my stomach and ran to the toilet where I heaved. I coughed and spat and wiped the bile from my lips with one of his towels, still damp. I threw it on the floor. I flushed the toilet and leaned against the wall, then I looked at myself in the mirror. I was white, but I had stopped shaking. My face was the last thing Sonny had seen. Well, the hell with him.

I walked back into the living room. Using a handkerchief, I rubbed down the arms of the chair I had been sitting in and I turned off the power on the stereo. The women stopped. Except for a fly buzzing around the lampshade, the room was silent. I looked out through the peephole: there was no one in the corridor. I let myself out, holding my hand in front of my face in case someone was looking out through a peephole.

I went down the stairs. The young mothers still lounged out in front with their strollers. They glanced at me but I walked between them quickly. The shot hadn't alarmed them. The fly buzzing in Sonny's living room stayed with me.

I found a working pay phone on Broadway and called 911. I muffled my voice with my handkerchief because they tape these calls and I gave them Sonny's address and said they'd find him dead. I said he had been a cop. I didn't leave my name. I had a train to catch.

20

Through a window on the porch, I could see her sitting in my firehouse chair in a pool of lamplight, slumped over a book. It was midnight. The cab I'd taken from the station had dropped me off at the bottom of the driveway. The night was filled with croaks and trills that would mask the sound of an approach.

I unlocked the door and entered quietly, the Smith & Wesson in my hand. Her shoulders rose and fell slightly in the rhythms of sleep. Thank God. I slipped the gun into my pocket, put my arm around her shoulder, lifted her falling hair aside and kissed her. She smiled dreamily and opened her eyes.

"I waited up for you."

"I see."

She kissed me again. I made some coffee. We talked for hours.

I told her about the backer's audition in the Soho loft and Kavanaugh's scams. I told her about Rina Hadley's background and her relationship with her brother. I tried to explain Lou's analysis of the emotional symbolism of the murder. I told her what Cheech had learned following Rina. Then I talked about the assault on Sadie and what I had found in the records and what my father had said they meant. I explained who Chen was and what she had overheard. I told her what Sonny had done in front of me.

I was all keyed up. I bounced from topic to topic. Moira

224

would ask a question about one person and that would trigger a chain of thought about another.

My narrative seemed to be a net of entangling lines of fact, and emotion, stretching back into the past, even to prehistory, moving in and out of focus, as the stories overlaid and contradicted each other, putting light on one but blurring another, throwing out lines of relationship or causality that led to another nexus, from where we could see more and yet more relations and causes. I was dealing with a world of facts remembered, distorted, misdirected and invented. Yet someone had really killed Peter Barrett, and threatened India and my father.

I told Moira what Lou had said: make sure I don't overlook the killer because of some flaw in my own vision.

"I'm not likely to have the same one, Ventry."

It was almost daylight when I finally got up enough nerve to say what I had learned about Cyril, that he was a black-mailer, involved with Royal and Kavanaugh. She simply didn't believe me. She got up and made some tea. When she could finally talk, she said Chen had plucked me clean for five thousand and what I had gotten was mispronounced hearsay. If what Chen said was true, somewhere Kavanaugh and Val were plotting to set me up for Hadley. I told her what my father had said about the citizenship market.

"Here," she said, "I almost forgot this." It was the package Jack had dropped off. When I opened it, I saw he had left me a good print and a complicated message. What I held in my hand under the lamp that night was a good facsimile, about 15 by 10 inches, of one of René Magritte's best works, one we had discussed over the years in our walks through the Museum of Modern Art. It was entitled, ominously, "The Menaced Assassin."

Just off center of the picture, in a room with gray walls and a yellow floor, lies a redheaded woman on a couch, naked, blood streaming from her mouth, a flimsy scarf across her shoulders. A well-dressed man, stands with his back to her, listening to an old fashioned gramophone, his head nearly enveloped by the horn of the speaker, one hand placed casually in his pocket, the other resting on the table. An overcoat is draped over a chair to his right, a hat rests on it. A small valise is behind the chair. There appears to be no connection between the listener and the corpse.

Beyond them is a window, through which we can see a grill work balcony, and past that, three men looking in at us placidly. Neither their purpose nor interest is clear. A mountain range looms behind them.

Closest to the viewer, on either side of the picture, out of sight of the man at the gramophone and the men at the window, stand two men, dressed alike in bowler hats, upright collars, black ties, and dark overcoats. Their shoes are well shined. The one on our left hefts a large, knobby club. The one on the right carries a fisherman's net.

The source of light would be outside the picture, from behind the viewer's left shoulder. It is intense and casts clear shadows.

I asked Moira what she thought it meant.

"It's about a murder. The girl's been killed. The crazy man listening to the record player did it and is about to be snared."

"How do you know he's not the detective?"

"I don't, but I thought the title referred to him."

"The man with the club may have done it. Perhaps our listener is the detective."

"Why should he carry a valise?" she asked.

"He's not carrying it. How do we know it's his?"

"Well, you tell me the solution, then, eh?"

"As far as I know, there isn't one. Magritte liked detective stories and he liked playing games, logical inversions, dreamlike contradictions."

"What's Jack trying to tell you?"

"He may just have wanted to show me what a real artist does with a crime: paint a picture. Or he could be suggesting that this crime will have no solution." I paused.

"There's something else, isn't there, Ventry?"

"No, I don't think so." But I did. This painting may not have been meant as a description of Barrett's murder, but as a warning to me of what may happen in the future. To Moira.

That morning we slept for a few hours, uneasily. I dreamed,

not of Moira in the meadow, but of Jack getting on a train with
his mother, and of me running after them, trying to get on,
them waving to me, their arms filled with rolled up canvases,
urging me onward, and as I tried to run faster and faster, I felt
like I was running in jelly, and I fell and tumbled down a cliff
like my poor drunken grandfather, falling and falling, until I
woke with a start. Moira was still there, next to me, asleep.

I lay back and thought of the Magritte as the sun rose
higher, until its rays fell on Moira's eyelids, which fluttered
and opened. She lifted her arm and we embraced.

Later in the morning, Moira and I sat in the gazebo overlooking the pond, sipping lemonade. It was a soft, still summer morning. A big bullfrog, spreadeagled on the surface,
floated happily by. Bluets and twelvespots hovered and
darted over the surface. The sun moved across a cloudless
blue sky, and a red-tailed hawk circled lazily, high above the
meadow. We listened as the fledgling catbirds harried their
parents with piteous calls for yet more insects. Moira looked
at home in a white blouse and cut-off jeans. Little beads of
perspiration clung to her upper lip. She lifted one tanned,
bare leg up onto the bench where we were sitting and leaned
her head back languidly, against one of the painted timbers
supporting the roof, so that the grape leaves climbing up the
trellis looked as if they were entwined in her hair. I knew I
should go see Jack again, but of course I was reluctant. The
contradiction between the idyllic surroundings and my inner
feelings could not have been greater.

At Moira's insistence, I finally called Jack and told him we
wanted to check some things with him. He said fine, but
didn't mention the Magritte. He said he looked forward to
seeing Moira again. I had no heart to talk to him about his
lies, but said we'd be by later in the day. Then there was
Conklin. I had his painting to return.

"Days like this," I said, lying back and looking at the clouds,
"I'd give anything to be a kid in the hills above Hannibal,
watching the steamboats go by."

"Wherever that is. What was your childhood like, Ventry?"
she asked me.

"I think we have more pressing things to talk about."

"I'm interested in you right now. You're my case. Let's leave Barrett for a moment and talk about us, about you. A respite before we go over to see Jack." That sounded reasonable, my mind was spinning. I needed to make it as calm as the pond.

"Hannibal is in Missouri, by the Mississippi River. My childhood was spent in books and drawings by a river, the one that flows by the apartment you're renting and by Val Royal's antique shop. You didn't read *Huckleberry Finn* in Tasmania?"

A bright red dragonfly drifted past us, looking for a likely leaf to settle on.

"What about your mum?" she asked insistently. "Why don't you ever talk about her?"

"My mother? Most of my past is boring, Moira, whatever isn't sordid or downright embarrassing anyway."

"Not yours, not to me. I've been up here thinking about you, dreaming you up. I need to find out if that person in my head is anything like the galoot in front of me." She wouldn't leave it alone.

"My mother? Mom and my aunt and the elevator man were my only company till I went to school."

"Did your aunt live with you?"

"Yes."

"Was it crowded in the apartment? I could imagine with two women there they'd squabble. Did you get caught up in that sort of thing?"

A new pickup truck went by and a startled woodchuck froze over some black-eyed Susans he was munching. I didn't see the driver because of the dust the oversized wheels were kicking up. For a moment, I thought it looked familiar, but I didn't pay attention. He turned onto the dirt road on the south side of the meadow and started climbing the hill.

I decided to tell her something I had never told anyone. "The truth is simple. Helen is my real mother. Pop seduced her and she became pregnant."

"My God!" she said.

"He was a very charming fella. His wife, Margaret, whom I call Mom, and my mother, Aunt Helen, were both large, strong and extremely beautiful women. My grandfather, old F. X.

Brunnock, had been a tugboat captain, a pretty tough guy; he ended up owning a small fleet of tugs. There was a lot of money. Their mother died early and they went off to schools run by the nuns, *mesdames,* they called them, where they learned obedience and French. Helen did well in drawing. They didn't know very much about men, I suppose. My grandfather died just before they got out and they were left a bundle. They met Pop in some club a classmate's older sister took them to. Pop fell hard for Helen and seduced her, but it was Margaret who married him before anyone knew Helen was pregnant."

"Why didn't Helen marry him?"

"The way I understand it she didn't want to and Margaret did. Of course, Helen didn't know she was pregnant with me."

"How old were you when you found out the truth?"

"I was about sixteen. And, actually, by that time I wasn't upset. You see the way I looked at it I had grown up with two mothers, and very loving ones at that."

"Where are they now?"

"Far away from my father. They still live together and run an Indian jewelry and crafts shop for tourists in Taos, New Mexico. I spend Christmas with them every couple of years."

"I'd like to meet them."

"The squash blossom kids? Sure. They go out on dates, and all, but I think they're content with the way things are. They seem happy."

"What about your father?"

"He never sees them. When I grew up and left, the household broke up. They went to New Mexico. Pop stayed in the apartment, but I never went back there. When we meet, he tries to take over my life."

Half a dozen crows lifted up off the spruce trees on the hillside beyond the meadow, cawing angrily. The woodchuck raced into his burrow.

"So your peculiar parentage never really bothered you sometimes?"

"Everyone has fantasies about being switched at birth. It was just that I wasn't switched, my mother was. When Helen and Margaret got sloshed on their rum and cokes, sometimes they would talk about it with me, but, you know, it wasn't something I was obsessed with. I thought it was natural. Maybe it is."

"Thank you, Ventry. This means a lot, you telling me this."

The timber behind Moira's head exploded, and then I heard the loud echoing boom of a rifle. I grabbed her arm and wrenched her on to the floor. Two more shots slammed into the bench where we had been sitting. Whoever had driven by had spotted us, then taken a position up on the hill where he had disturbed the crows. The sun was behind him on his left. He had all the time in the world to sight in on us, probably using something like a 30.06 with a four-power scope. He would be in that clump of white pines two hundred yards away, with his truck parked just beyond. Now I knew why the truck looked familiar. It was the truck I had last seen Merkle drive away on Vesey Street.

Another shot, hitting the post again, sending fragments over our heads. I had watched deer in this meadow from that spot. He could take us down before we had run one step to the house. We could only lie there and hope there wasn't a second shooter coming closer while we cowered there. None of my neighbors would pay any attention to the noise of rifle shots. Too many of them practice shooting. I had no weapon. Moira started squirming beneath me. "I can't breathe, Ventry." I moved off her. "What the hell is going on?" She didn't seem to be hurt.

"It's Merkle's truck. He's up on that hill with a deer rifle."

"Why?"

In the distance I heard a regular whoomp, whoomp beat like an air compressor or the drumming of the ruffed grouse. The sound was getting louder, closer. Another bullet whizzed through the gazebo, just inches over our heads, slamming into the barn behind us. The next bullet crashed into the bench, followed quickly by two more, splintering the wood, making us press our bodies into the floor as hard as we could. I could hear the noise getting louder. It was a helicopter! It must be coming low over the house toward us. Who was it? One of them? Did they have rockets for us too?

I saw the sheriff's decals. I had to go out there, even though the shooter might have a clear shot. I hauled myself up. "Stay here, Moira," I shouted. I jumped out of the gazebo and raced into the meadow, hunched over, legs pumping, waving frantically at the same time. The sheriff's deputy at the controls of the helicopter on the Marijuana Eradication Patrol saw me and brought the chopper low over the pond, whipping up droplets of water that splashed onto my face. I dropped down and pointed over to the hillside. I saw the plume of dust rise up from the truck racing away at top speed on the dirt road. The deputy brought the helicopter over to my side of the pond and settled it down. I ran back to the gazebo and grabbed Moira's hand and pulled her up.

"Quick, into the house." We trotted into the rear yard and went through the back door. "Stay here," I wheezed. Then I ran, shoulders down, out the front to the chopper. I bent down low and, gasping, told the deputy that I was just trying to tell him I thought there might be some herb growing up south of us on that hill. He still wore the mirrored lenses he had on when he had dropped off the Van Deusen police files. Officer Berry took off his sunglasses and gave me a strange look, a thousand yard, disbelieving stare.

"You okay, fella?"

"Saw some strange plants up there," I said. I don't know if he believed me. He didn't say anything about the shot-up gazebo. I guess he didn't see it. As much as I just wanted to drop this in someone else's lap, I knew this was not the right guy or the right time. I had to let him go.

"I'll check it out," he said. "Ten four." Message received.

I said, "Ten four," too. I crept backwards. He lifted up. I dashed, hunched over, back into the house. It was time to go see Jack. To finish this. I don't know why but I put on the yellowed linen jacket I'd gotten from Val, and dropped the .38 in the side pocket.

When we arrived at Jack's studio this time, I slammed the car into the small driveway and jumped out. Jack was kneeling next to the goldfish pond, tossing in pellets of food. He stood up, looking alarmed. I strode over to him. Moira followed. "Giresse, you lied."

He looked up at me, shocked. He frowned, saw Moira, shrugged and said, "Yes. I did. I lied to you."

"Why, Jack?"

"Come on." He led us to a tiled court, just outside the studio, filled with large ferns sitting in terra cotta tubs. We could look out on the small fountain spraying the goldfish pond outside the open windows. He pointed to two wicker chairs. We sat. My clenched fists rested on my knees. He took another chair, pulled it over next to me and sat down. I glared at him.

"What was I to do?" he asked. "These men are killers. You're not. I wanted you to stay away from them."

"They killed Peter Barrett."

"Yes, probably, and others as well. They would not have hesitated to kill you or me. This isn't some kind of game. No."

"You didn't see the pictures, Jack. Not the murder scene," I shouted at him. "You didn't see Peter Barrett trussed up in his own studio with his eyeballs burnt out. You didn't see that, Jack!"

"If I had, it wouldn't have been any different," he yelled back at me. "I would have taken one look, and pffft, vanished."

"Don't you fucking care?"

"Yes. I care, kid. I care about a lot of things. Death, *that* I don't care much for."

"Well, what are we going to do? Continue to tell lies to each other?"

"Nothing," he said.

"What do you mean?"

"Nothing. I'm not going to do anything."

"For God's sake, why?"

"Maybe they will leave us alone. Maybe they won't. But if you continue to snoop around, they'll kill you."

"I'm in it, Jack. I can't get out. I told them I was some conman. I'm in their net. They're setting me up, Jack. They're going to take me out and Moira, too."

"I have known about people like this all my life. What are they to me, eh? I must take the world as I find it. In 1940, my mother and I ran from them. We ran here. And here we want to be left alone! I knew Kavanaugh was mixed up with something. They are all the same. I'm not going to go hunting after a man like Kavanaugh. What would I do if I found him? It would be like the swallow landing on the crocodile's nose. We have nothing to do with one another."

"I'd hate to live in a world like that."

"My coltish friend, you do live in a world like that." Wait. That was a wrong word to hear flying up in conversations about killing on successive days. "Coltish"? That's what Chen had said Kavanaugh had called Val? Had Jack used it before? Had he been talking to Kavanaugh?

"Why 'coltish' Jack?"

He glanced sharply at me. "It's just a word. Impetuous, charming, American."

"I see."

"This is a bad business and we have work to do, other real work," Jack said.

"You wouldn't consider going to the police, at least?"

"The police? Have you been listening? The police work for politicians. Kavanaugh and his friends know all about politicians."

"Listen, Jack, I'm not naive . . ." He rolled his eyes upwards.

"Maybe I understand only some of this, but the man who had Barrett killed doesn't deserve to live. Why the hell should he?"

"Calm down."

"I am calm."

"You're so sure of everything are you? Why did Kavanaugh do it? What did he get out of it?"

"I'm not sure yet."

"I thought you wanted to paint?"

"I do."

"So, paint. Forget all this. Tell them all to go straight to hell."

"It's too late."

"Maybe, but you should. Believe me. It's worth a try."

We sat there, the three of us, for a long minute. The bronze patina of the fountain looked good against the bricks of the garden wall. A corkscrew willow threw intricate shadows across the grass.

"My mother used to tell me about Picasso," Giresse began finally, "my father used to visit him in his studio in the Rue des Grands-Augustins at the beginning of the war. In the middle of the preparations he was making for her, getting the cash, the paintings we would take with us, the tickets, my father asked Picasso why he didn't flee. The Nazis hated him. Their friend Franco hated him. There would be no place for him in the new European order. Picasso knew all that. He said he would stay. Why? 'Because I'm here. I have no desire to leave.' You see. For him, his desire, which was to paint, was all there was. The Germans and their armies and police could go to hell for all he cared. He stayed and painted. He didn't go out and shoot anyone. He painted his girlfriend, Françoise Gilot. You understand?"

"A very uplifting story, Jack, with a pointed moral. Trouble is: like many pretty stories, it's probably not true."

"What are you saying?"

"Your father was a collaborator, wasn't he, Jack? Picasso would not have let him past the door. Yes, Picasso stayed and painted, and your father stayed and looted. You didn't walk through the night with your mother into the passes in the Pyrenees to escape Vichy France. You were probably driven in a Mercedes." There was a big silence.

"Those times were hard, confused. Survival meant everything. How could you understand that?"

"Oh, I'm learning about survival."

"At least, don't drag the girl into this."

"What do you know about Cyril?" she asked. "Tell us."

"You've been talking to Kavanaugh, haven't you? Recently, Jack?"

He half closed his eyes and wagged his fingers in denial.

"You talked to him about your 'coltish' friend, didn't you?"

"I didn't want any harm to come to you, boy."

"What have you done? Did you kill Peter Barrett?"

In his eyes I saw the certainty that our friendship had died and sadness that it had to be so. He said finally, quietly and simply, "No."

"Why did you send me the Magritte?"

"To tell you that we were close long ago. That I loved you. That you should stop because you know nothing and would learn nothing."

"What was your true relationship with Peter Barrett?"

He rocked back and forth in his chair slowly, a rumble started in his chest, his face turned florid, his eyes tightened up, his fists were clenched and he pounded them on his thighs. "True relationship," he roared. "I'll tell you about 'true relationship.' Yes, yes, yes, yes, yes," he shouted over and over, "Yes! You want to know? I'll tell you then. I *was* Peter Barrett!"

Moira and I looked at one another. "What do you mean?" I asked.

"We become what we create. When I worked for Peter Barrett that winter after the war, I had a pitiful whiner with a broken leg on my hands, but what an opportunity! It was I, Halevy Giresse who painted all those abstracts while he lay there. What did I care that he signed his name to them. What a jerk. He was a fraud. So what? I did a job. I got paid. It was a lot too at a time when I needed it."

"But you never worked in abstraction?"

"I proved I could do anything."

"How did you feel when Barrett's show won all that acclaim?"

"Sick with the irony of it. I could have killed him then," he said with a tight grin, "but I didn't, not then or later."

"What happened, Jack, later?"

"I might as well tell you. Kavanaugh came to me a couple of years ago. God, he never forgets, never lets go. He needed some connections in the art world for this project of his. He also wanted respectability, like a whore who marries a banker. He blackmailed me, essentially. He said he would have my mother deported and tried in France for what my father had done to get us out. Not only stealing paintings. Terrible things. She's Jewish, herself, of course, but I know the French. A Jewish woman on trial? Some of them, enough of them, would say: 'What could you expect? eh? *une juive*'? " He paused. "She's old, Ventry."

"Go on."

"I knew Kavanaugh was capable of it. I told him about Peter Barrett and who actually had done the abstractions. I told him India Barrett was rich and knew all the right people. He took it from there. It turned out he knew her from long ago. He sized up this girl's cousin, the Hart boy, as a kid on the make and recruited him."

"What went wrong?"

"Everything. Principally, after getting Peter's wife and her cousin, Hadley, interested in his project, Kavanaugh decided Peter should paint for it. Great publicity. This would be fine if you wanted some paint smears which is all poor Peter would be capable of. So the old fraud could do only one thing . . ."

"He called you up and you did the paintings."

"Yes. Yes, I did them. I came at night with my own gear, my brushes and tarps. No one saw me but him. He wanted no one to know, not even the caretaker. It hurt Barrett, my being in his place once again. He really believed in the Dawnwalk project. Remember how I told you he would talk endlessly in the old days about the past, about the artists of the tribe. This was a chance to get in touch with all of that. He had a box full of Indian dolls he would play with, rattles and things.

"He was bitter, frustrated and paralyzed. Drunk and angry. He just lay on a cot, moaning when I was there. Maybe he was convinced in the end that he painted them himself." He paused. "They're good, aren't they?" he asked.

"Maybe," Moira said pointedly, "you're a better painter as Barrett, doing fakes, than you are as Jack Giresse." Jack looked away, his moment of self-adulation punctured. Moira was hard at the core and taking nothing from him that day.

"Why did Kavanaugh kill Barrett?" I asked.

"I never said he did."

"Did he?"

"He could have. He *likes* death."

"I know."

"He told me to say nothing, and I haven't, till now. He didn't boast or anything. He is a cool one. He talked about a change in plan, like a director making a change in a movie script. I gather Kavanaugh is shifting his attentions more to Hadley, who has more money than India Barrett."

"They're plotting to kill Hadley, and, I think, they plan for me to be part of it. What did you tell him about your 'coltish' friend."

"I told him you were student of mine long ago. That is the truth. I would not have them hurt you, boy."

"I need evidence to convict them, Royal and Kavanaugh."

"I won't help you there, not while my mother is alive."

"They tried to kill Moira and me an hour ago."

Looking at Moira, he said entreatingly, "Leave America. It's not safe for you."

"I won't leave Ventry," she said. "Tell us who killed Peter Barrett. Ventry thinks it was someone trying to make it look like the Crucifixion of St. Peter. Someone who knows art, like you."

"I . . . I did *not* kill him. My art has nothing to do with killing. My work is about living and seeing. As for St. Pierre, I think the one who knows is, maybe, your friend, Conklin."

"Why Calvin? Because of his father and the citizenship scam?"

Jack looked surprised. "How long have you known about all these things?"

"Until this week I knew nothing about any of it."

"*Alors*, the mystery was not solved because Van Deusen did not solve it. He did not do so, not because of a lack of zeal or perspicacity but, I think, I do not know, it remained unsolved because he was *told* not to solve it. Conklin's father was powerful enough to have done so. Whether the son is . . . maybe, but as for why he should, you must ask him yourself."

"Conklin's been helping me. He wants a big story. I think he's honest. Why would he cover up the investigation?"

Jack gave me a pitying look. "Go find out. I expect he will have much to say. Before you do, go to Val Royal. Bring that revolver I see in your pocket. Threaten him. He is weak and will perhaps betray Kavanaugh, who may have killed Peter Barrett and who may kill you all."

21

As we drove away I kept alert for any sign of the pickup truck. I was both angry and fearful. Calvin's painting was in the back seat. A plan started to form in my mind. First, I needed to go into Chatham and leave Moira and the painting with Calvin. Then I was going to see Royal. Chen, Sonny and Jack had all told me in different ways that my efforts at deception had been less than perfect. Kavanaugh knew about me. These people, Kavanaugh, Jack, his mother, India and Peter, had been players for decades, changing positions as the currents of Kavanaugh's greed and mania washed past them.

I crossed the Interstate and passed the teepee-like structure where the highway crew was working in the heat of the summer to store the salt they'd sprinkle on the roads during winter storms. I hoped I lived to curse the damage it would do to the already corroded undercarriage of this car. No, I wouldn't curse anyone now. Go to it, men.

I parked around the corner from the paper. Calvin wasn't in his office when we arrived. His assistant recognized me and told me we could wait inside. We went in, and, when Moira sat down, I gave her the painting of Jeremiah Oster-houdt to hold.

"He should be along in a minute. While we're waiting, I'm going to call Sadie, but I don't want to use this phone." I didn't explain why and she didn't ask. I didn't want to use that phone because I wasn't calling anyone.

In the anteroom, I scribbled a note to her on a classified form. "Gone to Hudson to face down the bad guys. Be safe. Stay with Calvin. I love you. Ventry." I folded it over and wrote Moira's name on it.

"If my friend asks for me, give her this, will you?" He nodded, and I ran out of there.

There was the pain in the darkness. Inside my head. Throbbing behind my left ear. My cheek burned. I opened my eyes. There was a naked bulb dangling from a wire. I was tied up. My wrists were behind my back, wrapped around a beam with what felt like wire. I was sitting in dampness. My feet were free. Beyond the bulb was a rock wall. I could hear water running through a septic pipe. Someone else was in the house and using the toilet or running water. I rubbed my cheek against my shoulder. Blood came off on my shirt.

I was in the cellar beneath Royal's shop. The last, clear memory I had was of walking up to the entrance. Something had hit me in the darkened foyer after I entered the unlocked door. I'd been coming to and going under for a while. I could still feel some sensation in my hands. Judging from the tightness of the wire, soon the feeling would leave my fingers. When that went, so would any hope.

Can't think that way. I pulled on the wire and twisted my wrists, trying to get some slack. Houdini broke out of straitjackets this way. Slack. I had to think of something. Eric White. That was Houdini's name. No. Weiss. That was it. Named after Houdin. Not Houdon the sculptor. Houdin the wirecutter. Oh, God. Wire stripper. Linesman's pliers. Oh, no. A cramp in my shoulder. Jack pointing to a model. The latissimus dorsi. Can't stop. Got to pull. Stretch. Twist. Ignore pain. Pause. Go down into the darkness. No.

Get angry! Pull harder. Behind me? Noise? Pull. C'mon, do it! Back hurts. Eyes filling with sweat. Burns. Salt. Cheek. Basilio. Do it. Hook! Hook again! Twist it. Turn it. There! Oh, God, yes! The wire separated.

Oh lord, my back hurts. My arms by my side, hanging. I can't move them. Numb. No feeling.

I swung my right arm forward. The wire was still twisted around the wrist. The skin around the wire looked like two worms crawling in tandem. The skin would burst if I touched it. The pain would come again when the blood flowed to my hands. It would be bad. I had to get up somehow. I was free.

"You did that very well," came Royal's voice behind me. I turned, painfully. He was standing there at the base of the stairway. Merkle stood at his side, holding an over and under shotgun. It was pointed downward. A bucket was between them.

"Ernest and I consider ourselves privileged, Ventry," he went on, inexorably, "Privileged to have witnessed such a *triumph* of the will over the body. It must have hurt very badly. We were just about to rouse you," he pointed to the bucket, "when you came to and started your struggle. It would have been wrong to waste an opportunity like this. I'm sure, under other circumstances, you would agree?"

"Ernest?" It was all I could manage.

"The importance of being and so on . . . not Merkle henceforth but Ernest."

I couldn't focus. What resources I had brought to this were depleted. It was over.

"Now, Ventry, you probably think I'm a sadist who wants to do you harm? Eh?"

"You won't . . . You wont get away . . ."

"Oh, come, *come*, Ventry! Let's *not* have all this. Stay with us. Don't lose it all just yet. Please?"

"Bastard."

"If I were in your position, and I do not intend to be, I would be a tad more polite."

"That's what Vinnie my trainer told me," I said. "Do what you want."

"Oh, Ventry. If only we had met years ago. Then, oh then, we could have really explored this notion of 'doing what I want.' It would have been meaningful. Now we have more pressing concerns."

I swung my arms back and forth. "Get it over with," I said.

"Ventry, you are really going to have to make the effort. Get with the program. Raise your level of consciousness. Focus, man!"

I had been conked, bound, and beaten. Now, new age babble.

"Ernest, cut those wires off him, will you?" Ernest walked over to me, while taking needlenosed pliers from his back pocket. He pushed one end under the wire and snipped it off. I dropped to the floor from pain. He took the other hand and snipped its wire off. I slumped.

"Here's a little helper. Ernest?" Ernest opened my mouth and put a pill in it. He took a cup from the bucket, dripping with water and gave me a drink. The water was delicious.

"It's just a black beauty. Some dex to get you moving."

"What's on your mind?" I asked.

"Good. Signs of life."

"I don't think I have very long," I said.

"I admit you are not at your best right now. Okay, let's face that and build on it. Perhaps you feel the three of us are under some sort of compulsion, hmm, to act out some terminal scene of violence and death. Eh, Ventry? No, no, no. We are free agents. We are beyond that. Ernest here, for one, would be *sickened* by hurting you. Wouldn't you, Ernest?"

"Yes," he said, stolidly.

"You perceive this situation in terms of stereotypes, I suspect. Bad faith, Ventry. Okay. I admit, yes, there is a certain *frisson* in being seen as a sort of dark angel of the Waffen SS, jackboots gleaming, my prisoner cowering and my henchman by my side. The basement, the fear, all the poses. Ah, well, I'll just have to save up the memories."

I touched my wrist. Pain shot up my arm. "Where's Moira?"

"Another country heard from. In good time. Now, I will tell you what's on my mind, Ventry. Survival. That first. Then, money. You see the way Ernest and I have figured things out, he and I are really in a *very* difficult situation. What do we want? To grow old together and really establish a lifestyle that would see us fixed in one another's eyes as significant, morally feeling, sensitive and loyal. We have talked about this at great length and this is what we want."

"Terrific. I'll just go home. I'd just get in the way here."

"Just wait, will you? There are some obstacles, you see. Well, one major one, really, and some less acute."

"What are they?"

"It. Him. Kavanaugh. He deals in death, that man, and he is a threat. If things continue the way they are, Ernest and I will never have our life together."

"So, kill him," I said.

"I am impressed, Ventry. Your principles are so delicate. Trouble is, we don't want to. Ernest, now, is working very hard to overcome that in him which makes him, well, a thug. We agreed," Royal said, as he reached over to take the shotgun from him, who let it go with indifference, "We agreed today that Ernest would commit violent acts no longer. None. He was very upset after firing at you with that deer rifle of his this morning. I can't tell you how much. You realize, don't you, that he could very well have killed you and that woman, Moira? Sounds like a Japanese dish wrapped in seaweed, doesn't it? Believe me, Ernest is so much happier, though there's still a *lot* of work that we need to do with him."

"Why did he shoot at us?"

"To get you moving."

"He could've tried the phone." The speed was clicking into my bloodstream. I felt the rush.

"Well, Ernest wanted one last fling. He was still a trifle put out after the bang up you gave him. He says you can really punch."

"What was he doing following me in Soho."

"He was *looking* for you. He wanted to give you a message from me. He said he waved to you and you pulled a gun on him. You frightened him badly I should say."

"What was the message?"

"To come up and talk to Hadley about doing his portrait and then Rina's, as Kavanaugh told you in his study. That's gone by the boards, now. Lovely plan, though."

"Who clipped me?"

"I did. After target practice, Ernest followed you in a highway gravel truck. He works out by the Interstate occasionally on the road crew, as do so many of his relations, and when he saw you go by, he took off. One of his innumerable cousins is the foreman, I believe. Quite a family. Curious history, as you know, I think. Basketmakers. Learned it from the Indians with whom they were rumored to have interbred."

"So?"

"So don't call him 'chief,' sport."

"That was it? That's what set him off?"

"Indeed, yes. Anyway, when he saw you leave the news-paper office he called me and I was waiting with this, a genuine nineteenth-century sap." He slapped his palm with it. "No jokes," he cautioned. My head throbbed.

"I don't want to kill," Val said, "but if I have to, well, there you are. It would be stupid for us to go up against Kavanaugh. We can't let him go on, though. He really is getting unhinged. But even were I successful, the cops would be on to me right away. I'm sure of it. I am not going to do any time."

"That's what everybody says."

"I would have liked to gently remove Hadley's fingers from the death grip he had on his fortune without getting involved in Broadway plays and monuments in Western Alaska and all the glare of the attendant publicity. I'm afraid Kavanaugh is a moth, and I am a bat. You are going to do the crime," Royal said.

"Me?"

"Yes, you are going to kill Kavanaugh."

"Why?"

"Because I won't and Ernest doesn't want to."

"But why me?"

"That's what they all say, isn't it? Look, do the world a favor. Kill him."

"Why should I?"

"Ah, the big question. I'll tell you. Let's be logical about this, shall we."

"My head hurts."

"Listen or it will hurt more. I can either kill you, here, now, or let you leave. We don't want to kill you for the same reason we don't want to kill Kavanaugh. An absolute dread of incar-ceration. But I will. If I have to. As for you, it's clearly not in your best interest to be killed. What is? Why, to be freed, but is it in ours? Only if it helps Ernest and me to achieve our life goals: Kavanaugh dead, the two of us, free, together, rich and unbothered by the police. So we free you, if you can convince us you will help us out. Is that in your best interest? We believe so."

"Can I stand?" I didn't like the idea of sitting on the floor in front of them. In a street fight to be down on the ground meant to be kicked, often and hard. Ernest helped me to my feet. I staggered. He caught me, and leaned me against the post.

Sorry there aren't any chairs, but we won't be here long in any event. Where were we? Oh, yes. 'Why *you*?' and '*Why* you.' We've been sizing you up. From the beginning. You would be our wire controlled rocket to penetrate Kavanaugh's defenses and kill him for us. What potential you have. We saw how you handled Ernest that day. I saw what you knew, and your poise, your knuckleduster, roustabout charm, your instincts, your gift for ingratiating yourself." He sighed. "Who called India and my father?"

"Merkle and me."

"Who actually killed Barrett?"

"Who killed Barrett? Did you suspect Mrs. Barrett, Ventry? Women are capable of the most depraved brutality, the cunts, much more so than men. She might have killed him out of jealousy or something, maybe she caught him rubbing the wrong titties. No, not Mrs. Barrett. If she killed him, why hire you to come sneaking about, pretending to be some kind of hood? I mean you *were* in *Art in America*. Ernest and I aren't Philistines. We keep up. No, Mrs. B. didn't do it. Morsel Moira? Lovely thought, see what interesting places logic takes us? Does that bother you? But, uh-uh, no, she was in bloomin' Australia. We'll come back to her in a moment."

"Leave her alone."

"Oh, we will." He laughed and Ernest smiled lopsidedly.

"Speaking of women. Hey, maybe my sister? Rats! She was with Hadley and me all that night, first the opera, Aliberti and Alfredo Kraus in *Lucia*. Rina got through it with coke. Then off to do some serious partying—Molucca's, Club Up!, Woggles—then off to the Hadley apartment, some downers and beddie bye. The three of us were together all that night."

"Does Merkle, I mean Ernest, here, enjoy Donizetti?"

"No, and he didn't kill Barrett, actually. I can read Ernest's character. I know when he lies. He didn't kill him. He was there that night, though, twice."

"Where is Cyril?"

"Ah, Cyril. He was very greedy. I don't admire that in a man. Here was this lovely operation spinning along with all the delicacy and inevitability of a piece by Balanchine. Anyway, Barrett, himself, killed Mr. Greedyguts. Does that surprise you?"

"No."

"He was quite strong. Hit him with a hammer. How impetuous you artists are. Ernest saw him do it. He told me about it that night, several times. He couldn't shut up."

"Where's the body?" I asked. "Who killed Barrett?"

"Try to stay with us, just a little longer. We excluded all reasonable suspects. I had sent Ernest on an errand. He was, as a matter of fact, bringing Barrett the very basket you later identified so expertly. Cyril had told me Barrett was gaga over Indian artifacts. He thought it would help him with the big Dawnwalk pictures, so I thought the old man might buy it from me. He had wads of money. I really did know it wasn't Shaker when I showed it to you, but I thought Barrett might take it for an Indian basket and, after all, what Ernest had told me about his family making them did seem improbable. I know Ernest better now. I called Barrett up and he said to send it round."

"Who killed him?"

"But Barrett couldn't have used it. Do you want to know why? Did you know the cause of this uproar was a burnt out old fake! Someone else was doing the pictures. Hah!. Art is such a crock."

"Did Jack Giresse kill Barrett?"

Val looked at me in wide-eyed wonder. "Ernest, the game's afoot! Our sleuth has actually discovered something. Tell me, did you use a magnifying glass or your oh so powerful powers of deduction?"

"Did he?"

"No. He didn't."

"Who did?"

"To push on. Hadley had told Kavanaugh that Barrett was getting antsy about the project. Acting weird. When he stopped by, he was drunk, weeping and shaking a Seneca gourd rattle. Hadley didn't know the reason. He thought Barrett was important to Dawnwalk because of the murals, so Kavanaugh should know about his behavior. No one had told Hadley about Giresse. I suppose after all those years to see Giresse back in his own studio did something to poor Barrett's sense of *amour propre*. It's all very well to get in touch with yourself, I mean, look at Ernest here, but if the self is a fraud, well, who wants it rubbed in, eh?"

"Kavanaugh killed Barrett, didn't he? Why?"

"Ventry, Kavanaugh is a very different person. That is one strange mode of thought he's got. I *think* he felt that Barrett alive would be an uncertainty. That made him nervous. Ah, but Barrett dead, that he could control. Think of Kavanaugh as a memorialist. A non-living Barrett would serve his purposes even better than a living one. He deals in death. He is close to it. He's happier with it."

"So he killed him?"

"No."

"No?"

"Isn't that extraordinary? He participated, yes, but it wasn't him our shy, lurking Ernest saw that night."

"Who?"

"Who, Ventry, was linked to Kavanaugh's past? Who knew that Giresse painted the murals, and Barrett would be no loss? Who would have the taste to want to steal the de Koonings and the Klines? Who would keep them in his bedroom and not sell them? Who would have access to police reports? Who tracked Detective Van Deusen's vain efforts to find him? Who was all too eager to help you pretend to be an itinerant folk portraitist by providing you with a picture to deceive Kavanaugh and me? Who could Kavanaugh control by blackmailing him over his father's reputation?"

"Calvin Conklin." I had left Moira with him. "I've got to get out!"

"Of course you do, dear boy."

"Where are they?" Why hadn't I seen it before: Calvin!

"Calm down, there's time."

I sucked air down into my diaphragm. I needed to maintain control. Royal watched me coolly. "But why are you so sure Conklin did it?" I finally asked.

"Ernest saw the whole thing."

"He watched Barrett's murder?"

"This is how he told me the story. When he pulls up in his truck, he naturally drives round the back, as he had when visiting his cousin, and parks next to the kitchen. When he gets out he hears Barrett and Hart arguing. This excites him. He creeps to a side window, partially open, with ferns hanging in front of it. He wants to peek in. A character flaw, but there you are. He's done a lot of that sort of thing.

"Barrett bludgeons poor Cyril. And there Ernest squats, transfixed and unseen. Barrett makes a call. Ernest knows he should leave, but Barrett doesn't call the police, nor his wife, but Conklin, who shortly arrives. Ernest watches them get drunk and taunt one another. Ernest told me it was like watching a movie. He sees Conklin kill Barrett, and Ernest decides it's time to leave and come back to me. He gets in his truck and lets it roll noiselessly down the driveway with the lights off.

"Later Conklin called Kavanaugh for help. Not the best career move you can make, I'd say, letting that one get something on you. Kavanaugh called me, and I had Ernest go back. He was quite unwilling, but in the end agreed. Cost Conklin the price of a truck."

"The hell with the truck. I've got to get Moira away from Conklin."

"It's six o'clock now. That lovely morsel, Moira, is safe for the moment. Kavanaugh and Conklin are waiting for you. Hadley will be with them later on. They want you to come to them, so they can kill you, and stage that Verdian scene of love and revenge you have so dutifully cooperated in by screwing my poor sister, who is, come to think of it, no longer poor. Is that the story that Conklin intends to get his Pulitzer for? What are the bounds of human ambition, Ernest? Eh? No matter."

"What do they plan to do with Moira?"

"After setting up the *mise-en-scène*? With your bullet in his heart and his in your head? She'll join her cousin."

"Where?"

"A lime pit on the Conklin estate. Ernest put Cyril there that night."

"He watched Calvin do those things to Barrett? And did nothing?"

"He was very upset, really. It took me a long time to calm him down."

"Why don't we call the police?"

" 'I have wasted time and now doth time waste me,' wrote the Bard. You have no time for phone calls, no time for explanations. Save your lady, Ventry, 'face down the bad guys.' "

"Conklin called you."

"He read us your note. I said I'd get you heading back to your farm at the right time."

"That's where Moira is."

"Course not."

"Go to the police."

"Not our way of doing things I'm afraid." He came closer. "Too bad you're getting that jacket soiled. It does become you, though you look like Tennessee Williams after a three-day drunk in Key West."

"Call the sheriff."

"I have a terrible background. No police. Anyway, we thought Kavanaugh suspected we would make a move against him. This is not healthy. Be a good Joe. Kill Kavanaugh. Solve our problem. Peace will be restored to the kingdom, calm to the people's hearts."

"Fine. Let me out of here," I said. He looked at his watch, the Patek Philippe.

"Soon."

"Where is she?" Oh, Moira.

"Now, I know you will want to call the police when you're free. Go ahead. There's a phone upstairs. And you know what? They'll launch into action with their usual celerity. They'll send a sheriff's deputy over here to see what's up.

Grass will be growing over Moira before they get it sorted out."

"Where is she?"

"Kavanaugh has lost control. He doesn't only want to memorialize these Indians, he wants others to join them in death. He is one spooky person. If you leave soon, you can dust him before he dusts your girlfriend."

"Where is she?"

"Go!" he shouted. "Save your woman!"

"Where, Royal, where?"

"Your car is out front!" he pointed. "The door is unlocked. The keys are in the ashtray. We filled the gas tank. Your pistol is in the glove compartment and a deer rifle, a 30.06 with a 4x scope, is lying under a blanket on the backseat. It's the one Ernest used on you." Ernest mumbled something. "What?" Val said, impatiently. "That doesn't . . . Okay, okay . . . Ernest said it's sighted in at a two hundred yards. Get closer."

"Where?"

He smiled. "She's in a cabin just past the highway garage by the Interstate, near where the salt mound is? Ernest owns it. We've used it often. Ah, nights of bliss. They'll keep her there till sundown, then bring her to your farm. I'm to keep you running around till then. Get the jump on them, boy."

I started past him toward the stairs. "Give her my regards, will you? We really must get together." I kept going.

22

Bruised, battered and with no confidence in my ability to drive or shoot straight, I pulled out of Hudson, heading for the Interstate. The amphetamine that Royal had given me made me roar up the highway, passing cars on blind curves. As I raced to the northeast, past apple orchards and feed stores, I knew finally what had to be done. Hard as it was, I put my foot on the brake and turned off the road, onto the shoulder, next to a field with waist-high corn. What I had to do was stop for once, and think.

Why should I believe anything Val Royal told me. What was the likelihood of my going up there, finding Conklin, shooting him, only to learn it was a hoax perpetrated by Royal? Pretty good, judging from the way I had been manipulated in the last few days. If Hadley was in fact to die and Rina be his heiress, why would Royal want to jeopardize a comfortable future, a lifetime of villas in Tangiers with Moroccan boys, paid for by his grateful sister? Why risk that with involvement in multiple homicides? I'd been to Royal's shop twice and had been assaulted both times.

If Royal's story were true, Cyril was dead. Maybe that should be checked. I was regretfully related to someone who did that sort of thing well. If Calvin and Kavanaugh had taken Moira to Merkle's shed until the hour was ripe to bring her to my farm, where to suit their purposes Hadley and I could both be cut down like this field of corn, then I had some time to look into Royal's story.

That was my trouble. I hadn't been able to look. I just kept asking questions and moving on, working on the answers people gave me with no time for verification. It was time to check the facts. I started up and drove into the next village. There was a pay phone next to the storefront post office, I parked. Calvin killed Barrett. I hadn't been able to see it. Now I had to turn to my father. I got out to make the call. Pop answered.

"Vince Ventry's Broadway Beat."

"I need you to check out some stories."

"Fine."

"Sonny killed himself. I'm upstate. I need to know if India Barrett's cousin Hadley is still alive and where he is and if Calvin Conklin is in his office at the paper with or without Moira Hart. Talk to them personally. I need to know for sure. Call me back right away. There's no time to explain." I gave him the number and hung up on him. I got back in the car and waited. That was hard. The red sun was starting to sink in the west.

There were a lot of sleazy deals running through this case. Crossing over one another, hiding one another, going off and turning corners and twisting, coming back again.

As in Pop's theory of criminal motives, there was money and fear and revenge and the scouring, nerve-searing emotion we call love. So many victims: Peter murdered. Moira's cousin, dead. Sadie locked in her apartment in Brooklyn, terrorized. There was loopy Rina whose hippie-dippie mother had such sweet dreams. And Sonny dead. And Jack, my closest friend, who I never knew at all. The phone rang.

My father's message was unmistakable. I told him who to call next, at what time and what to say.

I got back in the car and headed for the interstate, and the shed that lay near a pasture beyond the work crew's garage. I drove by it and pulled over, around a curve, a couple of hundred yards further on. I decided against bringing the rifle. The .38 was in my pocket. That would do for what I had planned.

I walked as circumspectly as I could back to the garage. There was Calvin's car, covered with dust, pulled behind the shed. I stepped into the garage, where the front end loaders were kept. The first one I looked at had the keys in it. Who's going to steal a twenty-ton Tonka toy? I figured I had twenty minutes or so until Pop made the first call. Maybe less. I took out the revolver, spun the cylinder, five cartridges. I wondered if what they said about garlic rubbed on the tips was true: blood poisoning and slow. Probably not these days, and I had none. I thought about my garden and the pleasure I took in the solitary moments I spent there, even the weeding, even the pests.

I circled through the scraggly stand of poplar and sumac. I crawled up to the shed window. Inside, I could see Moira sitting in a chair with her hands behind her. There was a red bandanna wadded into her mouth and another tied around her neck to keep it in place. Her eyes were bulging and there were welts on her face which was bright scarlet.

Kavanaugh wasn't in the small room, but Conklin was seated at a small table, facing Moira. There was a gun on the table beside him. I went to the front of the shed and crashed through the door, falling on top of Conklin and sweeping his pistol onto the floor. I hit him hard once on the side of the neck. He slumped over onto the table. I quickly took the gag from Moira's mouth. She gasped.

"Are you all right?" I asked. She took a deep breath, sucking in the air and nodded vigorously. What could I say. There was no time to be tender. I went over to Conklin. I pulled his head up by his hair. He groaned.

"Where's Kavanaugh?"

"Ventry, who . . ." I slammed the gun barrel into his right kidney.

"I have some oven cleaner in my car. Kavanaugh. Where?"

"He took my car . . ." he sputtered, "to get something . . . for us to eat."

"Did you kill Hadley?"

"No. He's still alive. We were going to tell him to come to your farm at midnight. He thinks you've kidnapped Rina."

"He's got the key to the handcuffs in his right pocket, Ventry."

I took it from him and released Moira.

"Big dodgy, that." she said rubbing her wrists. "Out of here, Ventry, before that blue-eyed bastard comes back with the chips."

"No."

"No?"

"No."

"Ventry, are you crazy? Let's get out and call the coppers."

"No. We can end it here. Watch for Kavanaugh's car."

Conklin moaned as he sat slumped on the table. I put the cuffs on him. His eyes opened. I pulled up a chair and sat close to him, my face a few inches from his. I could smell the whiskey on his breath.

"Calvin," I said softly, "Hey, Calvin. This is Ventry. You awake? You want to talk a bit, hm?"

"Ventry . . . my neck hurts." He lifted his cuffed wrists, then dropped them.

"Talk to me, Calvin, we need to talk. Do you know where Cyril Hart is?"

"Dead."

"Oh no," Moira said mournfully behind me.

"Did you kill him? Did you? Calvin, come on, talk."

"Barrett."

"Barrett killed him? Why?"

"Hart knew his secret and thought he could get money from him. He didn't like Hart. He called me."

"Who? Barrett? Barrett called you?"

"Yes."

"Why?"

"Needed help. He sure did."

"When did he call you?"

"After Hart was dead. He hit him with a hammer."

"Poor Bulk." She began to cry.

"What did Barrett say when you showed up?"

"Thought I could help him. Straighten things out. Get the story right. Square the police."

"Why didn't you?"

"After the fight he had started in on a bottle of scotch. He was drunk when I got there. Raving."

"Why'd he call you, in particular, Calvin?"

"I used to stop by his place. Talk, have a couple of drinks. All the time. Didn't know that, did you? Don't know anything. Afternoon drinking cronies. Better company than you."

"When did this start?"

"When he came up here. Went over to do a story on him. Big shot comes to small town, you know. I knew of him. Always had. He had done a painting of my mother before I was born. Beautiful. Hangs in my bedroom. Had to meet him. Never ran the story. Got drunk. Pattern we fell into."

"What happened?"

"He had some good stories. People he'd met. Enemies he'd made who kept him back. Liked talking about himself. Arrogant bastard."

"Then?"

"Got hard to take, all this self-praise. I started slipping the needle in. Occasional questions. Like how come you only had one big show in your entire life? He'd get mad. It was fun."

"What happened the night Cyril was killed?"

"Barrett was out of control. Saying things he shouldn't have said. Shouldn't have even thought."

"What did he say?"

"Should have kept his mouth shut."

"Come on, Calvin, what did he say?"

"I told him that the best thing was to stop drinking and call the police. Tell them he thought Hart was an intruder. Wasn't expecting anybody."

"What did he say to that?"

"Said I was useless. We went into his studio where he had another bottle. I'd been drinking a bit that night, too. Those big paintings of Jack's were there. I told Barrett no one would miss him. He hadn't even painted the pictures in his first show. Kavanaugh told me that. I said to Barrett I wasn't even sure he had painted my mother's portrait. Asked him if Giresse had done that. I couldn't stop saying these things, Ventry. If only I had shut up and left. Anything."

"What did Barrett say then."

"Got angry. Furious. Called me a miserable good for nothing, lying son of a bitch. Then he started crying. I thought I should get out, but I waited, thinking maybe I should call the police from there. Then Barrett started raging again. The last time I was going to listen to it."

"What did he say?"

"Got me angry. I'm sorry. I just lost it. Went out of control. 'Kid, you're pathetic,' Barrett said to me. 'You live in a dream-world when you're not in a stupor. All the time you're talking about that goddamn family of yours like they're royalty. I got news for you, kid. That congressman father of yours was a crook. I've seen him with more envelopes in his pocket than the merry fuckin' mailman. Took more bribes than he took drinks. 'Nothing for nothing' was his motto." Conklin was taking large gulps of air.

"I told Barrett to shut up. He wouldn't, Ventry. 'And that mother of yours. Hah! She was some piece of work. Couldn't do without it. Got knocked up, of course, so her family had to pay Conklin to marry her. They knew their man, all right.' How do you know? I yelled at him. You're making this up, I yelled at him. 'I am?' he said, 'I am? I had her myself, kid, dozens of times. That dress I painted her in? Couldn't keep her in it. Tied her to the easel, once, and had her standing up. She loved it. You know I might even be your old man. What do you think of that? Going to help me now, kid?'"

Conklin brushed aside the hair from his face with his manacled hands, then dropped them on his lap.

"I picked up a knife from his palette. I remember it was short, a paring knife, and stabbed him in the back. I really stung him but the knife couldn't go in far enough. He pulled away with a scream, and he turned around, looking at me. I stabbed him again, and he grabbed for my arm. God, he was strong, but I managed to stab him a third time, below the center of the chest. That slowed him down. He staggered away. I followed him and stabbed him from behind in the side of the neck. He fell to his knees. I pushed his head down and stabbed him in the back again and again. I kept on going. It was like punching him. Pounding away at him for those things he said." Conklin nodded his head vigorously at the memory.

"The blood was warm. It was spurting out, so I guess his heart was still pumping. Tough old guy, you have to give him that. He was unconscious. There was some cord there. I lugged him over to that big easel with the ball bearings, tied him on to it. Like he tied her. Gave him a spin or two, and then his eyes opened. Glaring at me. There was a spray can there on the palette. Oven cleaner. I sprayed his eyes. He thrashed around, making the easel turn. Croaking sounds came from his lying throat, but blood was choking him and I guess I had pretty much ripped up his neck. I gave him one last punch in the heart with the knife. That was about it. It's not as if I had a plan. Dad said you have to improvise."

"What did you do then?"

"I called Kavanaugh."

"Why him?"

"I thought he could help me. We had met him at Hadley's. He told me my father had helped him as a young man, and he would always return a favor. He stopped by whenever he came up here. He hinted he'd like to invest in the *Vigilant*. The story about Jack doing Barrett's work came out one night when we were talking about his Dawnwalk project. Anyway, I called him and told him about Hart and killing Barrett."

"How did Kavanaugh react when you said you'd killed India's husband?"

"He said, 'Maybe I'll marry her after all,' and then he laughed. He's a good guy to have in a tight spot. It's as if he planned all this. He said to put the knife in my pocket, turn out the lights and leave. He didn't know about the spray can. I wiped it clean. He called Val who was going to send Merkle over for Hart's body. Make it look like the Australian kid did it and ran. Nothing should be done about Barrett. The last thing Kavanaugh asked was if the big paintings were damaged. I told him I didn't think so. Then I thanked him for his help."

"Where are the clothes you wore that night?"

"I burned them in a 55-gallon drum behind my house."

"And the knife?"

"Burned the blood off in the drum, then tossed it into the trash. It went off to the dump."

"And the paintings that were stolen."

"First-rate pieces, Ventry. I put them in my car while waiting for Merkle. He came and we brought Hart's body to my place. Buried him."

"Oh, Bulk!" Moira cried, "No!"

"Did Van Deusen ever ask you what you were doing that night?"

"You kidding? I'm press. He answered my questions."

"What are you doing here with Moira?"

"Kavanaugh said if everything works out I'll get to keep the paper. It would kill me to sell it. Then too, he helped me out of a jam. He likes to remind me about that."

"What did you do after I left your office today?"

"Read your note. Called Kavanaugh and Val, then took Moira for a drive, saying we'd catch up with you. We came here instead and met Kavanaugh. We didn't hurt her, Ventry. Did we, Miss? We were just waiting."

Moira came over to me. "Ventry, let's get out of here. Kavanaugh will be back soon." I stood up.

"I want to settle this."

"But we should warn Hadley," she argued. "Come on, Ventry. Let him tell his story to the Sheriff." Conklin started to get up. With a firm grip on the pistol in my right hand, I pushed him back down. Then I looked at Moira who was facing the door. Before I could say anything, her eyes widened, her mouth started to open.

I turned, dropped and fired in the same motion. One moment Kavanaugh was standing there, a greasy bag in one hand and an automatic in the other, and then he was staggering backwards, out the door, a red stain spreading across his stomach. He dropped the bag and lifted the pistol. I shot again. He toppled backward. Blood gurgled from his two stomach wounds, as wide apart as a pair of eyes.

I stood up. Conklin was sitting there, tears streaming down his face. Moira was white. I walked over to Conklin and pushed him back into the chair. "It's over," I told him. I gave the gun to Moira. "I don't want this anymore. If he tries to leave, stop him."

"Ventry . . ." I cut her off. "Just one more thing," I said. I walked over to the garage and started up the front end loader.

I drove it over to the hill of road salt and lowering the blade, bit into its side, then, lifting up maybe three cubic yards of the salt in the payloader, I reversed, turned the machine around and carried the load over to where Kavanaugh lay on the ground. I upended the salt over him, covering yet another slug.

In the distance the sirens wailed, obedient to my father's summons.

23

Moira sat down on the bench under the cherry tree next to the pond. The wood of the seat had warped.

It was almost October. The trials and the testimony were over. Cyril's remains had been exhumed and buried in a cemetery facing west, overlooking the Hudson. Conklin confessed, pleaded guilty and was doing life in a prison his grandfather helped build.

The carp nudged up to the surface looking for a handout.

When I had left Royal's shop that night, he and his Ernest slipped out of town till events were played out one way or another. Then they decided to head for Brazil, safe from extradition, though they were certainly accessories to the cover-up of two murders and deep into the plot against me. Rina and Hadley joined them there. Perhaps someday she'll find the forest pool of her daydreams.

Moira hugged her arms to herself as if it were a cold day, instead of a humid, September afternoon. We had had three good months together. The bees flew languidly among the stalks of the Queen Anne's lace that dotted the meadow, droning among the pollen-soaked florets.

The Dawnwalk foundation faded away, and I never heard of it again. I hadn't heard from Jack either. Not surprised. Chen had sent me a postcard from Florence.

The goldenrod was in full bloom, nodding saffron heads filled with the summer's sunlight. Weeds flourished in the humus-enriched soil of my garden, but plump red tomatoes were sunning themselves on the plants sprawling in a tangle unstaked.

India Barrett had given her husband's paintings and a million dollars to the University in Albany, and the trustees said they'd try to find a place for them. The de Koonings, the Klines, and the other paintings stolen the night of the murders were recovered from Conklin, undamaged, and were to be auctioned. She had mailed me another check for twenty-thousand dollars. Now I had enough for at least another two years up here.

"Ventry," Moira asked, "Ventry, what do you want?"

I had known this was coming. It didn't bode well. "Oh. Stay up here," I said, "Paint. Clear the weeds out. Turn over the soil a bit. Shoot back at the occasional sniper. Who knows? Maybe try sculpture. I was thinking of picking up some plaster and wire. Things like that."

"That's what I thought," she said.

"Is it so bad?"

"No," she whispered, "no, it's not so bloody bad."

We looked down at the hungry carp. I put my arm around her. She leaned on me.

"Ventry, you see . . . Lately, you seem to have some kind of dialogue with yourself going on. When I ask you a question," her voice rising, "it's as if I'm interrupting you half the time."

"Moira," I began.

"But the other times are pretty good."

"For me too. I'm trying to think things through."

"I understand, really, I do. I want just two things."

"Okay."

"No more sagging muscles in the drawings of me."

"We'll get some helium."

"Ventry . . ." she punched me in the arm.

We sat there for a while, the sun sinking lower in the sky, already turning the light in the meadow a soft yellow. I could hear the distant grinding of a chainsaw, the neighbors cutting deadwood to add to the woodpile for winter. High overhead, a broad-winged hawk, circling in an updraft, let out a cry. It was time to join others of its kind and head south.

"What else?"

"Do you remember your grandmother, the one who believed in retribution?"

"Yes."

"I may have to go to Brazil. Will you go with me, if that time comes?"

The flowers in the meadow in front of me swayed, abundant and bountiful, rich purple asters, blue chicory, nodding sunflowers, and in the woods, the late afternoon sun lit up the trees, the maples, the ashes, the hickories and oaks in their autumn dance, reds, yellows, browns and golds, all glowing in the light.

"Yes," I said, "I'll leave with you when you need me."

"That'll be right, then."

Moira rose and walked up to the house. I continued to sit. I took the small pad and pencil stub from my shirt pocket. I heard the clatter of the screen door. There was so much work to do. I started to sketch.